LOVE

BY INVITATION ONLY

by

CHARLOTTE BINGHAM

The beautiful Lady Georgiana Longborough and her friend Jennifer Parker-Jones, 7th Marchioness of Pemberton, are finding life a little too dull in deepest Wilt-shire. Jennifer's answer to all her problems it seems is to give a Summer Ball.

But the social life of the County Set is rarely if ever that straightforward, for while shopping for her ball gown Georgiana re-meets her first lover, Kaminski, the great and famous film director, while at the same time her aunt, the Countess - who is helping Jennifer arrange her ball - finds out that in fact Jennifer is bent on double crossing her.

The Countess in turn plots to teach the young Marchioness a lesson - but will she be able to manage her revenge? Will Jennifer discover the true father of her buxom neighbour's children? Will Fulton - the gay husband of Lady Tizzy the buxom neighbour - ever manage to make Lady Tizzy stop straying? And will Bloss, Lord Pemberton's wily butler, manage to get his get his new car? Will life in Wiltshire ever be the same? Not as long as Charlotte Bingham's famously wonderful characters inhabit this neck of the rural woods.....

*

Charlotte Bingham published her first book - *Coronet Among The Weeds* – at the age of nineteen. Since then she has written and had published forty further works of fiction, including the international bestsellers *To Hear A Nightingale, The Business,* the award winning *A Change of Heart, Grand Affair, Love Song, The Kissing Garden* and *The Blue Note.* She has also written over one hundred television scripts, plays and films with her husband the actor, playwright and painter Terence Brady, most notably *Upstairs Downstairs, No-Honestly, Yes-Honestly, Nanny, Forever Green* and *Pig in the Middle. Belgravia* is the first in a four book series of romantic social satires.

Charlotte Bingham has a son and a daughter and Lives in deepest Somerset.

Films with Terence Brady:
LOVE WITH A PERFECT STRANGER
MAGIC MOMENTS

Stage Plays with Terence Brady:
I WISH I WISH
THE SHELL SEEKERS
(adaptation from the novel by Rosamunde Filcher)

LOVE
BY INVITATION ONLY

ISBN 9781500951597

Originally published in Great Britain
by Doubleday, a division of Transworld publishers as
BY INVITATION
Doubleday edition published 1993
Bantam Books edition published 1993

ENGLAND IN
THE 1980s

LOVE BY INVITATION ONLY

1

In many places across Wiltshire early this summer evening people could be found staring at the green swathes of their lawns and wondering whether or not they might get away with not cutting it for another day, and if not then rolling up their sleeves to walk behind or mount their various cutting machines before rewarding themselves for their labours with a long, cool glass of Pimms.

Jennifer, the wife of the seventh Marquis of Pemberton, was no exception. She too was staring at the immaculate turf of the garden belonging to the Hall, but for a very different reason.

'A raised floor, you say, to cover all of this?' she asked, picking up her tapestry and thrusting a needle through the canvas.

Fulton, acting as her amateur party organizer, smiled, because he could see that already Lady Pemberton's heart was going out of the whole idea of giving a Summer Ball, and since he had just suggested a peach silk-lined marquee with peach flowers, peach food, peach napkins and peaches for dessert, he really didn't want her enthusiasm to sink with the already setting sun.

Silently he thanked heaven that the whole thing had been her idea in the first place, and that she had called him over to the Hall to adjudicate at her decision-making.

'It's very easy,' he told her in a soothing tone, 'much easier than you would first think, really. What happens is a little man comes along and covers the whole lawn with a floor, and then they tent the entire garden, flower beds, everything, they all become part of the decor. Sybilla Adelstrop did it for the 'Brass Hearts for the Aged' last year. It was very successful. Except the pelargoniums didn't *quite* match.'

'I'm not doing anything *for* anything,' Jennifer put in, with the sudden force of someone who felt she might be taking on too much.

'No, of course not. Particularly anything in aid of the Cathedral.'

'Especially not the Cathedral. Anyway, what on earth is Sybilla Adelstrop doing giving old people brass hearts?'

'Oh, I don't know. 'Parently they're like food coupons, only they didn't want to offend the old dears, so they called them something else. Elliott thought 'Brass Necks' would be more fun, but no-one took him up on it.'

'I think,' Jennifer continued, warming to her theme, 'I think the modern spectacle of charity organizers who do nothing but buy their wretched evening frocks and feed their families for the next millennium on the backs of poor starving people is, to say the least, a disgrace.'

She stopped, suddenly wondering if Fulton's stunningly cut safari jacket had been purchased on the back of the Brass Hearts Ball, but, seeing it had a rather old-fashioned half-belt at the back, decided it wasn't.

'I see you too are going for a daisy lawn.' Fulton looked down at his feet.

'It's for the children,' Jennifer told him absently. 'Nanny likes it. You know, daisy chains and things.'

'We ourselves, at Flint House, we too have gone for a daisy theme. Daisies in the lawn, marguerites in the beds, daisies in dahlia form, for later on. We're getting a tiny bit excited about it, as you can imagine.'

Fulton was referring to the imminent arrival of his wife, the former Lady Tisbury's, second baby.

'I heard about that from Lady Tizzy,' said Jennifer, her expression warming. 'Such a lovely idea, Daisy Marguerita. Charming names. So much better now they can tell which sex Baby is going to be. Two girls. Couldn't be more lovely.'

She placed a hand on Fulton's. She thought it was wonderful that he had married Patti. Everyone in Wiltshire thought so. And then to let her have not one but two babies was generous in the extreme, particularly since everyone knew that the first one could not have been - Jennifer stopped, wondering suddenly if 'sired' or 'fathered' was the better word. Unable to decide, she dropped the thought and went on to another.

'You're a hero, Fulton, really you are. And Elliott. Lady Tizzy is a very lucky girl.'

She sighed slightly, as Fulton smiled slightly. Lady Tizzy was a very lucky girl, but then he and Elliott were very lucky boys. They were friends, he had a wife, and now they were about to have two daughters, the Misses Benedict-Montrose-Cavanagh. What could have been a disaster of a minor sort had turned into something rather different -which all went to show that nice things could happen sometimes.

'Real heroes,' said Jennifer again, tactfully avoiding the question of the paternity of Lady Tizzy's children. A question which hung, and would always hang, over the nursery at Flint House, as all Wiltshire knew.

'Do you know, Fulton, our babies see each other so much nowadays, they've even grown to look alike, Nanny says.'

Fulton gazed straight ahead of him after this last remark, and then rose from the garden bench with some alacrity. Since the seventh Marquis was the father of all the children in the nurseries of both the Hall and Flint House, his alacrity was understandable.

As he rose to his feet he could feel that the complicated pattern of the ironwork of the bench had imprinted itself upon his derriere. When he undressed that night he would doubtless be able to continue to admire the pattern of Tudor roses and scrolled ivy leaves that made up one of the many garden benches at the Hall.

'I fear I have thrown out a clout before May is out, and I'm going to pay for it,' he said, shivering a little. 'We must continue our little plans towards the end of the week. After.'

'Of course. After Patti's inducement.'

'So we'll take it as read it will be private, by invitation only -'

'And matching.'

'Of course.'

Jennifer quickly put her tapestry into her basket, and they trod back across the lawn to the house, during which time Jennifer thought gratefully that at least this year she didn't have to face an inducement of any kind, except to persuade Pember to pay for the ball. And Fulton reflected that their dearly beloved Marchioness had somehow managed to make the all too medical word 'inducement' sound quite charming, like a churching or a christening.

'Tally whack and tandem all over Wiltshire,' sighed Fulton, sinking into the large feathered cushions of the kitchen sofa. 'Lady Pemberton is giving a dance and I'm ordered to design it all for her.'

He raised his eyes to the ceiling and his hand to the glass that Elliott was holding out to him.

'Well, that was just about the only thing I wanted. How did you know?'

He gazed happily first at the contents of his glass, and then at Elliott, who had gone back to making his very tiny mushroom pies for their fête champêtre to be held in the garden the following day.

'I knew,' said Elliott, neatly flattening his pastry with his glass rolling pin, 'I knew from the way you drove the Golf into the gate rather than through it that a serious drink was needed.'

'How's Lady Tizzy?'

Elliott sighed and raised his eyes to heaven, and then sighed again and lowered them back to the rolling pin and the pastry.

'She is *impossible*,' he murmured. 'Her feet have swollen, she says. She doesn't like having babies in the summer, she says. She never wanted this one in the first place, she says. That's how she is. She won't come to the fête champêtre tomorrow unless you buy her a new dress to cover her turn, she says, and even then she'll only come if she's allowed to sit down under the apple tree and people are brought up to her one by one, she says.'

'Did you tell her it's for the Cathedral?'

'Yes, and she said if she had to go to one more thing to do with the Cathedral she'd be sick.'

'I know how she feels,' said Fulton, stretching out one elegantly shod foot in front of him, 'we all do. But that's how it is.'

'Not with Lady Tizzy, it isn't.'

'So. It's being a naughty Patti, is it?'

'Naughty? She's like my grandmother faced with a bad kipper.'

'Fined. Fifty pence for the Cathedral. No similes to be used until the end of May.'

'Oh, very well. But tell me, tell me please about Lady Pemberton and this *thé dansant*, or whatever.'

'No *thé dansant*, because this is all whatever. A tremendous whatever, one enormous huge whatever. I'm to design it all, inside and out, special colour for the tenting, special tenting for the house, the house to match the flowers, the flowers to match the napkins, the napkins to match the waiters, and the waiters to match the guests, the guests to match the weather, and the weather to match the hostess, the hostess to match it all. Game set and match.'

'Sounds terribly tiring.'

'Tiring. I tell you it's going to have us all in such a spin you won't believe.'

'But so unlike Jennifer.'

Elliot raised his rolling pin and set it carefully aside. He hated people, particularly people he knew, doing things that weren't like them. It was muddling and strange. Everyone knew that Jennifer, whatever her drawbacks, which were many, was not a social person, that the mere thought of going to London was enough to send her into a three-day migraine, and equally the thought of London coming to her. She never received weekend guests unless she was absolutely forced, and yet here she was preparing to tent her lawn, and ask a great many people to dance and dine and be very careful of her flower beds.

'It's all a bit strange, for Jennifer,' he said slowly. 'You must admit.'

'Now you're not going to do one of your Inspector Remorses about this, are you? Because if you are, I refuse to let you. There is nothing sinister about the Marchioness of Pemberton giving a dance. Full stop.'

'She must suspect,' said Elliott, turning from the Aga suddenly. 'She must suspect what Pember and — to what Lady Tizzy and Pember are up — to. To what they are up. Have been up. To. If you know what I mean?'

'I hope not,' said Fulton slowly. 'I sincerely and totally and absolutely hope not.'

'We can't shut our eyes to it. Every day, week in week out, before lunch and after tea. I mean he's hardly managed to get out into the garden. Apparently Jennifer complained, and only last week, to the Village Voice, that they'd never had so few bulbs at the Hall, and that Pember had put it all down to a plague of mice.'

'Very biblical.'

'So what's Lady Tizzy's been up to, but that doesn't make it holy.'

Elliott stood back to admire the last tray of pies. Very tiny and very sweet. He could just imagine them sitting under the apple tree tomorrow looking festive.

'I can't take it. I can't take one more drama. Not with another baby on the way. We've got Nanny in the guest wing, the night nurse in Nanny's room, Victoria in the day nursery, the new baby when it arrives in the night nursery, and that is drama enough for six weeks for me.'

'And me,' Elliott agreed, 'but it has to be faced that if Jennifer ever finds out who the father of our children really is and they divorce, then Pember might feel forced to marry Lady Tizzy and Lady Tizzy might feel forced to take our children from us.'

'I know, I know,' sighed Fulton, pouring a great deal more vodka than was strictly necessary into his glass, and then topping it up with far too much tonic by way of a penance.

'I know only too well, but what can one do? Face it, one can only cross one's fingers and pray, because there's nothing one can do.'

'It's not crossing her fingers that Lady Tizzy needs to do -' Elliott muttered.

'Please.' Fulton held up his hand. 'Please. No, please. None of that. I'm going through a religious phase, and I can't take rude asides.'

'Aside from that we're going to have to keep an eye. One eye each, at least. Really. The future of our children depends on us keeping things terribly straight.'

'I've got a feeling that it's a little too late for that kind of talk.'

Fulton inhaled the top of his drink, and Elliott watched him with some interest.

'I was thinking of sending her away, you know, after the baby,' he said, having finished his short inhalation.

'So you have been worried?'

'Of course, of course I've been worried. Victoria's our daughter. She bears my name. Of course I've been worried. We're all worried. I keep staring at my curtains at four o'clock every morning and falling asleep saying my prayers that there will be some kind of outcome that will make everything easier for us, that will stop us worrying, but I can't think of any, except pushing Pember off a bridge.'

'Not bad, but I'm superstitious over murder. You know how it is, people's faces coming back to you in the night. Voices shouting 'alack, alack' just as you're dropping off into a nice post-prandial siesta. It would be better if it could be arranged naturally for us, by God.'

'I'm not sure you can pray for someone to fall off a bridge accidentally. I think that's sort of cheating. Anyway, we like milord, don't we? We just wish he wasn't quite so randy, really.'

'Where's Lady Tizzy now?'

'In her bedroom eating tinned peaches.'

'She will eat tinned. Remember last time?'

Fulton sighed. 'Last time she ate so many tinned apricots I was quite sure that Victoria would be born with a Del Monte label round her turn.'

'I suppose I should go up?'

'You don't have to. She's quite happy eating peaches and watching re-runs of *Pogley and the Pegtops*.'

'What a good idea to give her her own little recorder. That was certainly a good idea.'

'It was desperation,' said Fulton quietly. 'I was beginning to feel I was a Pegtop.'

'Shall we go through to the sitting room cum drawing room with its tasteful display of mixed antiques, and dine quietly in the window overlooking the lawn?'

'Why not?'

'It's only going to be very quiet dining, Chicken Kiev and funny pink lettuce.'

'As long as the lettuce doesn't match anything I shall be quite, quite happy.'

Fulton followed Elliott and his tray. The vodka was beginning to take effect. The last of the spring flowers could be seen through the French windows. They would sit in their own little window and picnic. He had been right in his earlier assumption: in between all the other bits, life, after all, could be really very nice.

Georgiana lay upon the sofa and contemplated the stucco ceiling of her drawing room. The sofa upon which she lay was, she knew, full of fleas, but at that precise moment her real concern was with a cobweb at the end of which hung a money spider. The money spider dropped upon her arm, and she let it tickle its way down to her hand before shaking it off into a crack between the floor boards. She then lifted one of her legs and looked at it. It was perfect - slim ankle, slight tan - altogether perfect. She lifted her other leg. It too was perfect. She had a pair of matching legs, satisfactory in some ways, indeed a pair of perfect matching legs would be enough to satisfy many girls she knew, but she herself felt demonstrably unsatisfied. In fact 'less than happy' would perfectly sum up the owner of the perfectly matching legs.

She was living with her lover Gus and George, their son, at Longborough, and they all enjoyed living at Longborough, and she knew it ought to be enough, but she was aware that it ought to be enough yet wasn't. The truth was she wasn't happy just living. It just wasn't enough.

She had thought about dried flowers. In fact she had thought about dried flowers a great deal lately, and then become depressed. Just the phrase 'dried flowers' was so, well, dry really. And just thinking about them made her feel as if she had turned the wrong corner in her life.

Of course dried flowers made sense, of course they did, they made a great deal of sense, and that was the trouble, they were sensible, incredibly, horribly sensible. It was natural, of course, to think about dried flowers, goodness knows they grew enough of the real things at Longborough, it was only sense to dry some of them, but even so, every time she thought about putting them into artistic little bunches, and hanging them upside down,

Georgiana found that something happened to her, there was a tightening of her throat muscles, her back began to ache, and she wanted to scream. Perhaps if Gus were not away painting in Israel at the invitation of the government, perhaps if it were not beginning to be such nice warm weather, perhaps if she were preparing to take a picnic with wine down to his studio, perhaps she would not be lying on her back lifting each of her legs in the air, one by one, but as it was she was, and he was, and there was very little that she could think of doing to relieve this unremitting feeling of boredom, of being someone about whose whereabouts no-one knew, or cared.

She could make a Symingtons table cream of course. But she could only make it if Nanny and Gus's mother were out of the kitchen, and had taken George for a walk, otherwise they would watch her and criticize. When she was a child she had always made a table cream when she was bored. Sometimes her mother had found her and smiled distantly from the kitchen door, and sometimes Nanny had found her and told her off for 'waste'.

She glanced at her watch and then sat up quickly. It was four o'clock. Four o'clock was one of the highlights of her day. Time to go to the post.

She retrieved her shoes from under a chair and put them on. They were made of thin gold straps. Kaminski, her first lover, had bought them for her. She still loved them with a passion, as he had loved her, and then left her because she was young and boring. Now she was nearly twenty-five, and probably still as boring to someone like him.

Last week she'd been to see Kaminski's latest film at the Cinema Club in Berridge. They had all watched the film, and then, afterwards, the Club President, wearing a collarless denim shirt and tin glasses, which meant that as far as Berridge was concerned he was dangerously intellectual and had left-wing tendencies, had promoted a discussion about it. Most members of the Berridge Cinema Club, annual subscription two pounds, had not understood the film, and Georgiana had been among them. There had been a great deal of play with 'reality' and 'non-reality', and the actors had been used to portray actors who were really portraying themselves when they weren't actors, at least that was what the Club President had said, and since he had tin glasses and a denim shirt no-one present had been prepared to argue with him. Even so Georgiana had returned home wondering what on earth the film could be about?

It had been a lonely experience, driving home wondering how it was that at nineteen she could have been so interesting to someone like Kaminski, because she had been interesting to him, for those few weeks in London. But then, probably because he must have known that she would grow into the sort of person who wouldn't understand his films, he had left her and gone back to Los Angeles without a backward glance, and she had been left alone with just the memory of what it meant to be something special to a great man, a man that people wrote about constantly in newspapers and magazines, a man who was seen in the company of interesting, as well as beautiful, women.

Even now she could remember how she had cried when he told her that all great love affairs must end, and then how he had made love to her, and she had been left standing at the window of his apartment looking at him being driven off with his partner in their limousine. At nineteen she had been the dusty past, and he had seemed to be the vibrant present, and she had wanted to kill herself for being finally so deeply uninteresting to him.

Just lately she had started to wonder if she wasn't just as uninteresting to Gus as she had finally been to Kaminski. It was an unavoidable thought. Gus used to paint her, now he no longer painted her. He painted his mother and George, and landscapes and other things like water that seemed to hold a fascination for him far greater than Georgiana. And all this in between 'earning a crust', as he called doing his syndicated 'The Lady Loves' cartoons for America, and doing 'pretty ladies' for the birthday card business that Georgiana had encouraged him to start, which was being run very successfully by his brother from a small printing works in Devon.

She sometimes found it quite funny that he had never bothered to marry her, or even asked if she might like to marry him. Sometimes she found it quite funny, and sometimes she found it quite beastly of him. After all, to someone like him, a Lady Georgiana Longborough should be quite a bargain. But Gus didn't think like that. It wasn't that he even rejected thinking of that kind, he just didn't even begin to adopt such a line of thought, it was utterly foreign to him. Occasionally his mother, dear Nan, would remonstrate with him.

'You gotta marry Georgiana, Gus, because of your boy. George is gonna get teased in the playground else, if you don't, you just gotta marry his mum. It's only right.'

But Gus would only smile and pour himself another glass of wine, always forgetting anyone else in the room might want one, and light another of his strong-smelling French cigarettes, and then rub his bottom lip with his thumb, a habit of his he always observed when he had switched off.

Georgiana never mentioned it, of course. She wasn't that keen on marrying someone who wasn't that keen on marrying her, and nowadays she wished that Nan wouldn't bring the subject up. She was far too proud to do so herself. One marriage and divorce had been quite enough for her. Besides, men seemed to change so when they became husbands. Her first,

Stranragh, had been really perfectly all right before they got married, but afterwards he had become like the monster from the lake, practically growing long fangs and sucking the last drop of blood from her veins. No, now that she knew that Gus wasn't fascinated enough by her to want to marry her, she had become convinced that she too wasn't fascinated enough by marriage to want to try it again, really -at least not for the time being, anyway.

By now Georgiana had reached the post box at the end of the long drive. The walk had done her good, not a wholesome kind of boarding school 'good', but a proper kind of enjoyable good, and she was able to slip her hand into the wire cage in which the postman left their letters without feeling a sense of dread. She would even be able to face the fact that Gus had not written to her yet again, not even a card, and for the fourth week. Instead of a card from Gus there was a nice stiff white envelope among all the nasty buff floppy ones. It was quite childish but Georgiana felt her heart give a little leap, and she allowed it to as well. It was an odd dizzying kind of feeling, and one that she hadn't had for ages. It was an invitation. She turned her eyes quickly away from seeing the handwriting on the envelope, or the postmark which would tell her where it was from, and started the return walk back to the house.

Suppose the invitation was something exciting, she wondered? Suppose it was to the kind of occasion to which she had always been used to be asked - one that would demand an evening dress with a long Winterhalter-type skirt. It would be incredible if it was. She stopped walking suddenly, and her heartbeat slowed to its normal pace. It could just as well be an invitation to a wine-tasting. Lately vintners had grown into the habit of sending out stiff cards in stiff envelopes, and only last month she had had an engraved invitation to a party to view Italian sheets, of all things. This could be another one of those. Well, whatever it was, she decided she wasn't going to let Nanny or Nan or anyone else for that matter see it. This was going to be one secret she would keep from them. She stuck it up the front of her old darned cashmere jumper as she walked back into the house, deliberately throwing all the other envelopes down on the silver salver in the hall, so that she could have the pleasure of watching Nanny, who was a great deal less deaf than she liked to pretend, leafing through them all, searching for some kind of letter from Gus, and then see her smiling when it failed to materialize.

'Nothing from Mr Gus again, I see, Lady Georgie,' she would mumble, and then go quickly down to the kitchens to tell Nan who would shake her head, laugh, and pretend to be shocked, when all the time she knew that Gus had never written a letter in his life, unless it was to enclose a bill for one of his pictures. Nan had no illusions about Gus; he was her son, and she'd made him that way, and it was something of which she was proud.

'You'll never change Gus, Georgie,' she would say when she was on her second glass of cooking sherry of an evening. 'He's the spit of his dad is Gus, and he never wrote to me in his life, except during the war to ask for something, thicker socks or the like - the rascal. No, there's nothing you can do about it, girl, just stick it up your jumper, and get on with your life.'

Just at that moment, as she slid carefully past Nanny, Georgiana hoped that the invitation, which was by now getting quite warm down the front of her jumper, wouldn't find its way to the floor.

'No letter from Master Gus,' mumbled Nanny, but by that time Georgiana was up the stairs and down the long corridors to her own suite of rooms where she quickly closed the doors, and locked them.

It was wonderful to smuggle things past Nanny once again. When she was little she'd smuggled dog biscuits, particularly the black ones, up to the nursery to share with her toys; now and how strange she found it – now it was invitations.

Just lately Georgiana had become convinced from the way the two old dears seemed to follow her everywhere that Gus had asked them to watch her every move while he was away. For apart from being very much himself, and doing exactly as he pleased, Gus was violently possessive. He might not want to marry Georgiana, he might not paint her any more, he might not pay attention to her from one day to the next, sometimes not even speaking to her for hours on end, but nevertheless he wanted her there, permanently, for him. She was his person in waiting.

Georgiana slid her nail file under the crease of the envelope, and neatly slit it open and pulled out the stiff invitation, for invitation it was, a lovely hard engraved invitation. She shut her eyes quickly and tried to trace the words and the name on the card with her finger, before opening them again. How heavenly, it was properly engraved, and with a name that was all too familiar.

The Marchioness of Pemberton.
By Invitation Only

Georgiana gazed at her old friend's name. A name that might have been Georgiana's, if she had taken John Pemberton up on his marital offer. All too easily the invitation could have been coming from her, and not from her old friend Jennifer. It could have been Georgiana's name written on the piece of stiff engraved cardboard with the tissue paper across the top. She daren't think how long it was since someone had been at home *By Invitation Only* to her. Since installing herself, Nan and Nanny at Longborough following her parents' unfortunate demise, she had only received telephone calls by way of invitation, or little bendy cards with *Regrets only* scrawled across the bottom. This was going to be a real dance with real people of the kind to which she had been used to be used. She lay back against her large Victorian lace pillows. How wonderful, at last, after all these months, to be asked out somewhere proper. And how pathetic to feel so excited. It seemed that it wasn't so long ago when she would have turned such invitations away and accepted something more exciting than a married friend's dance, but now she was over the moon just because Jennifer had remembered her.

Then she remembered Gus and knew at once that she would not be allowed to go. Worse than that, she wouldn't be allowed to go for a really good reason. Gus didn't like socializing, and he didn't like Jennifer. In fact, he was violently opposed to it. Particularly if it had anything to do with anything to do with Georgiana's past. What was more, the mere sight of an invitation from the Marchioness of Pemberton would be enough to bring on one of his diatribes in which he would go to great lengths to describe Jennifer as something really horrid, and his mother as the salt of the earth.

Georgiana closed her eyes and let the invitation slip to the floor. Suddenly she felt proper tears welling up behind her closed eyelids. Of course Gus would never let her go, not in a million years. She wouldn't be able to have a beautiful evening dancing and forgetting all about Nan and Nanny, and whether or not to go in for drying flowers. Instead she would have to stay shut up at Longborough, just as if she was in exile, or banned from London by an old-fashioned husband, instead of cooped up with a bolshie lover.

Indulging in her silent tears Georgiana found to be rather healing. She let them drip upon the old soft cotton of the pillowcase, sliding gracefully, first cold, then warm, into white oblivion. Then she opened her eyes and stared, as she had so often as a child stared, at the painting of Lady Desborough hanging opposite her bed. Lucky Lady Desborough, she thought. She'd never had these awful problems. Losing a little at a game of chance, wondering if her husband was going to be late back from the club, or whether or not to reprimand the maid for bringing her the morning cup of chocolate late, those would have been her matters of concern, most definitely not dried flowers.

And then too she would not have had the awful experience of a lover, of all things, just a lover, trying to stop her going to a ball. He would have wished most heartily that she would go to a ball, and her husband would have gone too, and they would have met all sorts of exciting people there. Her husband would have met his mistress, she her lover, and they would have all enjoyed themselves in a most courtly way. But all that was foreign to Gus, insisting as he did on early-to-bed-early-to-rise routines, and a life about as exciting as that of a chartered accountant.

Until she had come back to live at Longborough with Gus it had always seemed to Georgiana that painters were very exciting, colourful people, and anything but normal, for that was how Gus had seemed to her when they were crouching in their little semi-detached house in East Sheen, London. But once at Longborough Georgiana had discovered to her great concern that Gus and his way of life were dull to the point of boredom. Just painting, and all day long, too. No wild moods, no slashing of canvases, nor orgies in hellfire caves. He never wanted to throw a party for other Bohemians, let alone dress up as one. Sometimes, particularly during the seemingly endless winter, Georgiana had found herself hoping that Gus would suddenly discover that he was Spanish and start painting all night like Picasso, or would cut off his ear in a fit of pique and send it to a rival in the post and cause the kind of scandal that inspired *in focus* interviews by *in depth* journalists, and Georgiana could be photographed in a harsh light wearing somewhat outrageous clothes. But nothing of that sort ever happened at Longborough, where the most exciting event of last winter was the Aga going out just when Nanny was making tea.

If only she hadn't had George she could leave Gus. It would all be quite simple, but as it was she loved George, and he loved her, and although he did look horribly like Gus he was nevertheless her son, and she knew one just didn't leave one's sons because one had grown bored with their fathers. Georgiana knew this. She knew it the way she knew how to sing *I Vow to Thee My Country*, and to always be kind to animals, and to keep your voice down in restaurants. No-one left their children, not ever. They sent them away to school, of course, but they didn't abandon them.

Georgiana leaned down to the floor, and picked up the invitation again. The ball looked twice as nice now that she knew Gus would never consider letting her go to it. Any day now Gus would be back from Israel, filling the house with his demands for black coffee and smelling out the rooms with his strong French cigarettes, and lecturing his houseful of women about everything he had seen and done. There was no doubt at all that he would have become embroiled in kibbutzes and things, the sort of stuff that would make his mother yawn with boredom and drink even more cooking sherry, things that Georgiana could only attempt to pretend to be interested in.

Then as everyone else slipped off to watch their tellies, she would be left leaning on her hand and smiling as best she could while Gus banged on, crossing and re-crossing her legs under the table until they looked like nothing so much as the parcel into which the rats had tied Tom Kitten. It was such a pity about the things that interested Gus, because he could really be quite nice when he wanted to, and quite a lot of people liked him, even country people, but he had become was and she had to face it - a little bit *boring*.

Georgiana jumped off the bed and flung open one of her wardrobes. All her old dresses from yesteryear hung there covered in plastic bags. Just seeing them made her sad – her dear sad dresses, and what lovely evenings she had enjoyed in them. Not they hung stiffly on their hangers with their petticoats stiff beneath them and their diamanté embroideries still faintly glowing.

There was the dress that Kaminski bad given her to wear for the film ball at Longborough, and there was the long evening coat to match. How marvellous they had been together, that dress and coat, and yet it seemed that that was the night when he had decided to

17

part from her, so she couldn't, after all, have looked quite good enough, and that was all there was to it.

Georgiana buried her head among her old dresses and prayed. Georgiana prayed quite often. Her God was a kind of heavenly godfather who had sent her some nice things now and then as well as some pretty disappointing things too, the way godfathers nearly always did, but on the whole she reckoned He meant quite well, even if He had made some slip-ups. She prayed to Him now. Please, please, please, help her to find a way to go to Jennifer's ball, then settled herself in front of her dressing-table mirror to stare long and hard at herself as if she was lunching with a friend. Since she had no friends who lived nearby, she had to advise herself – she had to be her own best friend as it were, and bang on to herself about herself.

The problem was that her lover would not let her go to the ball. Worse than that, if he knew she even wanted to go there would be a row, and Gus would go on and on about the things that meant a great deal to him, but not much to her. Gus had respect for things like socialism, but none for the things that meant a lot to her. Even so, physical beauty and luxury of a certain kind were very important to him, while oddly enough they didn't matter quite so much to Georgiana. What meant a great deal to Georgiana was everything being nice. She had always rather someone was kind first and beautiful next, and she didn't care for luxury nearly so much as she cared for the past, and what that meant – which is why she cared for Longborough because it was both kind and the past. It might also be cold and dreary and cost a fortune to heat most of the time, but it stood for something that you couldn't write down, something that was very difficult to explain to someone like Gus who thought his garden studio a great deal too small, and the light wrong in his winter studio, and had never once been allowed to see a central heating bill, because if he did he would probably burn the whole place down, or sell it to a foreigner who would put in double glazing, electric fires and wall to wall carpeting.

If only those were the only things that Gus went on about. He also went on and on about George and what he should be doing, and what he shouldn't be doing. He wasn't going to be allowed to go to private school on principle, although whose principle Georgiana couldn't discover. He wasn't going to be allowed to ride in case he was tempted to hunt. It was pathetic, Georgiana told herself. Her poor son was only just getting his first pair of wellies and Gus was insisting on them being red rather than green.

By now she had banged on to herself so much that Georgiana was beginning to bore even herself, yet she still hadn't formulated any great plan to deceive Gus, who after all she reasoned and not unreasonably deserved to be deceived, especially since he wasn't going to allow George to have a pony, only a donkey, and then if ever.

There was also another reason that Georgiana considered that Gus deserved to be planned and schemed against and that was because he would never allow Georgiana to read either Vogue or *Harpers & Queen* or even *The Tatler*. Georgiana of course could not do without any of them, yet purely on account of Gus's ridiculous attitude she had been reduced to reading them in the back of her car while parked in the municipal car park in Berridge. Many a long winter afternoon had passed away in secret dreaming and yearnings, and then she had been forced to drop the magazines into the litter bin before driving home feeling vaguely discontented and unfulfilled, much as she supposed anyone did after a binge of any kind.

But although she had no copies of Vogue to which she could refer, Georgiana knew what she should look like for Jennifer's ball. Her dress would have to be long and romantic and when she thought the thought she sighed because nothing romantic had happened around Longborough since Kaminski had filmed there. *Romantic*. She sighed again as she relished the word for even the word seemed to have a scent to it, not a suffocating one like lilies but deliciously delicate like jasmine. It was crushed silk, it was celandine and tiny wild orchids, it was the finest spun sugar.

She stopped by the door of her bedroom, and before inserting the key back into the lock she thought how exciting life had suddenly become in the last two hours. All of a sudden it was full of promise again, not stagnant and stale as it had been of late, or worst of all – all dried up. She knew why it was. It wasn't just that she had been invited to a ball by invitation only, it was because she was going to have the chance to be Lady Georgiana Longborough again. She had become a little tired of being just Gus Hackett's live-in lover, Gus Hackett's bit of posh, or plain Gus Hackett's bit.

That was exactly it. She was going to be able to be herself once more, and she would make sure she would stay that way. She would buy herself the most wonderful dress and everyone connected with it would be sworn to secrecy. She would buy equally marvellous shoes and they too would be bought in the highest secrecy, and finally she would go to the ball even if it meant wearing a mask if necessary for go she would, and she would look ravishingly beautiful and take the eye of everyone there – and then after the ball was over she would hide the dress and the shoes and every other accoutrement away, and resume her role of sitting sit smiling nicely at Gus across the kitchen table, but because of her success at the ball her legs would no longer be crossing and double-crossing themselves, mostly because she would have double-crossed Gus for once.

As Georgiana closed the door of her bedroom behind her she gave a small shudder of delight. The whole idea appealed to her as so utterly exciting, more than a little bit like being unfaithful, and even just a tiny bit like leaving someone too. She hadn't felt so exhilarated in months and she thanked the heavens above her that Gus hadn't bothered to write to her, not even a post card it, because finally it made everything so much easier.

2

There was no doubt about it, the Countess sighed, there was very little left of England now, just the monarchy and the National Trust.

She was gazing from the train on to the green strips of countryside that were flashing past the window. It was nice to see there was still the odd scarecrow, although why it was nice to see a scarecrow she really couldn't imagine, especially since so many people nowadays so closely resembled them. Still, it was nice - nice also to see that there were still villages and church towers, and horses grazing beside the railway track which was all very well but as the Countess finally decided not really quite enough.

Like everyone she knew that life behind the green façade of the countryside was changing and not always for the best. Only last week she had been informed by her housekeeper that the woman found it embarrassing to refer to the Countess by her title in front of her friends, and that she now she referred to the Countess as plain Mrs instead because otherwise her friends made constant fun of her. Time was when people had been only too happy to say they worked for a Countess, but nowadays it seemed it was a decided drawback, the Countess realised, it was something of which they were ashamed, something to hide from the neighbours as in the worst excesses of the Russian Revolution.

It was no good blaming any one person for the way things had gone, but one thing could be blamed, that there was no doubt. One thing alone had made the civilized world crumble, and that was communications. She had in fact written a letter to the local paper on the subject. If communications had not become what they were everything would have stayed as they had been which was undoubtedly much better than things were now. If people couldn't fly or drive or whatever to wherever they wished at a moment's notice, she reasoned, then the rape of Old England would never have happened. For rape it was with houses made of cardboard being built as in-fills in ancient towns and villages solely because people had driven to see them, and having taken a liking to what they had seen then decided to settle there, whereas in the past before the advent of so-called better communications, they wouldn't even have known about such historic places.

What good had this done anyone, the Countess asked herself. Just how little was plain to anyone with ears who had the misfortune to have to go to a post office to collect their just dues. There they would hear how unhappy everyone was, despite having pensions, health care, welfare benefits plus the free catering for every bodily need and function known to man, from elastic support hose to new tin hips. Yet all everyone did was stand around grumbling. In the old days none of them would have had pension. Quite a lot of them wouldn't even have had a post office, and as for new hips and tin legs, country people had made their own. It was absurd how life had changed so drastically, not that it would seemed to have changed for the better since now a letter took longer to be flown by aeroplane from London to York than it had taken by coach and horse – to the Countess that said everything that needed to be said about the current state of the country. Nor was it possible to send a telegram anymore. To the Countess' way of thinking there were many good and sound reasons why one should be able to telegram for something. Personally she had always used the telegram as the best means of escape from dire circumstances, when marooned and bored at some dreadful house party having all too frequently way sent herself a wire urging her immediate return home. But this was no longer possible due to the new Post Office regulations governing *communications*. The Countess found herself so suddenly piqued at this thought that she suddenly kicked the sole of Andrew Gillott's foot under the intervening table.

'You're snoring,' she told Andrew as he awoke with a vulgar grunt before sliding back down in his chair with his eyes once again shut tight.

Sleep and drink, sleep and drink, it seemed to the Countess that's all the wretched man did, either on the train like now or back at home. Looking at him fast asleep once more she found it hard to imagine and believe what a handsome man he had once been. Even Freddie, the Countess' late husband, had been a little jealous of Andrew Gillott's looks – and of course woman in London had made a play for him, with the sole exception of herself of course, because after Freddie had died she had remained resolutely unattached. Freddie had been everything to her as she had been everything to him, and the one thing she could honestly admit to was that, although she kept it as her best kept secret. Often she found herself remembering how they used to laugh and gossip together, and the moment she did she tried as instantly to forget it lest someone somehow managed to intrude on her thoughts and discover her weakness. She also came to realise that that sort of reminiscence was not at all constructive; that she really must put the past behind her and kick on. That was really the only way and the best way of managing things.

So there it was, and there was Andrew slowly sinking down again beneath the frightful plastic table so thoughtfully provided to make utterly certain of the passengers' discomfort. He hadn't even finished his first class breakfast, probably because he knew she would pick up the bill for it. The Countess's gaze returned instead to the countryside, like the past flashing by comfortably fast. She was going to meet her friend Lavinia for lunch. This was the reason she was wearing a hat. The last time Lavinia had won a hat and she hadn't, the Countess had felt underdressed, and she had gone away wondering if living in the country permanently as she did now - having let her London house for a fortune to who she considered to be some perfectly horrible foreigners – if her new life hadn't perhaps affected her fashion sense.

Life was too good for Lavinia that was her problem of course. Too much had gone her way. A wonderful lover late in life, holidays abroad on a yacht whenever she wanted, a vast dress allowance, and an account for flowers at Pulbrook and Gould that must sometimes make even her lover's straight hair curl. She also still had everything sent round from Fortnum and Mason's. It was incredible. Of all the people she knew, Lavinia still seemed to live in a way that no-one else did, just as if nothing had happened, as if London was still the London they had all known and loved. And she still spoke of everything in the same way too, as if nothing had changed.

'Lovely, lovely flowers,' said Lavinia, not looking at them, and leant her chin on her hand. 'What very lovely flowers. What will you have?'

They both stared at the menu. It was quite obviously going to be what the Countess always called bits and pieces food - an egg with a little sauce over it, one bean arranged decoratively, a stiffish sort of bean, or a mousse with sauce round the bottom that tasted like very pleasant green blancmange.

'I don't want any prawns that you have to pull to pieces because they make such an untidy mess,' said Lavinia firmly in reply to the waiter's suggestions. 'And don't read us out Today's Specialities - we all know they're Yesterday's Flops.'

'I shall have a little cold soup,' said the Countess. 'And you?' she asked Lavinia pointedly, because it was her way of making Lavinia understand that they would each be paying for themselves.

No sooner had Lavinia finished deciding than the Countess made a resolution. If Lavinia began by asking after her early tomatoes, she would leave. It was a put-down, and they both knew it. The moment Lavinia sat down she would ask the Countess about either her cabbages or her tomatoes, as if to ask after anything else would confuse the now country-based countess.

'I'm opening up the house this month,' she said, keeping safely away from vegetables and perhaps sensing the Countess's resolution. 'You must come and stay with Ozzie and me in late June when Lady 0's famous borders are at their best.'

'I'd love to,' agreed the Countess as they both tackle their fish mousses, served with tiny pieces of dried toast. 'But -' she paused, 'I am, for my sins, being coerce into helping with a private ball.'

Lavinia's eyes narrowed at the mention of a private ball. These were two words that Lavinia had not heard in many a long while. They rang around the Countess's head too, whirling round and round, dancing in and out of her imagination as prettily as a waltz tune when one strolled home from a dance.

'Oh, what a pity. The borders are really at their best in June.'

'I know,' said the Countess. 'You told me.'

Lavinia's purchase of someone else's famous house had become the bore of the century. The way she banged on about Lady Muzzeline Ottell's house and the garden that she had designed gave the impression the Lavinia had built and planned the whole thing herself, instead of just having a lengthy affair with the man who had simply bought it for her on a whim.

'But I am called upon, alas, to help out. There are to be three marquees, a small orchestra before dinner and a band afterwards, and we shall sit down to a dinner for two hundred before being joined by another two hundred. But the work, *the work*. I mean nowadays with the shortage of proper staff it calls for a committee, but alas there is none.'

'I suppose it's an old friend giving the ball?'

'No quite a new one, as a matter of fact, a new, young one. I like having younger friends nowadays. I find they do you good.'

'Yes, it is good for one,' Lavinia agreed, and then she stopped suddenly, hesitating before she said any more, and the Countess could see that she was wondering whether or not she should still be saying *one*, or whether in fact saying *one* was now a little *passé*. It wasn't a little passé for 'one' to be saying?

'Tell me - has one stopped saying one?' asked Lavinia finally, and really quite bravely.

'I'm very much afraid so,' said the Countess, giving her a gentle but patronizing smile that held more than a hint of correction in it. 'For quite some time now. One is not being said, although *you* and *me* and *us* and *you* are. *I* should still be avoided, of course, as much as possible. Especially in letters.'

Lavinia frowned, but only slightly.

'It's very difficult. Do you mean to say I have to write that *me* is very well, if one's to keep up to date now?'

'No, Just *we* or *everyone* will do nicely.'

'But supposing you're not a *we*. *We are very well* sounds a little grand for one person.'

'It's the principle of the thing, Lavinia. There's been far too much talking about oneself going on. Far too many people talking about one when all they mean is I, and covering up their wretched manners by so doing. Here in Wiltshire we are all working very hard to reverse the trend of modern egotism, and small beginnings can turn into large movements. Just look at the *Keep English Simple for the Simple Society*. It's booming, despite initial difficulties.'

'Are you trying to say I talk too much about myself?'

'No, you talk too much about oneself, and that's not good for any of us, believe me. We must make an effort to stamp out one and smother the I in conversations, and stick to you – as in *you look very well. You look very pretty. You look very good in green.* Much more pleasant, don't you think? Much more *au fait.*' '

Lavinia smiled suddenly.

'Do you really like me in green? I was a bit worried when we chose it. One is, aren't you? I mean we stand in fitting rooms with no-one to help us – you – one – and you worry and worry what we look like, until someone tells me - us. Now, in future, we shall be quite happy knowing I look good in green.'

Lavinia smoothed down her skirt, a look of relief spreading over her face as she realized that she had pretty successfully maneouvered her first real attempt at mastering the labyrinthine twists and turns of conversation seemingly now required by not using the first number in relation to oneself.

The Countess opened her bag and took out her box of Russian cigarettes. Lavinia strongly disapproved of smoking, but just at that moment what Lavinia liked or disliked was neither here nor there, since to the Countess most of what Lavinia thought anyway she considered utter tosh.

'So. There's to be a private ball and you are going to organize it?' Lavinia said, returning to the subject in hand.

'Certainly there is to be a private ball, and I am helping. There is no social secretary to hand, alas, but nowadays they get everything so wrong, I don't suppose it matters. So often the wrong type. Women who never quite made it ending up organizing other people's lives when they couldn't organize their own. How's your secretary?'

'Sacked. Found her reading Ozzie's love letters.'

'Yes. Yes I remember now. But why sack her?'

'Because they were private.'

'Private perhaps, but I seem to remember they weren't to you.'

'That's what made them more private. If they'd been to me, it wouldn't have mattered. No, if we split up, I shall need those.'

'Have you read them?'

'Of course. How else should I have known to sack the secretary?'

'Well, no, I don't suppose you would.'

'They're — how can I say?'

'Hot?'

'Red hot. Sizzling in fact. And I'm keeping every single one of them. In case he leaves me for someone else.'

'That's usually the reason someone leaves you.'

'No, it's not. You know it's not. Especially since we all got older, a great many people are being left for no-one at all. Personally I think that's worse. I mean it's so blatant. It looks as if someone would rather be with no-one rather than one, well - you. If Ozzie were to leave me for no-one that would be the end. Imagine the laughter. The mockery. One's friends. Our friends. I'd rather he left me for you.'

The Countess breathed two matching curls of smoke through two perfectly matching sculpted nostrils, and decided to continue the story of her ball rather than take up the issue of boring Ozzie.

'Anyway, we're not having a social secretary, even though the numbers can't be kept under five hundred. At least not as far as I can see, although we're telling her husband, poor dear Pemberton, that it is four hundred. Actually it doesn't matter because he won't notice, won't let him. On the night we'll fill him up with champagne so he won't be able to count how many, how much - and anyway men don't ever really notice those things, not at all, any more than they notice the flowers.'

'But you haven't told me - you still haven't said which exactly of your young friends is giving the dance.'

'The ball. No, I haven't, have I? How ridiculous. I wonder whether they're going to bring us coffee, or whether we'll have to scream for it? Waiter?'

'It must be a very dear young friend, or you wouldn't be helping her. You gave up all that sort of thing when you left London, remember? Or so you said.'

'Temporarily left London - '

'When you temporarily left London.'

'It's Jennifer.'

Lavinia's eyes narrowed once more.

'That plain fat girl who used to get on your nerves when Georgiana was doing her little Season thing?'

'No, not that Jennifer,' said the Countess hastily.

'Not the one that married - who was it? Yes. The Marchioness of Pemberton. Not Jennifer Pemberton surely - not the one who wears those dreadful home-made skirts and has no style at all and who you said you could never understand how she landed Pemberton and Georgiana your niece didn't? Not that one?'

The Countess drew on her cigarette holder, and then puffed out again.

'Oh very well yes all right - that one. That Jennifer,' she finally agreed. 'But she's changed a lot – a great deal, in fact. That's one of the reasons why she wants to give a ball, so that she can enlarge her social activities, show everyone how she's changed. A good thing, I'm sure. She feels she's fallen into a rut since having all her babies and she wants to stop being in a rut and get out more, out and about. This is a start, at least.'

'I never thought you'd be friendly with her. She doesn't sound your type at all. She doesn't sound the sort of young that you like.' Lavinia snapped the clip on her crocodile handbag so suddenly that the gold initials on it appeared to wobble uncertainly with the impact.

'She's not my type, but in Wiltshire one - we learn to get on with each other, as indeed we must; it's either that or spend the whole week in church doing the flowers. Anyway, the poor girl needs help. Doesn't get on with her mother at all ah and here's the coffee - at last. Anyway, her poor mother is a thorn in her side, a quite tasteless woman, a woman on whom no-one can rely, which is almost worse than being one on whom everyone relies. And by the way, did I tell you? I've been helping Jennifer with her hall at the Hall? We have been trying hard to introduce the more natural element. We have banished the dreadful African masks and the reproduction suits of armour, done away with the medieval look and returned to natural eighteenth-century simplicity. She's very pleased. We're both pleased in fact.'

'I know the sort of thing — Colefax and Fowler curtains, and I don't know what everywhere.'

'Not in a hall. Particularly not in a hall in The Hall. Far too drawing roomy. No - simplicity is the key note. Polished flags, a chest, of course, flowers in a big and casual display, fire burning, logs piled up, a club fender, you know the sort of thing.'

'I've got Colefax and Fowler in my hall,' Lavinia interrupted. 'And even Ozzie likes it.'

'I know, but your hall is not the hall of a Hall, yours is the hall of a small country house.'

'I know a great many halls that are smaller.'

'But I don't suppose the halls in the Halls are a small as your hall. There's a need for dressing up small halls. You were quite right to fuss it up with curtains.'

'I didn't fuss it up with curtains, you did. It was you who suggested them.'

'Well, I would. I knew that the fussy look would be most welcoming, but not as it happens in the hall of the Hall.'

'I think I had rather you had advised simplicity for me too. I think that sounds much more the thing. I think must come down and have a look at the hall of the Hall and see what simplicity looks like, even if my hall is smaller than the hall of the Hall.'

'But you can't come down, Lavinia dear, I've just told you - we're preparing for the dance. Busy, busy, busy.'

'I thought you said it was going to be a ball?'

'It is a ball.'

'I'm sure your young friend wouldn't mind in the slightest if I came down to her hall. She can't be that rushed off her feet, if you're helping her,' Lavinia reasoned.

'But she is. Babies and Nanny, and all those things, it takes it out of you.'

'Give me her telephone number, and I'll telephone her and ask her myself.'

'I haven't got it on me, I'm afraid.'

'Then, I'll ring you for it when you get back to Wiltshire. You'll have it in Wiltshire, surely?'

'I don't think - well, of course I'll have it in Wiltshire,' said the Countess, stubbing out her Sobranie Russian cigarette a little too savagely.

She suddenly knew exactly what Lavinia was up to. She was up to being asked down to the summer dance by Jennifer. The Countess knew how she'd do it, too. First a call to say how much she'd heard about her hall, that the hall of the Hall was such a success, and she was trying to remodel her own, and could she come and see it? And then once she was down, she'd make sure to befriend Jennifer in her most oleaginous way, and then she'd ask her across to see Lady 0's wretched borders, and before you knew where you were she'd probably be helping with everything, imposing her taste for dark colours and finger food, and Ozzie and she would be standing just behind Jennifer helping to receive the guests. That was how Lavinia worked and she was brilliant at it, the Countess had to concede. Her technique had to be admired because the moment Lavinia apprised herself of a situation she took it over, and in no uncertain manner. She would take over Jennifer, totally and completely, and before Jennifer could turn round everything would be dark blue and silver instead of cream and green as the Countess wanted it.

The Countess shuddered inwardly. There seemed so little in the way Lavinia and her getting Jennifer Pemberton's telephone number. Even now as Lavinia snapped her powder compact shut the Countess could see her working out how to get the Pembertons' telephone number from someone else, probably before the Countess even arrived back in Wiltshire. She gave Lavinia a sharp and piercing look which contained the proper amount of sudden, forgotten panic.

'Sorry - I'm going to be late for the chiropodist. You know how it is, toe people are always so terribly demanding, so must rush, so much to do before one - we totter back on to the evening train. Lovely to see you once more. We'll do this again, and very soon.'

She waved vaguely to the waiter for the bill, such was her desperation. She couldn't wait to leave the restaurant and hurry out to a telephone box so much so she was quite prepared to pay for lunch.

Once she was well out of sight of the restaurant she would ring round everyone she knew and tell then not, whatever happened, not to give Lavinia Jennifer's telephone number, not until she had caught the evening train back to Wiltshire, and could sort things out the way she wanted.

The telephone box was quite disgusting. It smelt dreadful, of old cigarettes and new foreigners, and the floor was littered with newspapers, so much so that it was impossible not to spear a piece on the end of one's shoes. She dialled her daughter Mary's number with difficulty, and with the end of her diary pencil, and as she did so the diary pencil's tip broke just as she heard Mary's maid answering, then as she tried to push the correct money into the coin box with a gloved hand, everything slipped out of her glove at once, and she was left dropping coins on the floor, abandoning her pencil to the filthy clutter of newspapers into which it had fallen, and falling back out of the booth as a man in a long robe person carrying a funny little stick with wisps on it banged on the glass so impatiently that the Countess wondered briefly if the wretched man might have mistaken the telephone box for the gentlemen's cloakroom.

She backed uncertainly down the road, eager to be away from the telephone box, because the smell of it was so overpowering, and tottered off towards a cab rank. She would have to go round to her daughter's house, and make a series of telephone calls. Mary wouldn't like it, but it just couldn't be helped, particularly since it was Mary's idea that the Countess should rent out her London house in the first place, and live off the income, instead of trying to organize people's debutantes into some sort of ludicrous little Season.

But Mary was not in. The Countess could tell from the way Juanita, her Portuguese maid, was looking sideways all the time, as if she was afraid of admitting her without permission from her mistress.

'Never mind, Juanita. I only wish to use the telephone, and to leave Lady Mary a message, that is all. Nothing complicated, but you may bring me a cup of afternoon tea with lemon, to the study, please.'

It was with some satisfaction, and not a little sense of comfort, that the Countess sank into her daughter's study chair. Wherever Mary was, maybe even hiding from her round the house somewhere, it really didn't matter. Here she was in a newly scented study with stephanotis scenting the lamps, sinking into a chair covered in a nice neutral blue, and lifting a hand to a nice clean receiver that didn't smell of cigarettes, and putting her feet on a large Persian rug and not on fifteen old editions of torn up Sun newspaper. She looked around her daughter's study in the lull that followed her seating herself. Not a great deal had changed since Mary had become Lady Stranragh following Lord Stranragh's divorce from her cousin Lady Georgiana Longbourough. Not a great deal, but something had.

The Countess soon realised what it was. There was a new severity about the house, whereas when her former lover Lucius had been about the place there had been a certain fey casualness, a sense of ordered disorder. Now that Stranragh occupied the house instead having sold his London house handsomely, it was not quite the same. There were fewer flowers and much stricter lines. In fact everything was much stricter. There were fewer books left carelessly about, fewer messages placed at angles in the corner of things, no invitations stuck into the edge of the looking glass, everything was much more sparse and tidy. It was probably better in some ways, but for a second as the Countess started to press the numbers on her daughter's telephone, she thought with fleeting affection of Andrew and his tiresome ways, of the Sporting Life always spread about the morning room floor, of things carelessly set down - old race cards, stud catalogues, membership badges. He might be many things, Andrew, but he was certainly not an old maid, which as the Countess had now to admit, married or not Mary and her spouse were fast in danger of becoming.

The Countess's immaculately lipsticked mouth had just begun to form the word *Hello* into the telephone receiver when her eyes caught sight of a letter written in a vaguely familiar hand. She leant forward and tugged at it. It was halfway out of its envelope anyway, so it wasn't really private.

Dear Mary, it started, in a not too sensational manner. But then the writing formed itself in front of her eyes as being quite certainly familiar, and the writing paper, with its rather over-blue colour and its picture of the Hall and its locations firmly engraved, even more familiar.

The Countess re-read from the top. It was a letter from Jennifer to Mary. So it had to be read, and quickly.

I wonder if you could help us out a little? the letter continued. *Your mother, the dear old darling, has offered her services to us for our forthcoming ball. Of course we are terribly grateful, of course we are; but the only trouble is that we already have an organizer, and whoops! Two organizers is going to mean mayhem. As you can imagine! Of course it was my fault, I should have discouraged her in the first place, but I didn't because I'm very naughty, and I never thought it all out properly. I wonder if you could 'deflect' her attentions. Perhaps say encourage her to visit some of those Italian gardens she likes so much?*

The letter fell from the Countess's hand on to the desk in front of her. She couldn't believe it, she just couldn't believe it. They had had a long conversation only the day before on the very subject of everything to do with the ball. Jennifer must have written to Mary directly after the tea they'd had together where they had agreed to everything including the colour theme of cream and green. Yet now here was Jennifer banging on to Mary of all people, on her horrid writing paper, all about the peach colours that she and Fulton had agreed upon, and about too many cooks spoiling the famous broth.

The Countess finished the brief but personally insulting letter, and then, having abandoned the idea of a telephone call to anyone even the Queen, she stuffed the letter back into the envelope. It seemed really rather pointless now, leaving Mary a message not to pass on Jennifer's telephone number to Lavinia, since she personally wanted nothing more to do with the silly little Marchioness who had the impertinence to refer to herself as a *dear old darling*.

She couldn't help but admit to a deep disappointment in Jennifer. What could she mean? Why on earth should she pursue her own path in this when they had already agreed to agree on everything? She might have changed her mind about the colour scheme, as she hinted in lengthy PS at the bottom of the letter, but even so, wholesale treachery was simply not on. In the past she had always thought of Jennifer as being the kind of person who might make a social gaffe, or be little embarrassing in her earnestness, but not a person capable, as this letter showed, of connivance. She would face it all the moment she arrived back in Wiltshire, but for the time being she would hide Mary's address book, and with it the Pembertons' telephone number.

She looked round the study for a hiding place. It was not that easy now that the wretched place was so tidy. Her eyes finally came to rest on the Chi-Chi china dog in the corner of the room. She happened to know that the head was removable, since once upon a time it had belonged to her husband Freddie. It had been given to Freddie on his marriage by an eccentric aunt who had never married, but had ended up being an expert on that kind of thing to everyone's intense surprise, because before that the family had always imagined her to be just a bit of a bore.

It must have been nerves, after all that business in the public telephone box, but just as she began to lift the head off the Chi-Chi dog, it slipped from her hands and fell, breaking into two halves so its curved mouth that had once seemed to put a tremendous grin on its face was now a decided grimace. The Countess stared at it. She had never liked the thing, or she wouldn't have let Freddie give it to Mary, but now she'd dropped it she nevertheless wished that she hadn't. Besides, it would really look most odd when Mary returned. It would raise all manner of questions that might remain just a little difficult to answer.

She thought quickly, for there was no time to think slowly. She would hide the Chi-Chi dog behind a particularly luxuriant ficus, and leave by the back way. Luckily Juanita still couldn't understand a word of English, let alone speak it, so Mary need never know her mother had been in the house at all. Having done so the Countess then let herself out through the garden doc and then, hastily making her way down the path and past the little studio room at the back, she emerged eventually into the street, where, most uncharacteristically, she leant herself up against a friendly wall and sighed with a sort of exhausted relief.

Her mission was accomplished. Mary would never find her address book now, at least not for years, and when she did Lavinia would have missed the chance to obtain the Pembertons' number from her. It had been a terrible adventure, but she had, after all, achieved a little of the something she had set out to do.

She started to walk in the direction of the Kings Road. It had been a little like something in the war. In fact by the time she reached her favourite bookshop she felt quite like Odette Churchill and other wartime heroines, and it would hardly surprise her if she received a letter mentioning that she was up for the Royal Victoria Order once she arrived home. Certainly the whole day had been torture. The telephone box, the Third World person banging on the window, and all this while knowing all the time how quickly Lavinia must have hastened back to her house to call everyone to try to obtain Jennifer's ex-directory telephone number. No, it had been a perilous adventure and she would reward herself with a first class ticket and a nice pot of tea and a teacake on the train journey home to Wiltshire.

It wasn't until the four twenty-four had pulled out the station and was heading towards the beginning of the first small patch of green that the Countess remembered what it was that she had forgotten.

She had forgotten Andrew.

3

The Honourable Mrs Andrew Gillott

In spite of her impending divorce from Andrew, the former Mrs Parker-Jones, mother of the Marchioness of Pemberton, still loved to see her handle written across the top of an invitation as it was here on the card now in her hand' although the longer she regarded it the more Clarissa was reminded just how bad her daughter's handwriting was. Jennifer's late father Aidan had used to describe it as being like barbed wire entanglements and staring at the hand Clarissa one could well see why. For a start Jennifer had never learned or perhaps more correctly had never bothered to join up her letters so her hand had subsequently remained childish all her life. Clarissa sighed when she remembered all the money Aidan and she had spent on sending her to Grantley Abbey, money that had all been sadly wasted. Still, she had at least Jennifer had bothered to ask her own mother to her dance. For nowadays that was at least something.

Sometimes Clarissa still wondered it was wise of her to have stayed on here in Wiltshire; with her divorce from Andrew pending, and with him now living with the Countess as her lodger, she wondered whether it might not have been better to have sold up and moved back to Kensington. On the other hand Kensington had changed so much and seemed to be developing in so many strange ways, with she considered more than a touch of the Eastern bazaar about it. And she was at least someone in Wiltshire rather than just anyone which is what she would doubtless be in Kensington. After all, here in the village where she lived in only the last three months she had been made honorary President of the Mixed Fruit and Veg Society in the village as well as the Secretary of the annual dance held at the Forthington Hotel in aid of the Cats and Dogs Local Relief Society. She also provided an annual village cup for the largest gourd which she gathered was something that everyone appreciated very much, and which was great fun to present as it meant wearing a hat and making a speech. Last year she had even succeeded in getting her picture in the local advertising magazine captioned *The Hon. Mrs Gillott and A Big Un,* which though just a little bit rural in humour, she found was nevertheless gratifying because after all it did show her willingness to allow her name to be used for local events.

Now that Andrew had gone to live with the Countess some thirty miles away, the house had become much tidier too and so too the garden. She had been able to open the garden to the public on two days in June the previous year, and although her house was really too far out of anyone's way to merit anyone coming, nevertheless it had been more than gratifying to know that although no one actually came round to see it, even had they come there would have been none of Andrew's cigarette butts tossed into the middle of the Albertine, or floating in the ornamental pond or stubbed careless out of the tops of the stone urns.

In short Clarissa missed Andrew not at all. He may have seemed like the way out of widowhood at one time, but after only a few months he had proved himself to be merely a way into madness. She knew she had done just the right thing in encouraging his trip to China before then changing the locks on all the doors while he was away. Of course Jennifer had been no help, but then as she well knew Jennifer never was. On the other hand Jennifer's butler Bloss had been an angel, quite willing to give advice day or night, besides volunteering the information that the Countess had agreed to take Andrew on as a sort of lodger when he returned from the Orient, although it transpired the plan was not to have Andrew living in the main house. Apparently he was allowed in only during the day time, before having to return to his dog kennel at the top of her drive, as the gate lodge was referred to by the Countess.

Nightly he was to be allowed back in again to dine, and then on Saturdays and Sundays he was to be allowed in again for the joint watching of the racing on television and for Sunday lunch.

'He's become her walker,' Jennifer's butler had told Clarissa. 'Although perhaps it might be more accurate to describe him as being more of her staggerer.'

Even so, Clarissa had found sending Andrew away just slightly galling to have sent Andrew off and gone to all the expense of setting divorce proceedings in motion, only to find that the Countess had found a new use for him. If she'd only thought about it at the time, Clarissa imagined she could perhaps have followed the same kind of practice, perhaps housing the wayward Andrew in a caravan to sleep at night, since she lacked a proper gate lodge. She was worried that that the Countess in finding a new use for Andrew might be rather like a girlfriend to whom one gives a dress that one had hardly worn and never liked, only to see the said girl-friend her reappearing in it and making it look quite different – or maybe even giving away a painting to find out all too late it was in fact a minor masterpiece of some kind or other. It was most definitely something along those lines, Clarissa decided. After all and come to think of it she could have used Andrew as a walker just as well as the Countess.

Just lately, and she didn't know why, Clarissa had had the feeling that it was all Jennifer's fault that she had found Andrew so irritating. After all, if Jennifer had been more of a good daughter to her, if she had been more the cosy kind of girl that other mothers seemed to have for daughters, then she would have thought of it for Clarissa, instead of just sitting around in her dreadful old skirt covered in dog hairs doing tapestry and letting Pemberton have his own way in the garden. But there was nothing to be done now, Clarissa realised. Andrew was gone, and she was left with having to divorce him on the usual grounds of gross incompatibility.

She picked up the invitation again from her mantelpiece, and once more regarded the name at the top - *The Honourable Mrs Andrew Gillott*. She decided that because it looked so good she would definitely keep her handle on after the divorce. She would in fact insist on custody of it, seeing little or no reason for its return to her wretch of a husband, then she picked up the latest edition of Vogue off her coffee table and turned to the sections for the older and more sophisticated woman. It was some months before the ball so she had plenty of time to choose herself a dress. She considered a tangerine *peau de soie* with a bustle effect at the back, then an Alma Tadage evening gown with the new rising front, deciding that she was a little too mature for the Kleinstein Erstwhile collection with hand-embroidered shelling around navel, but certainly not too advanced in her years for some of the delicious confections illustrated in her magazine.

While she made her short list of selections she rang the little bell she kept on marble coffee table for her Mrs Divine her housekeeper, who as Clarissa liked to think of privately was *everything-but* -but who since she came in to clean for her three times a week Clarissa had decided to she preferred to think of her as a housekeeper rather than a simple cleaning woman. Mrs Divine seemed to sense her elevation and had taken to bringing Clarissa her morning coffee on a tray set with a cloth and a bowl of sugar with tongs, even though Clarissa didn't take sugar.

Mrs Divine always changed into bedroom slippers do the cleaning, a habit of which Clarissa disapproved, thinking that if someone came to call Mrs Divine could hardly be taken for a member of her 'staff' if found to be opening the door in a pair of M&S slippers. Clarissa had actually bought her a pair indoor shoes for a Christmas present as a hint as to what she should and could be wearing when she was in the house, but Mrs Divine having made the right sort of noises about them, then announced that she was keeping them for church on Sunday because they pinched, and went straight back to her pair of seriously scuffed and grubby *faux* fur lined bedroom slippers. Clarissa knew that Mrs Divine wasn't much, but had come to realise she was about all you could hope for in the country in the way of domestic help. Once summoned to make the coffee she would now take ages before reappearing with the tray, a tray that Clarissa herself would have carefully laid shortly before Mrs Divine had arrived for work. Mrs Divine would then reappear with it looking as if she had done all the work herself, having usually succeeded in spilling coffee all over on the hand-worked tray cloth that Jennifer had given her for Christmas, Jennifer having pretended that she'd embroidered it herself when as Clarissa well knew Elliott had had to finish it for her.

As she waited for her coffee Clarissa now picked up the latest edition of *Country Life* in order to study the property market. Life in the country was becoming almost alarmingly fashionable, as a consequence of which she had been delaying her decisions as to whether or not to return to Kensington. Ideally of course she would like to move nearer her daughter and cash in on the cachet of her being a Marchioness, and the owner of the Hall, a thousand acres and a butler. Clarissa envied her Bloss most of all, even more than the Hall and all the acres. For his part Bloss had promised to notify her the moment a suitable property came up which was near the Hall. Because of his potion Bloss very much had an ear to the ground and heard that of things long before they reached the ears of others, particularly the breed Bloss thought the most wretched of all – the estate agents. Bloss and his cohorts waiting at table, listening at hatches, lurking outside smoking room doors were apparently responsible for more house sales than any of the smart estate agents that people in the country used.

Mrs Divine having served the coffee shuffled off once again into the depths of the house, leaving Clarissa to sign and offer up a thankful prayer for all the help and invaluable advice proffered to her by her daughter's butler. At that moment Bloss was the one star in a rather dark sky.

The butler in question examined the end of his silver cloth and turned it around to find a fresh and clean spot. He had been seduced into buying a new sort of polish that promised to do many things to the silver at the Hall, but having tried it out he had discovered it seemed to not to be any better than his previous cleanser. This was irritating but hardly surprising since the bottle had arrived from some obscure trading estate in North Yorkshire, yet this was entirely Bloss' own fault since he had become incurably attracted to sending off to such places trading estates for domestic items that promised more than they could actually fulfil, and as a consequence since they were always as over-priced as they were ineffectual, he found himself being forced into being more imaginative with the household accounts than he would ideally have wished to be. Not that his lordship paid the slightest heed to such matters, but her ladyship unfortunately was most persistent. Nanny and he had to be able to eke out their household items as long as possible, Nanny even having to measure out the soap powder into a large glass jar in front of her ladyship, because Nanny was not allowed to do more than one wash a day for the nursery floor, and if she had any personal items that needed to be washed Nanny was instructed to borrow from Bloss's personal packet of soap flakes for very fine things. Not that Bloss minded really - he always put certain cleaning items down under staff refreshment/expenses which was one item her ladyship found very difficult to calculate, namely quite how many cups of tea or coffee a week they were all in need of consuming, particularly if there were others people working somewhere on the fabric of the building which they generally were.

For the umpteenth time that year Bloss thanks the heavens above for the constantly decaying state of the building. Every stone that needed re-pointing, each chimney that needed resetting, each window that needed rehanging all meant more entries in the staff refreshments/expenses column which in turn finally meant more soap flakes for himself and Nanny. Now he found himself wondering if the new and sadly useless silver polish could be under tea bags/various/workmen or whether it might be more sensible to hide it away under plant fertiliser/potted/indoor or in a small column set aside for extra postage/returns, a column often useful when guests were said to have left various items behind them in their wake which Bloss had been required to send on after them. Bloss found this a most useful column as it was something of which her ladyship was quite unable to keep track, always provided he did not exaggerate such costs. But then of course often when she did try to instigate one of her in-depth enquiries Bloss would only have to clear his throat and gaze out pointedly over the garden for her ladyship to colour and cease to enquire further as to what had been left behind and by whom. Happily his lordship was as generous as her ladyship was mean. He was profligate by comparison. The nightcaps for instance he insisted on sharing with Bloss were more than generous.

'Come on, Bloss – what the devil's wrong with your pouring arm?' he would complain. 'We're not at one of her ladyship's damn' social teas now, you know.'

This was in reference to the tea parties Clarissa had just instigated which Pemberton found appalling. Being expected to stand around having to listen to a whole lot of hens talk about nothing whatsoever was not Pemberton's idea of how to spend an afternoon. Tea to him as he was always telling Bloss was a meal that a man had either in the stable with the lads pulling his riding boots off after hunting, or when he was in the bath, or when he was behind his newspaper at his club. The very idea of asking in a whole lot of people to eat bridge rolls and sip cups of china tea was horrendous. Bloss however privately disagreed. The fact that her ladyship wanted to entertain at all was to him a miracle and one he considered needed to be encouraged because not only did it help with the creative side of his accountancy but it also helped in other ways. It helped him to keep track of all that was happening in the village. Most of all it helped to distract her ladyship from the fact that his lordship was not only having what was called nowadays what he understood to be called a hot thing with Lady Tizzy but had also spawned not only one but soon to be two children with her, which while admittedly fertile and manly, Bloss considered might be said to be going a bit too far.

Bloss had to keep control of every event. It was one of the duties of a butler. The principal event of which he had to keep control was that her ladyship must not find out let alone even vaguely suspect that the child or soon to be children of Flint House were anything to do with his lordship's aristocratic predisposition to beget offspring born on the wrong side of the blanket. There must, after all, be no divorce. Bloss was a strict Anglican, and even if the rest of the Church might be giving way at every turn, he was not about to do the same. He did not believe in divorce, and never would, not even for gain.

He started to pull off his silver-cleaning gloves, and then changed his mind. There was still the all-important muffin dish to do. He picked it up, and happily started to rub the new polish into it. Bloss was happy with his lot, so happy in fact that he decided he wouldn't swop places with the King of Mesopotamia - if such a person still existed – for anything, and as he was delighting in his situation the telephone rang in the snug where he sat. Bloss waited, considering the ring. He had mastered the art of answering the telephone many years ago, knowing that if it rang briefly it was generally trade, while if it rang long and insistently it was usually a member of the family who was being currently avoided.

This time the long ring revealed the caller to be her ladyship's mother which was a call Bloss was more than happy to fence. He knew she had a soft spot for him and that she listened to everything he had to tell her which at this moment on time Bloss knew was more important than ever. He knew he must encouraged Mrs Parker-Jones to think that very soon, in fat if what he had heard was true *any-moment-now* - there would be a small Georgian gem of a house for sale very near them here at the Hall. It was vital that he kept her dangling on the end of this particular line for otherwise if she lost heart she would return to Kensington, cease to annoy her ladyship, and as a consequence her ladyship might start to notice that his lordship was not always where he had told her he was going to be. No, no – he well knew that the mother, the social teas, the ball – which had of course been his quiet suggestion - they were all essentials to the continuance of a peaceful life in rural Wiltshire. Everyone could go on doing exactly as they wished as long as Mrs Parker-Jones remained there to irk them all.

Really, when Bloss thought about it which he did great deal, particularly after dealing with the likes of Mrs Parker-Jones on the blower, the Church of England really owed him. Persons such as he should be style Bishop-Butlers because in their own they helped greatly to keep everyone on the straight and narrow if not entirely on the paths of righteousness. It was probably entirely due to people like him, he had long ago decided that the Daily Telegraph still had decent sales, and that this little sceptre isle set in a silver sea still had its own identity and was not just one of America's many small off shore islands.

When he switched his concentration back to the telephone he heard Mrs Parker-Jones was still going on about her need for a new house. Bloss made soothing noises while sipping his pre lunchtime sherry. He then told her he had heard from a friend also in service that Moss House at Little Kingbury had a quite unnaturally old owner who might well be booking her passage to Florida in the very near future. He would pursue it, he told Mrs Parker-Jones. There was no guarantee of course, he reminded her, but things were looking promising he assured her as he replaced the receiver, the only odd thing about this piece of information being that for once it was true.

Bloss smiled happily. If he managed to move Mrs Parker-Jones as near as Little Kingbury, her ladyship would be driven up the wall and down again and regularly so, so much so in fact that Bloss knew there wouldn't be a second in the day when she would have the time to turn round and wonder where his lordship was, or to what he was up. He must pursue the matter with all speed. Meanwhile he remembered that the ball and all that it entailed was currently being discussed behind the drawing room doors, in which case he downed tools and hurried upstairs to make the lunchtime drinks but more importantly to stay abreast with all the news.

Jennifer was seated in the window with her embroidery. She liked embroidery in the drawing room, and tapestry for outside. Opposite her was Fulton, and next to him was the Countess. When he entered and saw the set up Bloss stiffened. He had let neither Fulton nor the Countess into the house so he knew they must have come up the drive and round the back to the garden without his knowing it. It was all too aggravating, particularly since from the ominous silence it was obvious something must be in the balance, something that he would have to strain to catch up with.

'There's no need to ask anyone if they want anything, Bloss,' said Jennifer sharply when she saw Bloss hovering. 'We've got lemonade.'

'There's every need,' said the Countess. 'Bring me a gin and tonic with two pieces of ice and one piece of lemon and at once please, Bloss.'

Bloss went to the drinks table. The Countess could always be relied upon in every exigency. He would take his time over the making of the drinks, and that way as soon as conversation was resumed all - as some would say – all would be revealed.

'Well,' said the Countess, relieved to see Bloss already at work slicing a lemon. 'There seems to be a somewhat unfortunate misunderstanding. And personally speaking I think I can solve it. Thank you, Bloss.'

She took a large sip of the extremely satisfying drink that had been handed to her, before she allowed herself to continue with the enthralling of Fulton and Jennifer.

'I think I should leave you two to cope with all the details, and generally now get on with it.'

Jennifer didn't like the way the Countess had just said they should just get on with it, considering it to have a slightly spiteful ring, as if the ball had suddenly turned into a hole-and-corner affair instead of being that rarity of all rarities, a perfectly private dance in aid of nothing more than pleasure.

'Then of course, if there is a problem,' the Countess continued, in precisely the same tone. 'By that I mean if anything goes wrong - which I am quite sure of course it will not- I shall always be on hand. Personally I think Fulton's idea to go for the peach tones is charming, really charming. It will give a wonderfully *passé* feel to everything. Positively Proustian in fact.'

Jennifer had no idea at all what Proustian could possibly mean and although not being bothered enough to enquire meant, she thought it couldn't be anything very complimentary from the way that Fulton visibly stiffened, and having removed a very small piece of cotton from his immaculate trousers, had risen to go and drop the offending piece of lint in the papier mâché Victorian wastepaper basket with a look of deep intensity. She further gathered the term *Proustian* must have been deeply insulting from the way Fulton's backside was remaining so tightly clenched, his cheeks looking less and less like a backside and more like two very new and overlarge tennis balls.

'Perhaps not peach,' Jennifer wondered in a low voice suddenly. 'Perhaps people would prefer the cream and green - perhaps it is more fresh and more country after all?'

She dropped her head quickly back to her embroidery which consisted mostly of tiny little leaves and flowers, so small she had to put on special glasses to see them. She wished she'd never started the wretched tray cloth for the Lord Roberts Workshop guest tray in the mauve and blue bedroom. She would have preferred to do it in drawn thread work, but Elliott had put her off. That was another thing that was someone else's fault. It seemed so much was.

'I have just had Twinks prepare three peach boards in varying shades,' Fulton said with audible edge. 'But if you *really* prefer cream and green, I'll leave straight away before she gets too far in.'

Jennifer looked hopelessly across at the Countess. Fulton was practically by the door, and still the Countess had not pronounced.

'We'll have to talk about which cream and which green, though,' Fulton called from the door. 'Or will you leave that to me?'

'Yes, yes of course,' Jennifer assured him. 'All left to you, Fulton, and no more to be said.'

'I suppose that's something,' said Fulton addressing the vast arrangement of cabbage flowers mixed with stuffed percherons, weeds and hosta heads that was dominating the hall after he had closed the library door behind him and stalked testily out into the fine May morning.

'Twinks will be furious,' he told his beloved metallic bronze Golf as he started her up. 'Simply furious. But then, that is always the way with the Hall. We at Flint House rescue them time and again, and they pour scorn on our least idea.'

Elliott was ready and waiting by the door as soon as Fulton entered, hanging his keys on the specially antique hook that was fixed under the stairs.

'So?' he asked as always.

'So,' Fulton answered as always, having calmed himself by watching his keys swinging to a standstill for a few seconds. 'She's leaving it all to us.'

'That at least is something.'

'But she no longer favours the peach. She wants to go for cream and green.'

There was an appallingly long silence during which Elliott's not very large jaw dropped before resuming its correct physical position.

'I don't *believe* it.'

'*Neither* - did I.'

'But the food? Does she realize what this means? Molly and I have already gone through fruit dyes for the *cèpes*. Molly had just reached a really perceptible peach tone, which is quite something on a *cèpe*, I can tell you.'

'Quite.'

'Did you swear when she told you?'

'No.'

'Did you curse?'

'No.'

'In that case better have a coffee and do it now.'

'I think I will.'

'You do that,' Elliott said, and hurried off to the kitchen to make the coffee.

'I'll have to go and break it to Twinks. She's even now out in the stable staining the boards with three entirely differing and very subtle péche variations,' Fulton called.

'Poor, poor Fulton,' Elliott told the coffee machine. 'The work. And what shall I tell Molly? She's done at least a dozen *cèpes*, and we all know what they cost.'

A hideous thought occurred to him. He hadn't told Jennifer anything about the *cèpes*, in which case the cost would all be down to him. He wouldn't tell Fulton about it. He'd just have to make sure he saved from the housekeeping somehow, and make it up that way - although trying to save from the house-keeping money had become somewhat of a joke, what with Lady Tizzy eating more than a horse in training, and Nanny and Victoria having good healthy appetites, likewise himself and Fulton, not to mention Twinks.

Poor Twinks, he thought. Fulton had scooped her up out of a nowhere place on the Great West Road where she'd been recovering from a terribly broken heart, and a man who had left her in favour of a woman who would marry him, which Twinks could never possibly afford to do having only a very small income from an equally small great aunt who had died just in time to leave her enough to be going on with, but not quite enough to be able to afford to keep a husband who might go off with half of it. Now she was living over the stables at Flint House, busy making papier mâché trays and wastepaper baskets in the Victorian manner, as well as helping them both out with their reproductions of lightly painted early nineteenth-century Scandinavian furniture.

Elliott laid the coffee out on one of Twinks's trays that had not been a big seller. It was one of her less good ideas, being of a classical nature and involving nudity, which made putting cups and saucers on it seem rather odd, which was probably why it had not sold, even as a magazine offer.

He was just going into the hall, past the old bronze bust, and into the drawing room when he heard a scream from upstairs. He paid not the slightest attention, but continued on his way to their own special window where they liked to sit. Lady Tizzy screaming had become just another sound of the countryside. No more worrying than the cry of a small animal in the night as the owl swooped, or the sudden lurch of the hay lorries against their old wall which unfortunately ran by a small road which led to the main highway. Elliott continued to pour the coffee as yet another scream floated downstairs to force itself to his attention. Then he went to the door.

'What now?' he called up. 'What now?'

Last week just such a scream had heralded the dreaded news that the ITV had announced its final re-run of *Pogley and the Pegtops*. Now, doubtless, Bede, her favourite character in *The Inside Outers* had contracted something dreadful and terminal.

Elliott looked up. High above him at the top of the stairs, draped dramatically over the banisters, was Lady Tizzy, and she was upset all right. Her long hair tumbling in its vast array of coiffured and tortured curls, her large poitrine shaking with emotion, she was, Elliott had to admit, a magnificent sight, if – Elliott thought – if this was the kind of sight that rocked your particular boat.

'Elliott, Elliott, Elliott -'

'Yes, dear?.'

'Something terrible has happened.'

'Don't tell me.'

'I've got to —'

Elliott thought for a second.

'Bede's been taken hostage again?'

'Bede's fine. As a matter of fact, he's just got out of hospital – you know - after having had his whatever reversed.'

'Poor Bede -'

'But, Elliott —'

'Yes?'

'I'm afraid you'll have to borrow Mr Burrows's four wheel drive to get across the fields on that short cut to the hospital what you worked out - 'cos I've only started!'

'Very well,' Elliott said, anxious to keep as much of his decorum as possible, particularly since he was never quite sure what *only starting* in instances such as these actually involved. 'Fine.'

He turned as Fulton came back into the house.

'It seems she has started,' he said calmly. 'Hence the screeching.'

'What?' asked Fulton. 'How do you mean?'

'I mean – she has started,' Elliott replied. 'As in *starting*. That's what I mean.''

'You mean she's started?'

'Yes I do! I do! I do!' Elliott suddenly screeched. 'Now what are we supposed to do?'

'If she's actually started,' said Fulton, inhaling suddenly and deeply while pointing up stairs vaguely in the direction of his wife. 'I just hoped with all my heart she has not *started* all over the very carefully chosen nineteenth-century and extremely rare kelim that Twinks gave us as a stable-warming present. Because if she *has* -'

'I'm determined on calm,' said Elliott, trying to draw breath. 'I'm determined on it.'

'Look,' Fulton said, pouring himself a quick drink. 'There is no need to panic. We've worked out an emergency route - all we have to do is cut through the three bridleways that we have spent all winter opening up, and we're there. We've been through all this before. Birth is perfectly natural. Everyone does it. Goes through it. It's quite common place. The suitcase is packed so there is nothing to do but get on with the show, and see to the kelim when we get back.'

'So why are you just *standing* there? What are you doing?'

'I am simply gathering my resources,' Fulton replied. 'Marshalling my strengths. Doing my best not to cry.'

'Don't be such an infernal *pansy!*' Elliott screeched and there was no other word for it. 'We have to get her to the hospital!'

Somehow – although afterwards neither of them remembered quite how, they managed the journey. In the purloined four wheel drive they trucked it across country via their emergency route, leaving Nanny and Twinks in charge of the house. It was no easy journey and for every afterwards Elliott could never see a pregnant woman without hearing Lady Tizzy's screams as they encountered the first bedstead thrown across their carefully worked out cross-country route which Fulton had insisted upon.

'Now what!' Lady Tizzy screamed. 'Now what!'

It was just as if they were responsible for the wretched bedsteads someone had maliciously or otherwise thrown across the bridleway that was meant to be kept accessible to everyone, especially those cutting it short across country to the hospital.

And then again -

'Now what!' as they were forced to make another and found themselves peering over a gate with a huge enormous bull and five randy-looking cows the other side of it.

And again –

'Now what!'

As they drove through barbed wire entanglements and burst through overgrown hawthorn hedges, while all the time Lady Tizzy's bump seemed to be sliding further and further down to her knees until not even Fulton could look at her without getting contractions of his own. In the end after their vehicle had become seemingly and hopelessly mud bound in what had once been a tributary of some river or other, seeing that the parcel was just about to be delivered Fulton and Elliott had both seized Lady Tizzy by the elbows and run with her, her legs sort of paddling over the ground, until they reached the hospital grounds where they forgot all decorum and burst in through an entrance marked Strictly Private, at which point they all three began to scream and yell.

'Being so near you seem to have left it a little late,' said the gynaecologist, when he finally saw fit to arrive.

Fulton shut his eyes and prayed, hoping that this time round the said gynaecologist he would really get going and really earn his fee, which is more than he had done on the last occasion when he stayed behind at home to deliver one of his prize cattle instead.

'Shouldn't be long now,' he later he beamed at Fulton. 'If last time is anything to go by, you'll have a nice little bundle to cuddle before you can say spoon.'

Fulton shuddered.

'A nice little bundle is about what he costs,' he said, going to the refreshments machine and pouring himself a small cup of lukewarm water, because at times of stress he could never hold tea in a paper cup without burning himself.

Fulton and Elliott walked up and down. It was just like last time, only a tiny bit less so. Elliott was right. They were calmer, despite having to abandon the four wheel drive in a riverbed just beside a mattress that had not only seen better days, but quite obviously some worse ones too.

'Hel--oooo?'

They stood to attention in a way they normally one did after the Queen's speech on Christmas Day. The gynaecologist beckoned them to the door of the delivery room.

'Afraid there's a little bit of a hitch.'

Fulton's eyes narrowed. She might be his wife, but he loved Lady Tizzy, and so did Elliott.

'What kind of a hitch?' asked Fulton coldly, his backside contracting in much the same manner as when he had lost the battle over the peach tones earlier that morning.

'It seems you've got a beautiful baby,' said the gynaecologist.

Fulton and Elliott looked at each other delightedly.

'And it's a boy,' he added.

They both stepped towards the masked figure, who had hastily pulled his mask up again when he saw their faces.

'What!'

'Yes,' the gynaecologist went on, speaking through his mask. 'A fine baby boy.'

'What!'

'A fine big, bouncing baby boy born at precisely three minutes after one.'

'A fine big bouncing baby boo-boo, you mean!'

'You said,' Elliott breathed out, his nostrils flaring as they always did when he was most especially indignant. 'You said that it was a girl. A girl. A girl. A girl.'

'Well I'm afraid it's a boy, a boy, a boy.'

'It can't be!' said Fulton.

'No, it can't be, ' Fulton agreed.

'We've re-done the Duc de Berry in very fine peach!'

'I don't suppose he'll mind,' said the gynaecologist, dashing back in answer to a summons into the delivery room. 'People put boys in anything nowadays!'

'We'll sue him,' hissed Fulton to Elliott as they walked up and down the corridor. 'How many scans did we pay for? Tests, tests, and more tests. The man should stick to prize cattle and pigs - he's nothing but a fraud with a buttonhole. Carnations indeed. He wouldn't know a baby girl from a baby boy.'

'I wonder what one sues under?' Elliott mused. 'Certainly not palimony.'

'The daisy garden, the marguerites. We can't call a boy Daisy-Marguerita. Dozy. We could change it to Dozy? Or Desi, like Desi Arnez?'

'Desi was Mexican. They don't mind what they're called. Besides, the daisies will still be there, won't they? What will Nanny say? Oh, what will Nanny say?'

Elliott sat down suddenly, and put his head in his hands. Fulton sat down beside him. 'I don't like boys. I never have done.' They both stared at the floor.

'Hel----ooooo?'

They both looked up again and saw the masked figure standing once more outside the delivery room.

'I do wish he'd stop saying that,' sighed Fulton.

'Mr Benedict-Montrose-Cavanagh?'

'Pretty near.'

'More good news.' He lowered his mask and beamed. 'A little girl.'

'What?'

'Thank heavens'

'You mean you got it wrong - '

'I mean Lady Tizpots has surprised us. One of each – a pigeon pair in one go. Bravo.'

'One of each of what?' Fulton faltered.

'One of each sex, both beautiful. Here's nursey. You can hold one, and you can hold the other.'

Alas Elliott couldn't. He'd fainted.

4

In the ladies' rest room, now with a newly painted sign declaring it to be a Persons' Waiting Room, Georgiana was pretending to read a very old book about Moliere. Given that she had really rather long shapely legs, and was not yet of an age when she could be called upon to knit or sew on a train journey, she had found that reading a really rather old book with a nice marbled cover, particularly on the return journey discouraged old sillies in first class from playing footsie with her all the way to Penbury.

Every time the waiting room door opened, which was all too frequently, Georgiana found herself looking up from her very old book on Moliere, and a part of her sinking right to the bottom of her heart if not to her feet as she imagined that any minute now Gus would appear, hoick her out of the waiting room, tear up her first class return ticket, and frog-march her all the way back to Longborough. She dare not even yet congratulate herself on escaping from Longborough, not until the train really did draw out of the station with her on board. In a way it was amazing that she had got so far. Her excuse had been that she had been called up to see the old family lawyer, and that she must go and see him, because it was all to do with making Longborough over to George. Naturally no one at the house had discouraged her in this idea. In the event of her premature and quite untimely death, Gus would be only too happy for their bastard son to inherit, and so would Nan and Nanny. So they had let her pack her suitcase and go without a murmur, and Georgiana had taken care to hide all the relevant papers from them in her absence. Even so, up and down went her head as each new arrival burst noisily through the waiting room door – expecting each and every person for just one ghastly second to be Gus.

The train arrived with the usual sense of drama that a train arrival brings, umbrellas attached to their owners, owners attached to over-labelled suitcases, suitcases being removed over heads, heads ducking out of the way of umbrellas - all sorts of activity what with Penbury being a country station. There were choruses of people beseeching others to wait as bicycle owners tried to load their precious old basketed jalopies into the luggage van in the short three minutes that the station master had deemed was time enough for the train to stop. His flag waved menacingly as the last wheel disappeared on board, and the last train door slammed uncertainly behind a latecomer, and finally the train drew out.

Georgiana threw her old crocodile dressing case up into the luggage rack and collapsed on to her seat, free at last. Soon the countryside would imperceptibly start to recede and slowly creeping towards the train would come first stockbroker villages, emptying their tired but perfectly suited occupants into the first class carriages, the suburbia where the waiting platform occupants fronting their stations would display a sartorial preoccupation with anoraks and rainwear, and finally would at last arrive past blackened city buildings and peeling billboards, its deceleration informing Georgiana that very soon her feet would be walking on pavements, and her life would once again be that of a girl about town rather than a prematurely retired young woman in the country.

She found it wonderful standing in the taxi queue to be able to see real people again - executive women in smart suits and men with properly furled umbrellas, not like Berridge where all the men hurried along smoking furtively while staring at the ground, and all the women shuffled by clutching small telescopic umbrellas in dingy colours and staring at nothing at all, as if there was nothing to look at, as if they were all alone in the world and not passing by anyone or anything at all.

She climbed gracefully into a taxi, knowing that at least half a dozen pairs of male eyes were eyeing her long slender legs and her high-heeled shoes, shoes that had had to be dusted when they were removed from their shelf. She sat back and stared with fascination at the neat parks and the late spring flowers all planted out so neatly and in such wonderfully bright colours then at the horses and ponies walking smartly out with their uncertain but perfectly attired riders, and at the horse guards sit-trotting through the sandy rides, and at the busy occupants of other taxis. Finally she gave one enormous intake of breath then exhaled just as boisterously. How much she had missed it all!

She shopped as someone hungry would shop, incessantly producing her cheque book and her credit cards, and she accumulated bags and boxes in such a short space of time she might have been a food addict cramming her mouth with so much that an onlooker could have been forgiven for believing her intake was so fast it would choke her, yet still she shopped on - always for clothes, or shoes, or little items that people in the country didn't even know were necessary to pretty girls, the exactly right shade of stockings, the exactly new scent. It was delicious, and lunching in glorious solitude, not having to listen to Nan and Nanny admiring the way George was dropping bits out of his mouth, or throwing his mug on the floor, was such a luxury it might have been a celestial gift. Even so she could hardly wait to eat her small plate of delicately arranged pasta, or drink her small glass of rough-tasting red wine, before she hurried on, to yet more shops.

Finally but not because she was tired or satiated, she stopped. She had to because the shops were shutting, the sales ladies throwing cotton drapes over the counters, or multi-locking the small doors that fronted the fashionable streets, leaving only curiously wigged models in their narrow windows to tell of their trade through the evening and the midnight hours, until dawn came and with it the milkmen, and the cats, and the early morning taxis returning home from night shifts.

Georgiana walked slowly to the hotel in which she had chosen to stay. It was small, and newly fashionable and she had read about it in Berridge car park in one of her glossy magazines. She walked in, her arms full, her head filled with the champagne of extravagance, the lightweight devil-may-care feeling that only spending money on yourself can bring. With each purchase can no agonies of uncertainty as to whether the recipient might like it, no self-doubts about taste, for she knew she had bad taste because Gus so often remarked that she had. So what if she had displayed her inimitable conservative but vulgar preferences? Only she was aware of it, and only she would know of it when she opened the boxes and the fashionably named shopping bag There would be no-one to mock her, no-one to hold her up to ridicule.

But she still hadn't even approached the business of buying herself a dress for the ball. She laid out the parcels on the bed, over-tipped the bell-boy because he looked her up and down so appreciatively, and then examined her room. The hotel, right from its entrance, had been everything she had hoped, and now so too were her bedroom at bathroom. The hotel as she had stepped into it from the fading sunlight outside had straight away declared itself to be not the sort of place to which married folk would come. It was just a little too dark, just a little too over-decorated, too expensive, too not-proper, and too filled with the newly rich to be designed for anything other than business or love, or quite probably both. None of the other clientele were anything except underdressed - none of the men wore suits, they just wore jackets – these were jackets of leather and suede, and open necked shirts that revealed perfectly and expensively acquired sun tans. At the small, discreet desk where she carefully wrote her name in the visitors' book as Mrs G. Hackett rather than Lady Georgiana Longborough and her place of residence as simply Wiltshire, there were no people in old school ties or pinstriped suits to remind her of the country, and of the people who hurried down to their estates to bray at each other at point-to-point meetings or shooting weekends.

In short the moment Georgiana had walked into the hotel she absolutely knew that she had booked herself to stay in her personal idea of heaven.

Once she had unpacked she lay across her small double bed in a silken peignoir, and gazed at the erotic prints around her with sensuous satisfaction. The walls were so dark they might have been lined with blackout material, the curtains wonderfully overlaid with gold, and her bed a riot of swirls and loops and yet more gold braid. She sighed with satisfaction. The day with its extravagances had brought so much to think about, not horrid things like menus, or Nanny not liking turnips, or Nan wanting a different sort of tea from everyone else, but nice things. The precise placing of a silk scarf, the angle of a hat, the right jewellery to wear with a suit that had braiding and buttons in gold, the seam of a stocking, the fun of a black silk slip that would make Nan raise her eyebrows when she ironed it, because the slits at the side quite obviously went a little too far up to the top of Georgiana's legs.

Eventually Georgiana chose a new dress to wear. Very little of it, all straps, black, and desperately expensive it shouted to her to wear it first. She just hoped that the bar to which she had every intention of repairing, did not have as dark walls as her bedroom, for if it did she would not show up at all against it, and she couldn't have that. She would either have to change bars, or change dresses She smiled at herself in the mirror, for it was certainly not a looking glass, and leant her head forward a little and then backwards too, to make sure her long dark hair was swinging as it should, and then she let herself out of her room and into the arena of the world outside her suite.

The room was a deep red, so she was quite able to remain there in comfort. She sat up at one of the stools set around the bar, her long slender legs draped in perfect arrangement. She would try to trick the barman, she thought mischievously. She would order a cocktail which he wouldn't know how to make.

'A California Dreaming, please.'

He looked at her, dark and Hispanic, his large black eyes remaining implacably unfazed.

'Yes, madam.'

Kirsch, pineapple, topped up with champagne - he knew how to make it exactly, and did so without hesitation. Georgiana smiled. In the pale rose mirror around the room she could see reflected couple after couple, staring at each other, into each other's eyes, letting their imagination roam ahead to intimacies already perhaps known, or yet to be discovered. Aloud they wondered whether to dine in at the restaurant next to the hotel, or out – whether or merely to send for room service while they occupied each other with things other than eating. There were business people too, but they were not the sort of business people Georgiana saw in the country – they seemed sharper, brighter and younger although more wary and less carefree in dress than the non-business clientele - all except one pair of males. Unlike the rest of the men sitting together these two were staring at each other, and talking and gesturing, not idly looking round the room but concentrating on what each other were saying until one of them, his face still in the shadows, stood up and still gesticulating somewhat emotionally came over to the bar, saw Georgiana's legs, looked up at her, and almost instantaneously allowed his face to break into a thousand pieces, as a plate might if thrown to the floor with terrific force.

'Dear God in all his glory - I just do *not* - believe this!'

Georgiana turned to face him. In the country, around Longborough, someone you had known all your life and who might even have some affection for you would only manage some sort of muffled greeting when they saw you. This over-extravagant greeting could only come from one kind of person - an American.

'Heavens - E.F.,' she said, factually and with great certainty because this the writing partner of Kaminski's whom she had known so well and so briefly when she had had her first affair seemed unchanged, except for a little grey around the edge of his hair, as if someone had tinted it carefully with a paintbrush. cotton wool had been left there inadvertently.

'Let me look at you, you little minx. You've dared to stay the same, dammit! You've dared to remain unchanged! How in hell could you!'

'E.F.,' Georgiana repeated, even more certainly, for she suddenly realized and it was a realisation that filled her with a dreadful panic-stricken excitement because she had seen that E.F. was not alone, and that the other man with him, the man whose long elegant legs were stretched across the carpet in front of his table, was surely and in fact Kaminski.

Kaminski had now seen her and was staring at her – sitting as he so often did with his hands in his all too familiar praying position with the tips of his fingers touching his nose. He was not smiling. He was just looking.

'This you won't believe,' E.F. said to him. Georgiana remembered that E.F. had always said such a thing that, particularly when he was pleased to know that he believed it very much. 'I just don't believe this.'

Georgiana looked at Kaminski, and smiled at him but just in her eyes.

'Hi,' Kaminski said. 'What are we drinking?'

E.F. seized her glass, and looked down at her. With his tall frame, his red hair, his freckles, to her he suddenly seemed like an old acquaintance if not a relative, and yet the time they had all spent together had only been such a very few weeks.

'You're very kind,' she murmured. 'But really, two California's Dreaming and I'll be anyone's.'

'Don't be anyone's, darling,' E.F. called back to her as he returned to the bar. 'Be somebody's.'

Then Georgiana did something which she knew was a mistake. She blushed, and thus was immediately helpless. Because of this feeling she avoided Kaminski's eyes, while she knew he very definitely wasn't even attempting to avoid hers.

'So,' said Georgiana, at last, and she raised her eyes to his. Kaminski didn't smile, because he rarely if ever did. Even Georgiana had remarked on this. But at that moment, which she felt was somehow unfair, she felt as if her silk and lace underpinnings had shrunk and that it would be very nice after all, to be staying at Browns and not here where Kaminski and E.F. were staying, and that by now she would by now be dining alone, and not saying *So* to Kaminski in a way that made him once more put his hands in that praying position.

Over by the bar E.F. was enjoying watching them both in the pink tinted mirror. Neither he nor Kaminski had forgotten Lady Georgiana Longborough. After all why should they? They had made a very successful picture around a character like hers, and to make it ever better, the picture had cost very little money and made great deal for the studio, which was why they were both back in town right now to research yet another picture but not so cheap and not so little.

Because he was eager to watch the events that might be unfolding behind him right there and right then, E.F. made a great play of forgetting his room number and then of trying to find some change to tip the barman just so he could go on watching. He hadn't seen that look on Kaminski's face in a very long time. It was most definitely not the look that he had when he was with Sofia, his present rather disturbingly beautiful mistress who was even now probably changing into something as exotic and disturbing as herself in Kaminski's suite and would most likely knife him if she came into the bar and found him talking to Lady Georgiana Longborough. Normally Kaminski only put his hands into the praying position when he was thinking out his next move at chess, or writing a script with E.F., or listening to E.F. explaining a plot point.

Eventually E.F. returned to their table with fresh drinks, but by that time, as he discovered when he looked up and caught the look that was not a look but a whole past being held between this fifty-year-old White Russian and the young beautiful aristocrat, he realized he had overdone the delaying tactics and that things had already progressed beyond the drinks stage. Although he was surprised that within half a minute they both got up and without a word left the cocktail lounge, leaving him with three drinks, at least two of which were not to his taste, he was not really that surprised and not at all shocked, for – as he thought enviously watching Kaminski following the fabulous Georgiana out of the room - Kaminski was famous and this was fame! Women would do anything to be with fame, and so would a great many men - but most of all women. He knew of a famous Italian tenor, of great voice and even greater weight for whom women of all kinds would crowd the bar in hotels all around the world, waiting patiently for him to finish with his little coterie of opera fans and critics, until, with some indication known only to him and the girl of his choice, he would rise to his feet, and leave with her for his suite for a night which he would forget as soon as he stood in front of his shaving mirror the next morning, but of which the girl in question would boast for the rest of her life. That was what E.F. called fame.

'Go to Sofia, and tell her I have been called away,' Kaminski had muttered to E.F. on his way out.

'Thanks, but no thanks,' E.F. had replied.

Even as he was left alone staring at Georgiana's cocktail and Kaminski's untouched vodka martini, E.F. started to write the scene that would now take place between himself and Sofia. First he would knock on the door, and then he would wait interminably for Sofia to open it. Finally Sofia would appear, probably thinking it was room service, but because she was brought up partly in L.A. she would make sure to open the door with the chain on –then seeing it was E.F. whom she hated and despised for taking up too much of Kaminski's time with work and more work, she would shut the door again, an make a great play of re-opening it to him, which was exactly how it happened.

'May I come in?'

Sofia nodded. Her hair was still piled up high into large white fluffy towel, and her body was completely enclosed by a large white fluffy towelling robe with the name of an American hotel written across the pocket.

'Yes?'

Sofia had a husky Italianate voice, which if you didn't know about some of her passionate Italianate scenes was really attractive.

'Yes?' she said again, still husky, still Italianate.

'May I say, first of all, how beautiful you are looking Sofia?'

Sofia walked away from him. It was a heavy-footed walk, and it gave E.F. time to notice that her toes were surprisingly stubby as she trod across the thick carpet.

'Yes?' she said again. It was obviously heavy dialogue for Sofia.

'Yes, Sofia, you are looking really beautiful. Your dark skin against that white towelling. I wish I had some ace photographer with me, it would be sensational really.'

Sofia turned her dark eyes on E.F. Normally she despised him and normally he mocked her. He had never attempted flattery before, and now he realized how stupid that had been. She looked instantly sensual just the mention of herself.

'You think so?'

'White towelling is - how can I say? It's amazing against that incredible skin. I tell you, that's how we must photograph you.'

Already he and Kaminski had had to agree, or rather E.F. had had to agree, to write a small, showy, near monosyllabic part to be written for Sofia in the new movie, to justify Kaminski's knocking her off, and also to allow him to get rid of her at the end of the picture, or whenever he became bored by her, whichever was the earlier.

'E.F., do you think that my part should be maybe written around this towelling robe, around my looking like this?'

'Sofia, I think this is the greatest idea, and now that I see you in that against the crimson of that bed, even more so.'

'You really think so? Fix us both a drink, will you, E.F.? Scotch on the rocks.'

E.F. went to the bar and did as he was told, all the while wondering that he still had not had to mention Kaminski or his whereabouts. Normally Sofia would badger him on this point, always suspicious that he was with some other girl, but now that he was with some other girl she seemed less than interested. More than that, she had parted the opening of her dressing gown and was now swinging a leg over the side of the bed, the rest of her magnificent and very ample body stretched out beneath the towelling.

'Do you think this would be a nice angle, E.F.?'

'Magnificent,' she was told, as he handed her a drink.

'Where is Kaminski?' she asked, after a thoughtful pause, and E.F. felt his heart sink. Now would surely be the start of a scene.

'He's been called away urgently, to see someone. You know some of the locations are going to be here in London. He won't be back until later tonight. He said you were to go on right ahead with the evening and he'd be back in about one, maybe two.'

'Sure, I understand, sure.'

Sofia turned her magnificent amber-flecked brow eyes on E.F.

'Perhaps we could work out something together?' she murmured. 'Are you free right now?'

E.F. nodded. 'Sure, Sofia, I'm free.'

'Good, so am I.'

She smiled, and picking up his free hand she placed under her robe where the rise and fall of her amplitude was hidden, but not still.

'Lock the door, and let's rehearse,' she told him. E.F. was only too glad to obey. He had rarely been so quick on his feet.

'Draw the blinds,' she commanded.

He did so, and as he did so he realized with a jolt that he too must be famous, for after all he asked himself - would she be doing this if he wasn't?

As Sofia's white towelling robe fell open it seemed to E.F. that he maybe might allow her four words in the picture, not just two. A little later he adjusted this to a dozen.

'Did you ever hear of the Irish actress who slept with the writer?' he asked her later.

'Sorry?' Sofia has wondered blankly in return.

'It doesn't matter,' E.F. had smiled. #You can let that one pass.'

Georgiana had forgotten just how dexterous Kaminski was at undressing not just himself, but her too. When they had first made love she had always thought it was something to do with his abilities as a director. But now it seemed to her that it had more to do with his abilities as a lover. He kissed her in a way she had forgotten men could kiss, with a sort of deeply felt concentration, but not so long that it was tiring. Her dark hair swung around her body, and her arms went up around his neck and her face to his neat dark beard. She laughed up at him.

'You're still ridiculously beautiful,' he said. 'No, worse, you are even more ridiculously beautiful - and I see you have had a child. It's given you a fuller figure.' He turned her round in front of him, back and forth. 'That is quite beautiful, the fuller breasts with the narrow waist.'

Still in her black silk and lace and newly bought slip, Georgiana felt her last command of the situation falling away from her. She was as helpless as she had ever been with this tall, dark, bearded man with his intellectuality and his strange films of which she understood not a word. She wondered briefly what it was that fascinated him, or her, about each other. But it was only a brief reverie for from the second that Kaminski touched her they were caught in a complexity of sighs and sensations, rushing through however long it was to the other side of reality, to where only love counts the minutes.

Kaminski allowed himself to be astonished. Not for a second could he, even if he had wanted to, not for one second as he made love to her could he remain outside himself, a detached observer of his own sensual activities, as he was used to doing with his many other mistresses. Georgiana's whole persona required his whole concentration. Perhaps it was her oddness, or her way of laughing at him, or her own seeming detachment, but when he finally lay back against the dark hangings of the bed, Kaminski was reminded of those weeks he had spent with her when he was filming all that time ago when he had found it so difficult to be ruthless with her, to leave the flat, not shut the door, but lock it and throw away the key, as he always did with women. Now as he looked at her beautiful face lying in his arms, her eyes shut, a slender white hand under one pale cheek, he wondered to himself something he had never allowed himself to wonder before - perhaps she really was after all everything he had ever wanted.

Fulton and Elliott stared at Lady Tizzy. They had waited until she had returned from the very expensive room at the very expensive private clinic that had only recently been built so conveniently near to Flint House, to approach the subject of Lady Tizzy's private life. But now that a decent interval had passed, they had both agreed that the nettle must be grasped.

'Although I'm not quite sure that is quite the right phrase or saying,' Fulton had murmured, as they proceeded up to her bedroom.

The way in which they had themselves passed through the really terrifying crisis that had faced them was magnificent they were both agreed. There was no other word for it. It was magnificent and it was undoubtedly the stuff of heroes. They had immediately hired another nurse to help Nanny, and now there was a tribe of starchily aproned people in the wing, the blue bird of happiness seemed once more to have settled on the roof of Flint House. Nanny had been an angel, and, as it happened, without effort, for while Fulton and Elliott had longed for two daughters, Nanny had been yearning for a boy.

'So much more affectionate, Mr Fulton, really. Nanny's really pleased with her present.'

So she was, humming happily as she changed nappies at what seemed half-hourly intervals, while leaving Daisy-Marguerita to the monthly nurses and Victoria, too.

'Of course she's quite abandoned Victoria now that we have a son. It's a shame, really. Not that Victoria seems to mind - she's besotted with the new monthly Irish nurse, and learning how to say cheers in Irish with her Ribena, which in this ever changing world should stand her in good stead.'

'I must say I still can't believe it, you know, not really,' said Elliott, sighing slightly, as if each time the realization made him just a little more tired than he had been before. 'You are going to tell her, of course? I mean you are going to be really, really strict about it?'

'Of course.'

'She won't like it.'

'Too bad.'

'Yes. Suppose it is really.'

Neither of them ever entered Patti's room without first either putting on dark glasses, or totally suspending their sensitivities just in case they happened upon something they might not like, or saw something which might make Elliott feel a tiny bit faint. This morning it seemed Lady Tizzy had awoke early, and then having executed her usual glamour over the room, festooning it with dropped diaphanous garments, retired back to bed in an enormous puffed sleeved peignoir that rose up round her ears in a way that was sensational, given that her hair was also piled up in extravagant mounds several inches above the sleeves, her mouth not just lipsticked but glossed, and every or of her eyelashes carefully spiked with mascara. She had acquired a very large diamond ring from someone who would doubtless prefer to remain nameless, but who Fulton and Elliott happened to know lived not very far from Flint House at the Hall. Quite obviously the arrival of the ring had coincided with the news of the twins' arrival, for the ring had arrived at the hospital anonymously - except that the package was postmarked Stanton, and very few people in Stanton, especially not anonymous people, could afford to send Lady Tizzy a ring the size of an ostrich egg made in entirely of very old, very expensive diamonds. Trade might be good for some, but not that good.

'Good morning, boys.' Lady Tizzy smiled at them.

'Good morning, darling,' said Fulton, and he leaned forward and kissed her affectionately, because he was after all her husband. Elliott just blew her a kiss from his fingertips, because he wasn't.

Ever since he entered the room he had stared right ahead at Lady Tizzy in the bed. Now he dared to look just slightly sideways, and around. These days the daily person who did for them came and did for Lady Tizzy's room too, because what with helping Twinks in the stable with papier-mâche reproduction trays, and the Cathedral fund, Elliott had found that he just hadn't the time to spend retrieving old Del Monte tins from under her ladyship's bed. The daily who came and went, Elliott quickly noticed, had done quite well, but she had fallen, as everyone did, by the wayside, and abandoned all hope, as even the bravest might, when it came to Lady Tizzy's dressing table.

It was an altar to the art of salesmanship. In the centre was a bowl of lipsticks, filled to the brim in a kind of plasti-clad confusion, a pot pourri of the old and the new in lip coatings. Then there were the innumerable plastic cases full of face blushers and powders, the small puffs, the big puffs, the half-filled bottles of scent, and even of perfume, clustered together in groups, small and large, old-fashioned and new. Like members of the chorus, they seemed to be staring around them wondering if they would be the chosen one when Lady Tizzy next visited the scene of her face before her dressing glass, while over everything lay not dust but a thin coating of face powder, because she dearly loved her largest puff, a lengthy affair on a stick with a ribbon on the bottom, and would wave it in a mad fairy gesture over her face before departing for whatever she had never in mind. It was a gesture that always mesmerized Elliott whenever he saw it, and he felt he would be quite unsurprised, if, as she finally finished, he had vanished.

'So how are we feeling?'

Patti looked momentarily saddened by this question.

'You sound just like that daft gynaecologist,' she sighed. 'Next thing you'll be asking me if I'm thrilled with my pigeon pair, and whether I've -'

'Oh no we won't,' Fulton and Elliott chorused.

'No,' said Fulton firmly, sitting down on her bed, and leaving Elliott to sit in the buttoned Colefax and Fowler bedroom chair. 'No, we have something else to talk to you about, which the doctor certainly won't talk about.'

'Oh.' Patti looked from one to the other surprised. 'You're not leaving me 'cos I had twins, are you? I didn't mean to,' she added, bursting into tears, but only a very little, not enough to make her mascara run.

'I certainly am not leaving you, and nor is Elliott, but we certainly are going to talk to you, quite strongly, about your position, our position, the whole family's position, and most especially the bank manager.'

'This is a deportation -'
'I think you mean deputation which it isn't but might well be if you don't listen.'
Patti looked away from them both, and her eyes, large and suddenly conveniently
blank, stared at a little bird pecking on her window sill.
'I know what you're going to say, you're going to say I've got to take a job to help
support the kids, that's what you're going to say.'
'No, nothing quite as bad as that,' Fulton comforted her, but his voice remained grave.
'But two things have got to happen. First, you have to tell certain people that there are grave
responsibilities attached to fatherhood, and our bank manager would appreciate some ass-
istance towards these crippling responsibilities, and secondly -' Fulton paused. 'Secondly,
someone around here is going to have to have an operation of - shall we say - curtailment?
Because three is quite enough, if not two too many.'
'You were quite happy about Daisy-Marguerita.'
'Of course I was, but being a father to a son is quite different.'
'I don't see why?'
Fulton got up and walked to the window.
'Because I shall have to sell my gold Golf and wear quite different trousers for a
start,' he told her after a pause. 'I shall have to start thinking about prep schools, and visiting
headmasters wearing a nasty three piece suits and sporting some infernal public school tie.'
'But you went to a public school —'
'Bad enough.'
'You went to —'
'I know where I went, thank you.'
'You were there with Pember.'
'I know. I just never thought I'd have to go back there, especially not to put the little
wretch down.'
'You can't put him down, I shan't let you!' Patti wailed.
'That's what you do for schools,' Elliott explained gently. 'It's not like going to the
vet. You just put them down so they can go up or be sent down, or whatever it is they do to
the next school, or to that school, and it's fine.'
'Well, and what happens after that?'
'Then they just grow up as stupid as everyone else, and get to wear a rather silly tie,
and keep quiet about it, except in front of headmasters or people who work in ICI. You
mustn't worry.'
'Were you put down, Elliott?' Patti asked him, sniffing.
'Yes, but not for long. I had very frail health so I was sent to Switzerland, where all I
learned to be was a pastry chef, the fees they charged were vast, but so long as I was away
and at school my parents were quite happy. Besides, it was much nicer. But we don't want
Beau to have frail health, so he must be put down immediately and then we can see, see?'
'Yes,' said Patti doubtfully, because she quite obviously didn't. 'And then what?'
'Well,' Elliott said. 'Beau then has to go away to another school when he's about
eight, to a really horrid prep school where the headmaster and mistress will be married and
pretending to be terribly nice, but actually waiting until all the parents have driven off so they
can rush upstairs and produce canes and whips and beat the poor little devils into such a heap
that when their parents come and fetch them after the first month, all they ever dare tell them
is how much fun they're having.'
'Elliott!' Fulton said sharply. 'Elliott's being very naughty,' he told Patti. 'Nothing
like that will happen to Beau.'
'Of course it won't,' Elliott agreed with a smile. 'But it can do if you're not very

careful and don't give fearfully large donations to the school rebuilding fund, or pay for the whole staff to go on skiing holidays.'

'But when we had Victoria none of this had to happen.'

'It's different for girls,' Fulton agreed. 'You can send them to very pretty places where nothing horrid happens and no one minds at all.'

'So why can't Beau be sent to a very gentle place where nothing horrid happens?'

'Because that's what people think does boys good.'

'Oh Fulton, you're right,,' Patti sobs. 'You're both right. None of this should have happened. I mean now we'll have to get a second nanny, won't we?'

'Don't worry. Fulton has already booked a young person from the village with suitable credentials.'

'Such as?''

'She used to keep pigs. No seriously - she's fine, the daughter of the district nurse, Twinks knows her, very suitable. She's quite ugly, and Nanny will scare her rigid and make her do lots of crochet when she's watching telly.'

'The poor babies -' Patti wailed again.

'Of course you could always look after them,' said Elliott doubtfully. 'You could help Nanny on her day off.'

Patti immediately stopped wailing which they both knew she would.

'Last time I did that she said she never wanted to see me in the nursery again,' Patti told them bravely.

'She was right. Now about the curtailment.'

'No, don't worry, I'll see to it. After all, something's got to be done, hasn't it?'

'That's one way of putting it. Of course you could just give up seeing each other,' Fulton added hopefully.

'Yeah we could,' Patti agreed. 'Except you know what happened last time. We didn't see each other, and then we did, and all of a sudden it was like one of those Saturday afternoon movies. We have no need to speak, we just look at each other, and that's it. Quite mindless it is.'

'Mindless and wordless and speechless,' said Elliott automatically, avoiding Fulton's eyes, while Fulton did his best to find something very cold to look at, and failed.

'Good. As long as that's all right, then that's all right,' said Fulton at last. 'Now we're off to the nursery. Want to come?'

'Not really,' Patti sighed, 'Nanny only really likes you two.'

'I'm not surprised,' Elliott murmured as he shut the door.

Fulton and Elliott walked along to the nursery wing in the usual stunned silence that always followed a visit to Lady Tizzy's boudoir.

'You've got to admit there's no-one else quite like her,' said Elliott.

'I'll admit anything as long as she calls a halt to the production line,' sighed Fulton.

He paused as he reached out to the beautifully decorated nursery door handle, all hand done by Elliott, little tiny bears and things with a matching finger plate with V for Victoria entwined within more little tiny bears. 'Nanny told me last night that we've had so many babies so quickly the village is beginning to suspect I'm a left-footer.'

'I'm going to have to re-do those finger plates to add D and B now,' murmured Elliott as they passed through into the nursery rooms.

Inside the nursery everything was a riot of activity. The two monthly nurses were laying the twins down in cradles only one of which was the reproduction of the Duc de Berry's, Beau's having had to be hastily borrowed and draped with blue ribbons while Victoria was running from one cradle to the other wearing a beautifully starched dress that Elliott had had made for her, and which certainly suited her lovely blonde hair.

'Daisy-Marguerita looks exactly like Victoria did at the same age, Mr Fulton, the spit of yourself.'

Fulton gazed down at his newest daughter.

'Miracles happen every day,' Elliott said.

Fulton gazed at the babies, but only briefly, before sitting down in the wicker nursing chair and looking round him in fascination. Flint House was not a vast house, but it was big enough, and now it had somehow even managed to accommodate not one new baby but two, and not mind. Everywhere there was a nice clean smell of freshly laundered linen. Elliott and Nanny had fallen into one of their deep discussions about drawn thread work and smocking. Things, after all, might be worse.

When Pemberton got a message from Bloss it was always in code. The only trouble was the code was sometimes somewhat difficult to read. For instance before Lady Tizzy got banged up for the second time, when as lovers they were meeting in the pool house at regular and very sublime moments, Bloss would leave out a bag of oats in the snug. If on the other hand she was unable to meet and had rung Bloss on the staff telephone, then at the usual hour Pemberton had only to pop his head round the snug door to see no bag of oats to know the score. It was a simple sort of code, and it worked.

This particular afternoon Pemberton had been feeling just a little ish-ish. Jennifer was in one of her preoccupied moods, all tatting and chatting about this infernal party thing she was insisting on giving. He had been happily gardening when she came out and started to pace the lawn, for all the world like a water diviner without a stick, muttering and murmuring about the size of the suspended floor and heaven knew what, with the result that Pemberton had had to go into the house just to get away from the irritation of the sight of her in her gardening shoes saying that something was wrong every fifteen seconds, and going back to the apple tree to start again.

It was while he was walking by the snug that Pemberton had popped his head round the door for no other reason than habit, and had seen the glorious sight of a bag of oats and so he had at once hurried off to the pool house in order to meet his inamorata, newly restored to her divinely curvaceous shape.

'What a wonderful surprise,' he whispered. 'You little darling.'

'I've missed you, Pember,' Lady Tizzy told him. 'I love Fulton and Elliott but frankly we just don't share the same interests.'

'Well, you wouldn't.'

'No, we don't. And I mean babies is fine, but after you've had them, and I mean they're all right and everything, who wants to talk about them all day long? They love it, but you know, there is a limit. And anyway Nanny only really loves them, she doesn't much like mummies, she always says they interfere with her work, so there's not much for me to do right now.'

'No, well, there wouldn't be,' Pember agreed, pausing in his act of kissing her deliciously soft white neck. 'Goodness, I have missed you. Your poitrine is like no other.'

'This is not a poitrine, Pember darling,' said Lady Tizzy, teasing him. 'You are funny. It's called a 'bustier'.'

'By poitrine I meant that which is within the bustier ,' Pemberton began but then stopped, seeing Lady Tizzy's expression of innocent enquiry, and turned with interest to the item in question.

Patti stopped him. Not that she wanted to, because she loved her Pember so much, and it was already beginning to be quite like the old days, but she knew her duty and that she must be loyal to Fulton. Whatever happened she owed something to Fulton, most of all not to have any more babies.

'The thing is, Pember,' she began, still whispering. 'I've not come here just to talk to you and all that. No, I've come to tell you about the twins and Victoria and everything.'

'Oh.' Pemberton's face fell. 'I see.'

He didn't of course, but he always said that he saw when he needed time. He looked up helplessly at Lady Tizzy's beautiful face. He did hope she wasn't going to talk babies like Jennifer. It would make him want to end it all if she did. Normally the magnificent thing about Lady Tizzy was that she just wanted to make love, she never talked babies. Sometimes being with her was just like being with a real friend, a person, not just a woman.

'I've promised Fulton, no more babies, see? So one of us, if we're going to go on seeing each other, one of us is going to have to do something, you know.'

'You don't mean not see each other?' asked Pemberton, shocked and panicked.

'No, you arse - do something as in go for a very little cheap little curtailment as Fulton called it. They do them everywhere now, apparently, Fulton says. Especially for men. There's even an advertisement in the Parishioner for it. You just ring up, and that's it. Plenty of oats and no more babies.'

'Jennifer reads the Parishioner from cover to cover,' said Pemberton doubtfully.

'Yes, well she would. So does Elliott, that's how come he read me out the ad. Here it is.'

Patti opened a handbag bulging with old love letters and handed Pemberton a tiny scrap of cheap magazine paper. Pemberton took out his half-moon spectacles, and placed them on his nose. He read *Men! You want it? Come and get it! Just ten minutes and the wife's best friend can really be that! Call Real Man for a carefree love life!'*

'Interesting,' Pemberton remarked.

'Yeah and it really works,' Patti told him. 'Really. So will you be a good bloke and go?'

Pemberton looked across at Lady Tizzy. The bustier was doing everything except contain her magnificent prow. He knew what she meant. To be really carefree there could must be no more babies for either of them. Altogether he now had six within two miles of each other, and on both sides of the blankets. His title was secure, his wife was virtuous, his mistress was divine, and he was rich. Considering everything, he had to face it - it was his duty to make sure that Fulton and Elliott should no longer suffer from his insane passion for Lady Tizpots.

'Very well,' he said. 'Very well, I will be a man, and go to *Real Man.*'

'I knew you would,' said Patti happily, then tuned to go.

'Not yet, please,' Pemberton whispered desperately. 'Please don't go - not yet.'

'Once you're a real man, Bloss can leave out the oats every day,' Lady Tizzy whispered back, before moving out of his reach, and referring to yet another piece of paper from her handbag.

'And yes. Yes next is putting Beau down for your old school and everything – there's the matter of endowments. Apparently Fulton just doesn't make enough from reproduction antiques, even though the trays have really taken off.'

Pemberton humbly he took this second piece of paper from Lady Tizzy. He'd do anything for her. It was no use pretending he wouldn't. Anything. Even go to Real Man *and* pay this long list of so-called endowments. .

5

As Georgiana awoke in her hotel room, without Kaminski by her side, she found herself wondering just a little - not just at herself, but at everything. She wondered at life, which seemed to be a continual set of either clashes, or engagements, or evolvements or, as in this case, re-involvements.

She sat up, her long shining dark hair falling over the sides of her shoulders, then very quickly she glanced at herself in the hand mirror that she always placed to the side of her bed, together with a small handbag-sized bottle of scent, and a comb. Sometimes she wished that she wasn't so vain, and sometimes, as now, she was very glad that she was. After all if she had not been a little vain she would not now be staring at herself with such satisfaction in the hand mirror, and she would not be remembering yesterday evening with quite the same sense of delicate, if sensual, delight.

She lay back against the pillows and sighed happily. It was terrible, it was awful – she knew what she had done was quite out of line but it was real and it had happened and she had let it happen and she didn't mind one bit that she had. It could hardly be called a one night stand because it had only been early evening. It could not be called the start of an affair because she'd already had one with Kaminski and anyway that had ended. It could not be called adultery because she wasn't actually married to Gus. It might be called fornication, but then to be called fornication she thought that surely you had to do it a lot, and she had only done it once. Once was simply not enough to be such a long and serious word. She stared at the ceiling rose, a rather ghastly affair in mock plaster picked out carefully in pink and thought she would have to find the word for what she had done with Kaminski before she stepped out of bed and into the shower.

Partied was too American, and anyway seemed to imply that other people would have been involved, so as she wondered she continued to stare at her reflection. It had certainly not been an orgy, and she could not ever consider, that simply wouldn't be her at all. Nor could she have done any of the things that Gus sometimes referred to such as having it off, ghastly things that made you think of alleyways and dustbins. At last the proper phrase to describe what she had done with Kaminski entered her mind, and like all proper phrases that were exactly right it was entirely simple. She had made love.

As soon as she realized what she had done Georgiana put her feet on the thick pile carpet and padded over to the shower. She knew she could not have got on with the day until she had found out what she had done the evening before, so quietly and so passionately with Kaminski. It would have preyed on her conscience all day if she had not been able to think of the right word or phrase. People who did not know what they had done were always a terrific bore. They got drunk and they made life difficult for other people, which was not the way to be. As long as you knew what you had done you could quite safely get on with the day and not feel guilty, or as if everyone was looking at you and knew what you had done, even if you didn't. To have made love was a beautiful thing, to have been made love to beautifully was a wondrous thing; Georgiana could now float through the day feeling wondrous, and beautiful. She dressed carefully, putting on a very simple new dress that had cost a great deal of money, but which she could pay for, since she had been saving up for what felt like years, and now it seemed to her it had been all worthwhile, not just because she loved new dresses, particularly when they were very simple and completely new, but also because she thought she quite deserved them. Her body after all was still fairly lovely, and so was her face. Not to be nice to them would be silly, like neglecting a building, or not polishing a piece of silver, and quite as wasteful. She stood in front of the dressing table and bent her knees. The dress was of a lovely rich blue. The colour reflected in her eyes. Georgiana leaned forward to the mirror and gazed into them. They too were very simple and extremely lovely.

Her train journey home was full of delightful expectation. She had lunched alone, wearing dark glasses, and thinking to herself how lucky it was that a lonely and unhappy childhood had made her appreciate her own company – no not just appreciate it - relish it. As she lunched she did not long for the company of other girls with their silly observations about their boyfriends or husbands and their prying ways as to her own good or bad fortunes, such as - *Gus still selling those funny little card things of his? Oh, he is, good. He must get awfully tired of them. You look tired. Terribly tired. I don't suppose you've had a holiday in years, have you? You certainly look as if you haven't had a holiday in years. You should put on some weight. It would suit you. Really.'* No, she didn't miss lunching with girlfriends. Nothing nice was ever said over lunch, certainly not at any she had recently been at, anyway. The only thing a person should ever be asked at lunch was whether or not they were ready to order.

Georgiana had most certainly been. She had been very ready to order oeufs mollets - soft-boiled eggs gone cold with a sort of pale green mayonnaise coating which were very good, followed by a tiny chicken breast carved into a fan on another sauce of a pale lemon colour with one or two beans to the side. It was utterly perfect, she thought, remembering how good it had all tasted, and how with a glass of cold champagne and white wine she had been able to sit back and savour her meeting with Kaminski with all its subtlety and nuance, and its superb passion. In the far distance, from the train window, she saw from the approaching water tower that they were about to draw into Penbury, her station. She sighed happily. That was the whole point of going to London, wasn't it? she asked herself. So that she could appreciate or re-appreciate Longborough and Gus, and even Nan and Nanny. By the time she had driven herself slowly home through the winding lanes they would all have changed for the better. And that too was what had to be said in favour of making love – making love changed everything for the better; it made you feel quite able to cope with things like dried flowers and Gus and his eternal quest for something that everyone knew didn't exist.

Georgiana sang a light snatch of Mozart, something she didn't even know that she knew - and in Italian too.

Kaminski stared at E.F.

'I don't believe what I'm hearing,' he said slowly.

'No, really,' E.F. stated. 'I read her last night, when you were otherwise occupied, when you needed me to keep her quiet, and she was really quite excellent.'

At that moment, as Kaminski turned and stared at him, E.F. was only too glad that he was a scriptwriter. Not a terribly brilliant scriptwriter perhaps, but not a terribly terrible one either, which was just as well in the circumstances. The circumstances were that Kaminski was now giving E.F. his number one deep director's look and not believing a word he was trying to say, and E.F. was remembering to look furtive, and to not look Kaminski in the eye, which would double bluff Kaminski, a quite considerable chess player, into thinking that EJF. was looking so underhand he must be telling the truth.

'Sofia read well? You have to be picking peppered pickles, as my old nurse would say. You're lying to me, aren't you?'

'No, really. She read really well, and - and she read long, I mean we read along together quite a bit, and she was - terrific. Really.'

'So what are we talking about? You want to put her forward for the part of whom?'

'The part she really impressed me with was the girl who comes out of the sea and seduces the marine biologist.'

Kaminski put down his coffee cup, and turning to the chimneypiece in his suite, he carefully lit a cigar, something he normally never did in the morning unless he had just been to a breakfast meeting.

'The girl who seduces Harris has at least seventy lines, and I don't think Sofia is capable of saying more than seven words on celluloid, and then only on a week by week basis, one word a week for seven weeks, leaving plenty of room either side for dubbing. E.F., tell me, please, what happens to you the moment I let you out of my sight? I was only gone a few hours - two hours in fact.'

'It was only an idea,' E.F. said, feebly, while all his insides trembled with the thought of what Kaminski might do to him if he found out that he had tasted of his, Kaminski's, private store of fruit. Never mind that he had been preoccupied with some other far more fatale femme, that he had been cheating on Sofia. Kaminski was an aristocrat, a White Russian, anyway in his own mind, and every slave girl within a hundred miles of his set was his by droit de director, and heaven help some overweight randy scriptwriter like E.F. who might come between him and his divine, utterly divine right. Directors. They got all the fun. E.F. sighed mightily. He had to get Sofia something or else, or else indeed.

'How was our ex-heroine?' he asked after a short pause.

Kaminski took a long draw on his cigar. They both knew who the ex- heroine was, she around whom they had written a very cheap, very successful film.

'She's changed. She's different.'

'Lost her innocence, huh?'

'No, not AT ALL. She hasn't lost her innocence – what she's managed to do was to gain even more.'

E.F. stared at Kaminski. For once he was interested in what he was going to say next. Being the egoist E.F. most surely was, he found he only really became interested in something when he was extremely interested in it. The rest of the time he was merely pretending to be where his body was, his mind being elsewhere, usually at some scene from the night before, preferably a good one. Because he was so interested, he said nothing, and merely waited until Kaminski chose to continue, which he knew Kaminski liked, and which he knew was very effective because he sometimes, not often, but sometimes, liked to use such pauses and phrasing in his scripts.

'What has happened,' Kaminski went on slowly, 'is that she's had a baby, and she's matured because of it, not because she wants to, of course - our heroine would never consciously mature - but the experience, quite naturally and simply, has changed her, given her more confidence, and made her aware, not of her charms, but of her own desires.'

E.F. frowned. Certainly to him Georgiana had looked, if that was possible, even more beautiful, but still very much a class act. He certainly hadn't noticed any overt self-consciousness.

'It was that good?' he asked Kaminski, giving him a wry look, and pouring them both some more coffee.

'It was a lot more than that good,' Kaminski told him. 'It was perfection.'

E.F. stared. It was unfair. Here was a man who could have anything, and usually did. Who could have the world's most beautiful women, for whom women lined up to be noticed. Yet it was not enough that he travelled with the kind of mistress that would keep most men in nights, he had also to take a couple of hours out to go and find perfection with a young British aristocrat.

'You don't really want to make this picture, do you?' he asked Kaminski, because he wanted to throw him, and because he felt insatiably jealous that this man was able to enjoy his life in such a way that he never even paused to think about someone else who might not be enjoying theirs at the same level, i.e. his best friend and scriptwriter E.F. 'I always know with you when you don't want to make a picture; your eyes go glazed when I mention it. They glazed over when I just mentioned *Harris* or *Jumby Island* - they become what the French call *en gelée*, they become set in an aspic of boredom. I-must-write-that-down.'

'It's not that good,' Kaminski told him as E.F. immediately obeyed himself.

'Not to you,' E.F. agreed, 'but to me it could be liquid gold one soggy, foggy morning in London Town when I'm in a white heat facing the white sheet, and not the kind I like, but the one that goes in the typewriter.'

Kaminski didn't even bother to shrug his shoulders, or to disagree with E.F. He knew, they both knew, that it was true. He was bored with making a picture about a marine biologist, but as Henry Fonda had said, and wisely, it was the *Sex and the Single Girl* pictures that paid for the *Twelve Angry Men* picture, and he spoke for all of them. Making pictures was a business. It might be a business that needed and used great art, and sometimes even great artists, but nevertheless it was a business, and if he had to make a picture about a marine biologist he would, and then next time round, as always happened, he would be allowed to make a picture about whatever he wished, and just so long as both were successful he would be all right, and that fat chump, the red-headed freckled face E.F., would be too.

'Come on, to work,' he told E.F.

'No thanks for keeping Sofia quiet?'

'No. Because you didn't. She woke me this morning with nothing but your promise, your damn promise, to give her lines. So, thanks to you, she will have to be written a part, by you, and then she will be given it, and I will have to shoot it, and then we will have to cut it. So your method of keeping actresses quiet is very expensive. It will now cost thousands of dollars to keep Sofia quiet.'

'But from the look of you, it will be worth every penny, huh? You are wearing your number one 'OK, give the kid some lines look', Kaminski. I know that look. You won't regret it.'

Kaminski said nothing. He knew how he looked. Tall, dark-bearded, slim, elegant, perfectly shod and perfectly clothed, yes, he knew all that, but he didn't know how he actually looked, whether he looked different, even if he looked different. He couldn't deny he felt different, as if every moment of his life now had added significance. That cup, the taste of the coffee mingling with the rich taste of the cigar, the way the sunlight was falling on the floor, just in front of the book-filled table, they were all being seen by him as if for both the last time and the first. He didn't believe in love, of course he didn't, probably because with the women at his disposal he didn't need to believe in love. That was what power did for you, it made it possible to avoid love as you would avoid the measles. Yet last evening, as Georgiana lay in his arms, something had happened to him, something he had never wanted to have happen to him: he held something, someone, in his arms whom he didn't want to leave and that he didn't understand sine he always wished to leave whoever it was he was with. He knew himself too well not to know that the panic he had felt as he dressed and left the room was the fear that he might have just made love to someone who was capable of understanding him. It therefore followed that he must avoid that person. Tonight, he resolved, he would make terrifyingly passionate love to Sofia. They would have a scene, not the kind that she loved to make, but the kind that Kaminski liked her to create. Only that way could he perhaps drown the memory of that dark-haired girl who had smiled at him as he let himself out of her suite, a smile that told him he was free, absolutely free, to go, and what was better, so was she.

'Back to *Harris,*' said Kaminski. 'Scene a hundred and eighty. He is just about to set up a marine biology station on Jumby when he discovers that the Republican candidate has vetoed -'

'Scene a hundred and fifty now, on the re-write,' E.F. reminded him. 'But maybe that is beside the point.'

What the point was going to be he didn't quite know, nor did E.F. quite care. He had won Sofia her little part and by so doing he had concealed from Kaminski that he had made a successful pass at his, Kaminski's, presumably prized mistress. Really, all in all, E.F. thought to himself, he had done more than well, he had been very successful, and what's more, judging from the way that the esteemed director of the picture was humming *Violets for You Fur,* E.F. could only imagine that he might have a chance of making another equally successful pass at the same lady some fine afternoon soon, if not soonest.

The end of the afternoon was always the Countess's favourite time of day, and now in late spring, looking at the lovely soft colours all around from the safe haven of her newly structured conservatory, it was proving even more satisfactory, and that despite the smell of Andrew's nasty cigarette which was drifting over the box hedge from the wild garden. Moving to Wiltshire from Sussex had, the Countess reflected, proved immensely successful for her personally.

Of course, she thought, watching a cat stalking something through a small patch of grass under the old apple tree, she was well aware to what the success of Wiltshire was due, and that was her quite astounding ability to hold on to those nearest to her, and attract their continuing irritation. After all, there was very little point in living to a moderately early old age if you couldn't enjoy the fruits of your own mischief, just no point at all. It would make not having a second gin and tonic at lunchtime, and not having a second glass of champagne at dinner, quite pointless, all that sacrifice for nothing.

She sighed a little with the satisfaction of everything. She had won a battle over Andrew, not just finding a use for him as a walker to the aristocracy , but also insisting on his smoking out of the house. She had won a victory over life at the Hall, by backing out of the private ball arrangements, and so early that both Fulton and Jennifer had been left gasping. That was something she knew from military history. Strike when the enemy least expects it, early, and preferably after a short ceasefire. It was always most successful.

It had been a terrible scene, of course, of the kind that the Countess really enjoyed. First there had been the call to Jennifer on the Countess's return from her horrid day in London. A short stilted conversation during which Jennifer had become perfectly aware that there was something wrong, that the Countess was mightily displeased, or she would not be requesting an urgent and important meeting of the ball committee - not that a private ball had a committee as such, but it certainly had to have steerage, and the Countess for one was determined that her hand was to come off the tiller.

Then there had been the now famous meeting – famous to the Countess and Bloss at least - during the course of which the Countess triumphantly gave everyone, that is Fulton and Jennifer, to understand that she would not be continuing with any help with the ball, she was bowing, or rather curtsying, out and leaving them to get on with it, as they wished, on their own, and never mind her, because it would be a far, far better thing that she did.

'But we've just changed everything from peach to cream and green,' Fulton had protested.

'Change it back, Fulton dear,' the Countess had told him, her eyes glittering with enjoyment. 'Let peach tones commence, what you will. I am far too taken up with my little charity for distressed field mice.'

'Distressed field mice?'

They had both looked unbelieving, astonished, and vaguely insulted at that, as if the Countess was mocking them quite openly, which she was, because she was actually still smarting from the dear old thing reference in Jennifer's letter to Mary.

'Field mice are becoming increasingly and distressingly rare. Myself and Colonel Bentley in the village have started a charity to conserve them. Hedgehogs have been well catered for, badgers are being assiduously guarded by those in the know, but field mice are suffering an alarming decrease in numbers. It's most important that we do something, and the Colonel and I are. We are establishing ideal habitats for the little creatures, protesting to farmers who spray and cut and maim our fields and set fire to everything. It is a very strong movement, a rural movement, a movement such as you would never find on the continent. Oh no.'

At that she had risen, snapped her perfectly worn handbag to, and stalked from the room, a friend of field mice, a foe of the ball. The effect had been alarmingly good, apparently. It had left everyone gasping, the Countess learned from dear Bloss, who had telephoned her a few days later to tell her that the early asparagus that he always let her have was ready to be picked up by her help.

'Her ladyship is so concerned, she has come out in a nasty rash at the back of her neck,' Bloss had told her after the usual exchanges to do with tips and stalks, and hot butter sauce versus vinaigrette. 'No, Lady Pemberton is not at all herself at the moment. She is something other, I'm afraid, your ladyship, she is - how can I say? - put out. Yes, that would be the word, put out by so many decisions. You see, Mr Fulton, as she explained to me only yesterday, Mr Fulton has his own worries and cares, the reproductions, the papier mâché trays and matching wastepaper baskets, they take up quite a little of his time, with the consequence that he really is not always available in the way that you, your ladyship, has always been available at all times. It's a quandary, if I may say so, your ladyship, and Lady Pemberton is not good with quandaries, they get her in a muddle. I've noticed it before. When the rose garden was altered she became so agitated, the doctor had to be sent for to prescribe a nice dose of herbal remedies. He's half and half, you know, Doctor Stillworthy, half herbal half lethal is what his lordship says. Still, they did the trick, the herbals, they got her on her feet and back out into the garden in no time.'

The Countess sipped her gin and tonic carefully. They were having the asparagus tonight. Very good it would be too, judging from the tiny tips of it that she had seen peeping through the top of the double boiler as Maria, quite rightly, fussed around them as if she had grown them herself. After the asparagus and tiny thin pieces of brown bread and butter they would have a little fish. Little pieces of fish that would go with the earliest of the Hall's tiny new carrots. Bloss was indeed a culinary godfather.

She must think of some way to help him in return for all his little back door gifts to Maria. Something she could do which would make him very happy, something that he lacked and she could bring about. The idea dawned halfway down her gin and tonic. Of course! If dear Pember cancelled the whole idea of the ball, refused to come up trumps with the wherewithal, and it could be seen to have been due to Bloss and only Bloss's invaluable manoeuvrings, if he could be credited with such a coup, then there was no doubt at all that Bloss would be in a position to indicate that so great a saving must be of benefit, and Pember would immediately order him up the new Peugeot *Starduster* to which Bloss had, it seemed, referred quite longingly to Maria only yesterday.

''E do so love he newest reggie, do Senor Bloss,' Maria had murmured affectionately. ''E say heet put 'im up with the rest if he drive he newest reggie. They no be h'able to look down on 'im in King's H'Arms when he parkies there, no he way hey do now with a banger - old Vauxhall H'Astra manual sheeft.'

As the Countess savoured the new young asparagus, while resolutely blocking out the sound of Andrew savouring his, she resolved that Bloss would get his Peugeot *Starduster,* come what may - and Pember would get his saving.

Having backed out of any responsibility for it, the Countess was resolved, perfectly resolved, that the ball must not go on. It would be quite wrong, for so many reasons, some of which were even now being given their bottles at Flint House. Pemberton, although his dear wife couldn't know it, must not give a ball, if only for the sake of his children. Six in all, at least four of whom were mistakes - there was no doubt about it, he had no trouble in reproducing, but then the Melburys never had, not since the Conquest, when as far as anyone could gather they seemed to have fairly inundated both Dorset and Wiltshire, and even been involved in the Cathedral when it first needed a fund in 1102. No, the ball had to be cancelled and soon, before the peach pleating for the inside of the hired tents had been done and well before Elliott had decided on the finger food.

The Countess dabbed her lips with her napkin. The second course, after the delicious asparagus, was just a little disappointing, as entrées so often were after really good hors d'oeuvres. Still, Andrew had chosen good claret, the kind of claret that made you gaze on the future with a great deal more certainty than you had in the past, the future being not just the challenge of the field mice, but the challenge of bringing about the demise of the ball. Mary would be of help, she felt sure, in little things anyway, persuading people who might like the idea, well beforehand of course, that the ball was going to be dull, that no-one great or grand was going to go to it, that it was not going to be a gold plate affair, that it would be little more than a hop, and a lot less than a ball. She would ring her in the morning. What would they all do without the telephone?

'Any more asparagus, Bloss?' Pemberton enquired of his butler.

Jennifer looked up. She wouldn't have minded some more either. The butter sauce had been really rather perfect, better than vinaigrette, and she and Pember had rather enjoyed dabbing their little pieces of French bread from the delicatessen in Stanton in it.

'I'm afraid there has been a small failure in that department,' Bloss told his lordship, in his best deeply regret voice. 'But Cook tells me there will be another supply in tomorrow.'

'I should say there should be, Bloss, another great grand one. Those asparagus beds were laid out by my grandfather and used to supply enough asparagus for a fortnight's guests, a whole house full. I should say there should be a great and grand and albeit continuous supply.'

Jennifer nodded vigorously as he spoke. Pember and he were as one on this, absolutely. After all, the asparagus season was only short, and if Pember couldn't have more when he wanted, then she too would want to know why tomorrow.

'Do you think he's been selling it off?' she hissed to Pember, after Bloss had withdrawn, taking with him his heated trolley.

'I don't know,' muttered Pemberton, reluctant to think less of his esteemed butler. 'No, I don't think so. Just didn't get Chappell to dig enough, probably.'

Nevertheless, he did wonder. It wasn't as if there weren't asparagus beds aplenty. But even as he wondered Pemberton was uneasily aware that he was not exactly in a position to quiz Bloss on the subject. If Bloss had had only a limited supply of asparagus he also had in his possession a little bag of oats. That little bag of oats had quite a tale to tell, and it wasn't the sort of tale that Jennifer would enjoy if she heard it.

'Yes,' he repeated quickly. 'Just didn't get enough dug, I should think.'

Jennifer stared across the table at her husband. He was looking really rather beautiful and handsome tonight. Blue shirt, blue tie, blue suit. She liked him in blue. He was, had been, considered one of the most handsome men of his generation, it had said in a small inset in

Harpers & Queen only last month. He was very handsome and very elegant in his way. A little wayward, which after all was only to be expected from a man of his wealth, power and lineage. His only problem, as far as she was concerned, was his reluctance to write a cheque to put into her allowance account, so that she could really get the Ball rolling. Without the wherewithal, now becoming rather blatantly and badly needed, as dear Fulton had pointed out this morning, they could not even order up the peach pleating for the tents, or retain a jazz group for the late night disco in the dungeons.

'Pember?'

'Yes, my sweet?' answered Pemberton, feeling inordinately fond of Jennifer as he always did, once he thought of Lady Tizzy and her bag of oats.

'Pember, would you like to come for a walk in the grounds?'

'Could do,' answered Pemberton, looking down at his lamb cutlet and then across at his wife. 'Might I finish my dinner first?'

'Of course, Pember,' said Jennifer graciously, 'but hurry. There's a full moon, and I want you to see the lovely dog fox coming down to the fish pond.'

'Lovely dog fox!' Pemberton's lamb cutlet turned to ashes in his mouth. 'You can't expect me to admire a dog fox – surely not with the amount of ducks and chickens we keep.'

'Oh, but I can,' Jennifer told him seriously. 'I have planted herbs around the fish pond, and he comes down to eat them. Mrs Chappell told Chappell that if there are herbs around the fish pond, Mr Fox will simply snip, snip, snip his herb dinner, and leave the chickens alone. It works. They do it in Australia.'

'They do a lot of things in Australia that I wouldn't want done here,' growled Pemberton.

'Why? What do they do in Australia that you wouldn't want done here, Pember?' '

'They wear corks on their hats! And I certainly don't want herbs here feeding foxes. I don't want to watch foxes either, they make me think of dead chickens, can't help it.'

'Very well, come for a walk anyway. New moon, lovely new moon to look at.'

Pemberton pushed his cutlet away. He might as well face it, it was a great deal easier to do what Jennifer wanted than not to do what Jennifer wanted.

Out in the garden Jennifer wandered ahead of Pember, looking and looking in the moonlight for somewhere quite private, somewhere very private.

'Pember?'

'How about here?'

'What about here?' asked Pemberton, staring at a lush piece of well grown long grass that set off some really rather mighty pampas grass he had planted, to his mind anyway, to perfection.

'How about succumbing to wild urges here?'

Jennifer dropped her gaze from the moon down to Pember's really rather well lit face.

'I don't think I want herbs here, Jennifer -' said Pemberton, looking puzzled.

'Not herbs here, us here, Pember darling,' Jennifer replied, giggling, but advancing on him with visible determination.

Pemberton's mind, at times lightning quick, at times quite the opposite, speeded up to its optimum. Good God! Bother the moonlight. He couldn't - more babies, Heathfield, Eton, heaven only knew what, he couldn't.

'My sweet, I can't, not here, we can't, not here.'

'Why ever not?' Jennifer wanted to know. 'Why ever not?' she repeated, still giggling, but now undoing the buckle on his belt.

'Because . . . because it's illegal, we would get arrested if found.'

'We shan't be found.'

'No, but we could be, we could easily be found, and by anyone. Chappell on a moonlit dig, Bloss - anyone.' Pemberton's voice suddenly reached to a higher pitch as he remembered just how much three babies, let alone six, was going to cost him. 'Anyway, I've drunk too much, much too much.'

'You hardly drunk anything — *drank* anything.'

'Before dinner I had three martinis, and it's given me whatever it's called - I can't, really.'

Jennifer let go of his belt. Thank heavens. And then she stood back and stamped her foot.

'Well really! When just for once I'm in a romantic mood you have to go and have three martinis. Well really!'

Pemberton watched her disappear up the lawn with a feeling of resignation, and of sudden passion. It would have been lovely. If only he had had the courage to go to *Real Man*, but the truth of it was, he hadn't. He'd made an appointment three times, under the name of Bert Ackroyd. He'd done it himself, leaving no telephone number or contact of any kind, of course, but each time the day and the hour had approached, he had found himself approaching the telephone and cancelling. Oh, dear, he groaned. Moonlight, love-making, even with Jennifer, it would have been what his nanny used to call *yumpty*.

6

On the train journey home to Longborough Georgiana had felt very beautiful. She had felt beautiful, and what's more she had felt desirable, something that she had not felt for a very long time. Even so she was still looking forward to seeing her little boy, and hearing from Nanny how he had been in her absence.

George was the spitting image of Gus. There was no doubt at all as to who had been his father, which was just as well really considering his father had never married his mother. He kissed Georgiana with great affection and she hugged him to her, thinking how much she actually loved him in return.

'I have something for you,' she said, giving him a parcel.

'You spoil him, Lady Georgie,' said Gus' mother, looking on jealously as the little boy unwrapped his present from London which Georgiana then showed him how to work. It was a spring loaded toy that when the spring was loaded and a button pushed fired pieces of coloured plastic up in the air, a simple thing but the sort of toy that gives young children infinite pleasure, a plaything that Georgiana had always longed to possess when she had been small, but which had always been denied her, so as soon as she had seen it in the toy shop she had determined to take one home for her son, and now that the coloured bits and pieces were flying around in the air with she and George chasing after them, she was very glad that she had.

'How's Gus?' she remembered to ask after the first twenty minutes of her return had passed in play.

'I don't know, love, he's been working all day – in his studio,' said Nan, shrugging, and then she added as if Georgiana had been away for years and forgotten where the studio was. 'Down the garden.'

'Then down the garden I must go,' said Georgiana, smiling, and standing up. Happily she had remembered to bring Gus back not one but two presents from London, not forgetting gifts for Nan and Nanny as well.

'It's not Christmas you know,' said Nanny in an accusatory tone – not that she liked of Christmas either, but even so she allowed Georgiana to open her present and helped herself to one of the handmade chocolates straight away.

Georgiana wandered down the garden and pushed open the studio door without knocking, an act she immediately regretted as she found herself confronted by the sight of a stark naked Gus standing by the studio chaise longue on which reclined a beautiful girl who was also stark naked.

'Oh,' Georgiana muttered. 'Gus. Sorry. Sorry - I didn't realize you were busy. Sorry. I'll see you later – when - when you're finished,' she added, before turning on her heel and returning to the house considerably faster than she had left it, convincing herself en route that Gus had been simply busy painting, hence the nude model, although as to finding the reason for Gus himself was also being naked she found more difficult, her final but half-hearted assumptions being that either he had stripped off due to the hot weather or simply to make his model feel more at ease. Then when she got back to the house she went straight up to her room where she locked the door and lay down on her bed quite unable to move or think.

Not much time elapsed before she heard her door handle being turned and Gus calling urgently from outside.

'Let me in, will you?' he called. 'Come on – love?'

She did wish he wouldn't call her *love* which she considered somewhat too working class for her taste, particularly when all things working class had long since ceased being chic.

'I'm just resting, Gus. I'll be down later.'

'If you don't open this bloody door!' he warned her. 'You'll be sorry.'

Georgiana sighed, finding it tiresome when men said things like that, particularly through closed doors, the implication being that the victim was going to suffer one way or the other, whether they opened the door or not. So Georgiana got up slowly off the bed and wandered across to open the offending door.

'What the hell do you think you're doing?' Gus demanded to know.

'Doing? I'm not *doing* anything, Gus,' she replied, wandering back to her bed.

'I mean by locking your door.'

'I often lock my door, I like locking my door.'

'And I don't. I don't like you locking your door. Okay?'

'Not really. It's my door and I think I can lock it if I want. Okay?'

'I don't know what you're playing at,' Gus seethed, following her across the room. 'Locking your door, barging into my studio without knocking.'

'Yes. Sorry about that,' Georgina interposed coolly. 'I didn't realise you were – you were working.'

'I've told you,' Gus said after taking a moment to find his balance. 'I've told you time and time again – you always have to knock when I'm in my studio. One interruption and inspiration can go forever.'

'I said I'm sorry,' Georgiana said, now going to her dressing table. 'What else do you want me to do?'

She picked up her heavy silver-backed hand mirror and her heavy silver-backed hairbrush before turning back to face him in her black silk and lace petticoat and black silk stockings, the same outfit that had achieved such an immediate effect t with Kaminski, although as Georgiana soon realised, it was not having the same immediate effect on Gus. Even so, hoping that her appearance might have some sort of calming effect on the raging Gus she stood before him slowly brushing out her lustrous dark hair.

'That painting might have gone, you know,' he said, apparently now slightly now mollified. 'An artist's inspiration is paper thin.'

'That would be quite awful,' she agreed. 'But then on the other hand it might be even better for the interruption. Neither of us can really tell, can we? And after all think of it - even you won't ever know.'

Gus walked over to her, but Georgiana backed off down the room, still firmly holding her hairbrush and her hand mirror.

'What are you backing away for?' Gus wanted to know. 'What d'you think I'm going to do?'

'Nothing. I'm not backing away from you - it's just that I wanted to give you your present,' said Georgiana quickly, worried for a moment that Gus had been going to hit her, grateful that Harrods still did presents up in big boxes so that she could bang the box in front of her and really shove it at Gus like a shield.

'Cashmere,' he said, having torn open the box almost savagely. 'Bit bloody extravagant, in't it?'

'Not really,' Georgiana said quickly, hoping to diffuse the moment. 'Bought you something else, too.'

She immediately presented him with another smaller box.

'God this is *beautiful*,' Gus said, this time hardly audibly.

Georgiana had surprised him with this one, a specially commission an enamelled box from *Halcyon Days* made from of one of his paintings, not a painting from his personally much despised but incredibly but incredibly successful *The Lady Loves* series, but from one of his current series of pictures, such as the one perhaps he and his naked model had been so-called working on.

Gus leaned forward and kissed Georgiana on the lips and his eyes filled with tears. Georgiana gazed back at him, happy now that she no longer felt frightened of him. She knew that the awful moment had passed, the moment when he could have beaten her and she was safe again, thanks to her sentimentality and to her abundant extravagance. She saw it had been a good thing that she had chosen this particular day to surprise him with the enamel box, the very day she had also surprised him with his model. She just wished that he didn't seem suddenly like a stranger to her, and that she couldn't wasn't behaving in such an obviously coquettish way that appalled her, although at the same time it also was slightly intrigued her as well. After all if she was honest, she herself had deceived him the evening before; well before Gus had even started to work with his naked model Kaminski had been making love to Georgiana, which was naturally why she had thought it only right and proper to make it up to Gus with his box and his cashmere sweater.

The worst of it was, she realized while recounting some minor anecdote from her journey home, she saw the worst part of it was that it had worked. Everything had worked - the presents, the deception, her behaviour since her return - everything had been successful which made one part of her glad, and one part of her sorry.

'Dinner,' she said suddenly. 'I think I hear Nan ringing the gong.'

Gus hesitated as he was pulling Georgiana into his arms, and seeing the hesitation in his eyes Georgiana quickly added that it was salmon en croûte, just the way he liked it in a white wine sauce – and greed instantly overcame Gus' desire just as Georgiana had hoped that it might. He let go of her, and as he released her Georgiana felt an overwhelming relief that managed to surprise her, a surprise she could not say was due more to how easy she had found it to manipulate Gus or to how powerful was the impact that Kaminski had had upon her - and in truth because she was too busy taking advantage of the moment, quickly dressing herself while keeping Gus busy talking she had not to time yet to decide. That, she thought as she got Gus to fasten up the back of her blue silk dress – could wait until later.

Jennifer gazed at Fulton. She hadn't realized just how handsome he was until now. He was looking particularly nice because he was wearing the same kind of blue that she favoured for Pember, but on Fulton, she realized with a slight blush the colour was even better, really making his lovely blue eyes stand out.

'It must be terribly difficult for you now, now that you have had to take on two nannies,' she said in her most sympathetic voice.

'Not so much two nannies, not as such, because old nanny is top nanny and the new one - now the monthly nurses have gone - is under-nanny. She's very young and very sweet, and quick to pick up things. You know, smocking and that kind of thing. Smocks like mad. Non-stop in fact.'

'I dearly love smocking. Another Pimms?'

'Mais certainement. Quite strong, aren't they?'

'Lovely and strong,' Jennifer corrected him. 'I made them myself,' she went on proudly. 'Added things, but not mint. They should never be served with mint – it quite kills the recipe.'

'One more of these in this heat and I'll be undone,' Fulton sighed happily.

'Fulton? Guess what?'

'What?'

'I've only got the cheque out of Pember!'

She had deliberately kept the secret settled in the shade of her favourite tree with a glass of something lovely in their hands and the sun beating down on them quite beautifully.

'This is good news.'

'I know. It's taken long enough,' Jennifer agreed. 'Not at all like my Pember who is usually so generous. Must be awful tax and things that have held him back from signing. But now at any rate we can safely say the ball will commence!'

Jennifer took a deep draught of her fresh drink as Fulton sighed with relief. He was beginning to feel quite guilty about the cheque for the ball, what with overtures having had to be made to Pemberton so recently about Beau and Daisy-Marguerita's school fees, and the applied for endowments and all those sorts of things. It was as if they at Flint House were more in the nature of poor relations, instead of real relations, albeit on the wrong side of the blanket.

But it had to be, as Fulton knew. This was the way of the world. If Melburys were to be brought up Melburys and everything in both their gardens was to be lovely, then come what mayhem Pemberton had to pay for his little indiscretions, but which they all hoped that thanks to *Real Man* would now instantly be at an end. Even so and despite all this, he and Elliott were actually very fond of Jennifer and they dearly wished the ball to proceed, not only because everyone was so fed up with the Cathedral and its fund, but more because they were looking forward to making everything beautiful for Jennifer, who it had to be said was awfully good-hearted and who by and large did not wish ill will on anyone, not even Lady Tizzy whom she must sometimes have suspected however dimly of having something to do with Pember's regular little absences.

'Fulton.' Jennifer picked up her tapestry, and eyed it a little woozily. 'You know, we've been friends for quite a long time now, haven't we?'

'Certainly,' Fulton agreed, gazing ahead of him and thinking he saw roses in the garden where there had been none before.

'Then you won't mind, will you - you won't mind if I'm a little honest with you, do you?'

'Yes,' said Fulton, really quite promptly, considering he had just realized that he was seeing the panoply of the Hall set against its lovely gardens as even the architect in his wildest dreams couldn't have seen it, namely double.

'I make a practice of never being honest to other people,' he slurred. 'And I like people to be the same to me, please, nice and dishonest.'

'No,' Jennifer said, holding up one hand. 'No but really a really, really close friend can surely really say some things, some things that might not be said even by one's perhaps mother perhaps.'

Jennifer paused, momentarily, because she suddenly couldn't think of one thing that would not be said by her mother to her, not one.

'You know what I mean,' she went on hastily. 'Least I think you do. I hope you so because I don't. There are some things said in kindness mind, with only you in mind – mind - that have to be said and I honestly think are best said as I'm sure I hope you do too, Fulton – when we all think about it. I honestly do think that perhaps lovely as these things are, and you know how we all love them, lovely and beautiful though they are, and fond as we undoubtedly all are and can be of them, I honestly think - you and Lady Tizzy have had enough children, don't you? If you know what I mean. Which I sincerely hope you do. Because I am not longer sure I do.'

63

Fulton turned and stared at Jennifer, and tears welled up in his eyes. She was so sweet, so innocent and knew absolutely nothing, he thought - nothing about anything and this particular subject in particular. She knew absolutely nothing and so was lovely beyond even his imaginings and all his means.

'How you are sweet, you are. Jennifer,' he managed. 'You are sweet so, Jennifer. Absolutely *sweet.*'

Jennifer looked at him, her head on one side, her tapestry now held at a dangling angle.

'You're very sweet Fulton too, ' she managed after a careful collection of her thoughts. 'You're a very sweet Fulton and I love children you see, you know, Fulton – that we have most certainly and definitely in common - we have that in common the both of us - but nowadays, two or three and with Eton, Heathfield, all that expense, let alone everything else, even rich men Pember like men feel it. They feel the *pinch* – they feel it as he remarked to me only last week the other day. They really feel it. So we must think of the best, I think, think for the best as to how much it costs then double it then double it again and again and that's, apparently I understand – that is apparently how much children cost us.'

'Do you know?' Fulton said, leaning very slowly forward. 'Do you know how Jennifer you are, sweet? You are very so sweet, Jennifer.'

'Do you – thank you by the way – do you read *The Parishioner?* I don't know if you ever read – *The Parishioner -* ' Jennifer straightened her head, dropped her tapestry, and lifting her backside produced a copy from under the cushion she had been sitting on. 'I don't know who reads it but I – I find it personally *riveting*. Anyway. Anyhow and in here – in here is a small a'vertisement to which I think we should all of us each and every one man Jack – I think we should all pay 'ttention. Because this – this is an a'vertisement – this is an a'vertisement that can change the world, Elliott -'

'Fulton,' Fulton corrected her. 'I'm Fulton. It's the other one way may be or may not Elliott.'

Fulton fell slowly forward out of his chair but Jennifer seemed not to notice.

'This is for the whole benefit of whoever, Fulton,' Jennifer continued. 'The good of the world, the good of each other, for the good of us. I have ringed it for you, Fulton, because we don't want to speak further about anything, or be indiscreet, and I know how much you and she love each other, Lady Whatsit and what a dear friend Elliott is to you both – Lady Tizzy. That's it. And there you all are smocking together and everything - so I won't, you know, I don't want to embarrass us both and you and I and bang on but. But you will see however what I mean when you read this. Page a hundred and ten something – always such funny numbering always – they do. One doesn't know where you are. Somewhere after the Motoring and Farm Machinery section. Anyway, you will see, as I say, not to bang on too much, you will see what I mean. When you get home. Time enough to tell. For I have ringed it. For you. Wait till you get home.'

Fulton would have tried to read it there and then had Jennifer not collapsed sideways in her chair to fall into a Pimms induced slumber with her mouth open. He stared at her for an equally Pimms induced moment, wondering whether Jennifer might perhaps have collapsed fatally until he saw she was still breathing and at the same time smiling happily. So he endeavoured to get himself to his feet without falling forwards once again and once he was steady enough made himself slowly to his car, clutching what he thought must be a red hot copy of *The Parishioner.*

As far as he could remember he got home safely, although he was later to wonder indeed as to how he had achieved such a thing, given the amount of Pimms he and Jenifer had consumed in their excitement. But before he could read the advertisement Jennifer had so

thoughtfully ringed for him he collapsed and fell asleep in the hall chair. In so doing *The Parishioner* slipped from his grasp to lie open at the very page that announced:
Men! You want it? Come and get it! Just ten minutes and the wife's best friend can really be that! Call the Real Man Curtailment Agency for a carefree love life in home from home conditions.

Jennifer half woke up in time to hear Fulton's soon to be part-exchanged Golf hiccoughing its way down the drive, feeling another sudden and overwhelming sense of fondness for him once again. Even in through her alcoholic haze she knew that he would read the *Real Man* advertisement and ponder. After all it was the only sensible solution, she thought, imagining by now by his own and Lady Tizzy's ability to produce babies as nauseam. *Real Man* would be the answer to their troubles, she smiled. Thanks to her they would now be able to enjoy a wonderful and quite carefree love life.

The thought made Jennifer almost sit up, but not quite. Another thought then crept inch by inch into her befuddled brain - perhaps this was the reason why Pember had been so timid with her in the garden by the pampas grass – perhaps he was afraid of his own virility and the thought of even more school fees and endowments had affected his normally healthy appetite. So perhaps he too – Jennifer realised – perhaps he would also benefit from a visit to *Real Man?* Jennifer lay back in her garden chair and closed her eyes to give herself time to think. But before she found the time to wonder whether or not she should advise her dear Pember to pay a visit to this *Real Man* Curtailment Agency so that he would cease to be so shy in moonlit conditions, she had once again drifted off into a bucolic slumber.

Elliott paused by the door of the nurseries. They were the sweetest sight, their babies - of that there was to him no doubt.

Every one of them was busy wriggling and gurgling, or crawling across the floor. Once in the nursery with Nanny and Bessie he was just beginning to enjoy himself when he heard the sound of the front door banging shut and so after another five or so minutes of nursery fun and games he made his excuses and dashed downstairs since he could no longer wait to hear all the news hot off the press about the ball
'Well?'

He found Fulton was fast asleep in the hall chair when he finally descended with a magazine spread open at his feet.

'Fulton?' he wondered, deliberately loudly. 'Fulton?'

Fulton awoke with a start, got up immediately then sat down again at once.

'Oh dear,' he groaned, shutting his eyes tightly. 'I think I may have a little headache.'

'Oh dear is right,' Elliott agreed. 'I wonder whether you should have driven home. Yes?'

'No,' Fulton replied, before opening one reddened eye. 'I drove home? Like this? Where from? Oh dear. I do hope I drove slowly. Unlike the dear vicar after he'd had quite a few. And drove home as fast as he could before he had an accident.'

'Come on,' Elliott aid, taking Fulton by both hands and easing him back on to his feet. 'I'll make you some strong black coffee. You go into the drawing room and sit down, and when I've made the coffee you can tell me *all* about it.'

Fulton nodded but did as he was told. Truth to tell he sensed that Elliott was more than a little miffed, the way people so often are when it was not they that had been plied with too much strong drink. He walked slowly into the drawing room where he sat in silence, trying to sober up and organise his thoughts .

He sat in the window seat and gazed out on to the lawn. It was a very pretty lawn, to go with their very pretty house. Fulton loved the garden and the house, but he felt a deep and nagging doubt about the place, namely that ever since they had moved out of their apartment in Bath and into Flint House their life seemed to have changed somewhat dramatically, and in the state he was currently in Fulton was not entirely sure it had all been for the best. Here was now not only a married man but a married man with *children* which was really something he could never ever have imagined. He shut his eyes tightly, hoping that when he reopened them he would find himself back in Bath and that all that had happened had in fact been one long and rather troublesome dream.

'One good thing,' Fulton said later, after two cups of Elliott's especially strong coffee. 'Apparently Pember has not stopped the cheque – which was something Jennifer thought he might well do when he came to his senses.'

'Don't be such a silly billy,' Elliott replied. 'Roll on the day when Pember *ever* comes to his senses.'

'There was a very good chance,' Fulton replied. 'Not of Pember coming to his senses but of his cancelling. At least according to Twinks. The Village Voice told her.'

'Twinks should stop listening to Mrs Dupont.'

'She can't. Mrs Dupont has it over her dreadfully. Twinks says it's because she always arrives with a collecting tin, and people with collecting tins always have it over one. I know just what she means – they make you feel that you should be collecting instead of them, and that however much you put in or don't put in, it's always the wrong amount. That's why they smile so kindly at you. They pity you, you know, for getting it wrong. 'Specially if you put in too much. No, you can't blame Twinks. Hers is a sensitive nature.'

'Not too sensitive judging from that last tray she did.'

They lapsed into silence, but Elliott knew Fulton too well and it wasn't long before he had out-silenced him, which he, in his turn, knew was something that Fulton couldn't tolerate for a single minute, even in his still semi-inebriated state.

'Well. There was something else. Actually.'

He looked around him as if for something lost.

'Might it be this I wonder?' Elliott said, holding up *The Parishioner.*

'The very thing,' Fulton sighed. 'Jennifer's ringed something somewhere. Page a hundred and something or other. Her solution for the troubles of this world.'

Elliott riffled through the pages, passing by the advertisements for people needing to exchange a Baby Belling for a nearly-new nylon fur and four cockerels and many other etcteras until he came to the page with a blue ink ringed advertisement.

'My life and tinned peaches, I don't believe it!'

'Believe what?' Fulton wondered. 'I've not read it.'

Elliott handed him the journal and Fulton studied the advertisement.

There was a small but telling silence when he had finished.

'Well,' he said finally. 'I suppose when you think about it we could take this as a bit of a compliment?'

They continued to look at each other for a moment longer in silence and then they both began to laugh, Elliott a little more boisterously than the still *souffrant* Fulton.

Mrs Parker-Jones picked her way up the Countess's drive. She had parked her car at the bottom, just in case there was nowhere at the top where it would be safe, or so she was prepared to tell anyone she met, while in truth her sole purpose for making her way so carefully up the drive was to see if it was as weed-free as her own short path, and now she was treading along its gravelled surface she could see that it was. There wasn't a dandelion or a daisy in sight and for some reason this disappointed her. It was exactly like when she heard that Andrew had been behaving himself very well ever since she had decided to divorce him. Even so the Countess had at least and at last invited her to tea. Heaven only knew it had taken long enough, and heaven also only knew what the purpose of her visit was going to turn out to be because Clarissa knew as only a mother, a widow, a twice a wife could know, there would have to be a purpose. The Countess would not have asked her for nothing. The Countess never ever did anything for nothing. As she lived and as she breathed Clarissa Parker-Jones knew there be a very singular purpose behind the sudden invitation to tea.

They had collaborated before, of course, over the girls, as both Jennifer and Georgiana were still known to them. They had made small plans to cover potential scandals and divert happenings that they thought might be about to happen, but never once had the Countess asked her to tea. As she approached the front door Mrs Parker-Jones straightened the top of her Jason Jonet lightweight non matching two-piece, and checked its colour coordinated belt. She judged herself dressed quite right - not too smart and not too country either - about right in fact with the just the right and discreet amount of class.

The Countess had watched Mrs Parker-Jones making her way along her drive from the moment she had alighted from her car, considering that even from the landing window, even from that distance the woman looked quite frightful. And why was the wretched woman walking up the drive for heaven's sake? she asked herself – why leave her motor car down by the gate of all places? Had it broken down? Was she walking for some health purpose? And why was she so early? The whole business reeked of *les nouveaux*.

She made her way down to the drawing room to settle herself in front of the fire that she always had Maria light summer and winter while her guest rang for admittance.

'Hey Meesus Parker-Jones!' Maria announced loudly from the door. The Countess enjoyed having people announced, even though it seemed such a thing had long gone out of style. The Countess still did but not only for her own enjoyment but for that of Maria as well.

'How do you manage with such a large house all to yourself, and Andrew in the lodge?' Clarissa Parker-Jones enquired once tea was under way.

'Like everyone else,' said the Countess, pouring tea. 'I manage so-so.'

She had no intention of elaborating on that most boring of country conversational topics, namely the problem of staff.

'Yes, but how many do you employ here?'

'I employ two in the house, and three in the garden,' said the Countess, having considered the question and the vulgarity of it before handing Mrs Parker-Jones a cup of tea, and the sugar bowl, and not bothering to ask her whether she preferred lemon or milk simply because she was already regretting inviting the woman in the first place.

'I see your drive is weed-free,' Clarissa then remarked. 'So I suppose you have no trouble with gardeners.'

The Countess closed her eyes and counted quickly to ten which was just enough to keep her calm and stop her having to ask Mrs Parker-Jones to leave. If it wasn't for the memory of that frightful letter of Jennifer's to her daughter Lady Mary she most certainly would have done, but just the memory of being referred to as a dear old thing was enough to make her determined to see the ordeal through.

'Do have some cake,' she said, holding out a plate of strawberry shortcake to her guest.

'Oh no, no I never eat tea,' Mrs Parker-Jones replied with smug smile, at the same time tapping her waist as if in indication.

'It's very good,' the Countess said, making it sound like a reprimand. 'It's Maria's speciality and it just melts in the mouth.'

The Countess picked up a little pearl-handled fork and ate her shortcake delicately, so delicately that after two or three of her mouthfuls Mrs Parker-Jones deeply regretted that she said she didn't eat tea.

'At our age,' the Countess began and unfairly according to Clarissa Parker-Jones since the Countess was at least ten years older than herself. 'At our age,' she repeated ruthlessly - 'We must stick together. We are usually - all of us at our age - completely in agreement with what is wrong with the world, and what is right with the world, are we not? We have outgrown all the hideous idealism of youth and can sit back and see what there is to be done and very often do it. Or,' she paused, sipping her tea and then carefully replacing her cup, 'we can see what is being done, and undo it. Would you not agree?'

Mrs Parker-Jones nodded. She knew very well that what the Countess was saying was true - they did both feel the same, and why shouldn't they? Although they might not be the same age, as the Countess had so unkindly insinuated, at least they had other things in common. They lived in Wiltshire, they looked after Andrew, and they both took the *Daily Telegraph*. None of those things could be considered to be nothing, least of all looking after Andrew Gillott.

'Is something wrong with Andrew?' asked Clarissa, essaying to come quickly to the point, knowing that since he was still her husband be it name only, anything he had done would undoubtedly have to be undone.

'As a matter of fact there is nothing wrong with Andrew bar his eating asparagus a little too noisily. No, nothing, for once. He's happy enough in the Lodge, and I let him out at night, as you know - although China has fallen through but then let's face it nowadays – which place hasn't? Even so, although China has fallen through he is hoping to take a small party of people on a trekking expedition to Western Australia. It's a new travel agency a friend of his has started *Nihilistic Tours,* their motto being *Nothing to see, nothing to do.* Apparently it's designed for people who live in inner cities. It makes the poor souls able to embrace the crowded life again once they return, having been so utterly *desolè.* Andrew maintains that once they have tramped across the scorched earth for days on end seeing nothing but the corks on their own hats, they soon stop complaining about conditions on the underground and the litter and everything. It really makes them appreciate civilization. Unsurprisingly they are booked out already, so Andrew says. Of course, as you can imagine, his only problem is how to get his copy of *Sporting Life* flown out, but apparently supplies have to be dropped daily anyway, so *plus ça change, plus c'est* very much the same old story, especially when it comes to holidays, I find. Everyone taking them and then coming back and telling you all about it in infinite detail, and of course sun tans are now so utterly *de trop* of course. Everyone has one. The gels at the supermarket check outs, one's daily help – even *les garagistes* – at least so Maria tells me. A deathly pallor is what one must achieve nowadays, as it was before, before everyone decided to try burning themselves to death. And then after taking all these holidays they all have the gall to complain how poor they are. Ridiculous. Time was when no-one but the Duke of Westminster could afford two holidays, and then only because he had his own yacht. But I digress.'

The Countess stopped, realizing she had gone too far.

'Not at all. I am completely riveted,' Clarissa replied.

'It's your fault, Clarissa,' the Countess scolded. 'You shouldn't have started me on this.'

Mrs Parker-Jones opened her mouth to protest that she hadn't, but shut it again when she realized that the Countess had called her by her first name, the first time this had ever happened. It made her feel odd – almost – she had to admit – actually a little moved.

'Have you been on holiday?' the Countess wanted to know, staring at what she suspected might be a sunburned arm.

'Gracious no,' Mrs Parker-Jones protested. 'I caught the sun simply from working on the mixed border by the bust of Beethoven in the sink garden, that's all this is. This is just a little Wiltshire gardening brown. That's all this is.'

'Your arm is so brown it looks almost foreign,' murmured the Countess accusingly.

'It isn't, I do assure you. I catch the sun just like that,' Clarissa said, trying to snap finger and thumb rather ineffectually. 'It fades almost as quickly as it arrives.'

'Where was I?' demanded the Countess, back to being ruthless because she really wasn't interested in talking about Clarissa Parker-Jones and her suspect sun tan any longer. 'I know where I was. I was just about to broach a subject.'

She put down her fine eighteenth century Spode tea cup carefully and arranged herself suitably for her new subject.

'Yes,' she then announced, hands now in lap. 'Your daughter. Jennifer. Such a sweet girl.'

Clarissa Parker-Jones's heart started to beat a little faster. So this was it, she wondered. This was the purpose of her visit. Jennifer must have done something frightful to the Countess, but what exactly? It must be something serious, she realized, for the Countess to invite her to tea here in the drawing room the Countess' own home with a fire lit and the fresh flowers everywhere, flowers arranged in carless and artless designs.

'Sweet is not how I would describe Jennifer,' Clarissa said quickly. 'Buxom, firm, opinionated, yes, and very like her late father Aidan certainly. She always was, too, never at all like me either in looks or character. No taste either, of course, none at all but then since she is married to John Pemberton she doesn't need to have any taste, does she?' Clarissa laughed, possibly a little too self-consciously she realised as she became aware of the Countess' expression. 'What I mean is when you're married to someone with fifteen racehorses in training and a private art collection, you have no real need of taste because everyone has it for you. Even so, sweet is not a word I would think of immediately when it comes to my dear daughter.'

The Countess studied Mrs Parker-Jones in silence. She was only too well aware of how frightful Clarissa was, but now she became doubly aware, considering that any woman who who that capable of running her daughter down in such a way should really not be tolerated. Unfortunately whether she had meant to or not, Jennifer had gone too far in her letter to Mary and the writing now on the wall, and so as the Countess then realised, tolerate the Parker-Jones woman she surely must – at least for a while longer.

'I see,' the Countess finally said, although she did not see at all and to cover the short but awkward silence that ensured she poured them both some more tea, before spelling out her proposed mutual plan of action.

When Clarissa heard what the Countess was proposing, so complete was their concord that it was not long before both of them were pecking away with small pearl handled tea forks at pieces of the delicious strawberry shortcake.

7

Bloss stared morosely at the Pemberton Cup. He knew it was historical, and he knew it was something that as the Pemberton butler he should be happy to clean, particularly since it was the whole reason why they now had a newly installed and over-effective burglar alarm, but for reasons which were all too clear to him nothing was making him happy that morning, and small wonder since he suspected that his master might be thinking of replacing him. After all Bloss' loyalty and patience let alone tact and forbearance rumour had it that Bloss was going to be replaced by someone called Bert Ackroyd.

Not that Bloss was a snob - of course he wasn't even if he did say so himself. He liked to think of himself as the very last person who could be described as such; for instance he didn't mind at all fraternizing with the lower orders down at the King's Arms and was ready to converse fairly freely with anyone back at The Hall and treat them all as fellow staff rather than talk to them as if they were servants, with the possible exception of a very bad tempered and over sexed young woman once employed as housemaid who in Bloss' opinion would have been far more at home in the stables. Yet in spite of having moved with the times as no other butler he knew in fact had, in his heart of hearts he knew he would experience the greatest difficulty in being replaced by someone with as common a sounding name as Bert Ackroyd.

He was curious to discover quite how Lord Pemberton proposed to bring about this revolutionary change of staff. How would he tell her ladyship for instance, Bloss wondered. They might not be the best of friends in the way that he and his master were, but nonetheless he and Lady Pemberton were agreed on many things, from how to deal with Mrs Dupont, the Village Voice, to how to keep the Countess away from the arrangements for the forthcoming ball, and while it could not be said that they enjoyed the easiest of relationships, nevertheless Bloss was quite certain that her ladyship would miss him should he not be there.

At least as he remembered his lordship had had the grace to look embarrassed the day before when someone had called the Hall requesting to speak to Bert Ackroyd. For himself Bloss was proud of the unselfconscious way he had handled the incident while interested to note how flustered the ever reddening Lord Pemberton had become.

Bloss himself had taken the call and told the enquirer that to his almost certain knowledge no one called Ackroyd either lived or was staying at The Hall.

'You're quite wrong there, Bloss,' Lords Pemberton had announced, appearing out of the shadows to seize the telephone from his butler's grasp.

'I am sorry, m'lord,' Bloss had replied. 'I was only speaking from my cognizance.'

'Yes, yes, yes, I'm sure you jolly well were,' Lord Pemberton had blustered, turning an ever deeper shade of puce. Let me handle this, will you?'

He had then proceeded to apologize unequivocally to the caller on behalf of the mysterious Bert Ackroyd, explaining that Mr Ackroyd had been unavoidably delayed in spite of being well known to his lordship, but that his lordship knew that Mr Ackroyd had every intention of arriving at The Hall any time now, and moment that he did his lordship promised to give him the message and urge him to call the agency back as soon as possible.

That was what did it for Bloss, the word agency. As soon as he heard the slip Bloss knew that he was for the chop. He was going to be replaced by someone cheaper. It was all too obvious – what with the spiralling cost of living plus the added expenses that were to become due thanks to the new arrivals at Flint House had all obviously been too much for his lordship, and he was being forced to cut down even on essentials such as himself. Bloss knew that in such circumstances he would always be the first to go since all the other staff lived in tied cottages and worked for a pittance at the Hall in exchange for having a permanent roof over their heads, free fresh meat off the farm, plus a corn-fed turkey at Christmas.

Of course he would have to tell Bloss immediately. That would be the only honourable and decent thing, as Bloss well knew that – but then he also knew that his lordship might be having second thoughts since after the famous telephone call he had heard him muttering that he couldn't do it, that he couldn't go through with it - which came as no surprise to Bloss given the length of his service at the Hall.

Bloss picked up the Pemberton Cup and began to polish it, knowing it was best to keep himself busy until the axe fell. He knew that given his pedigree he would have no trouble of finding another position but the idea of no longer being at the Hall was really very upsetting. After all he had been with his master for many a year and there were things he knew that no-one else knew - and they were things not just about his lordship either, information that he would of course take to his grave. Not for Bloss the modern habit of supplementing his income by ringing the gossip columns and informing on his employers, that was most certainly not in Bloss' canon, even now however hurt and wounded he might be, he would not stoop to such a thing. As far as Bloss was concerned, the buck stopped with him – but even so, he could not help feeling a deep disquiet.

The telephone rang. Bloss picked it up.

'It's all right, Bloss!' a voice said on an extension. 'I've got it!'

Bloss stared at the telephone in his hand, sensing even more dislocation since he knew that one of the very last things his master enjoyed was speaking on the telephone let alone answering it. This one act alone confirmed Bloss' deepest and worst fears – he was indeed finally to go, and if this indeed was the case then he would prefer to see his master down rather than learn his fate second or even third hand. .

His lordship lowered his copy of the *Sporting Life* and stared at his butler who had now gained admittance to his study.

'Want something, Bloss?' he asked, his mind more occupied with finding the winner of a nursery Stakes at Sandown Park. 'I'm really quite busy, don't you know.'

'Your m'lord,' Bloss replied then cleared his throat. 'I shall come straight to the point, if I may.'

'Made it even quicker if you can, Bloss,' Lord Pemberton replied. 'Damn tricky card this afternoon.'

'In that case I shall come right out with it, m'lord,' Bloss replied gravely. 'Please be aware that I am in full cognizance of the position with you and Mr Ackroyd, m'lord.'

'Damned if you are,' Lord Pemberton replied, staring at him over his newspaper. 'You been at the nose paint?'

'No, m'lord, I have not. I am truly and perfectly sober and here to tell you I know about Mr Ackroyd *and* the agency.'

Pemberton dropped his newspaper on the floor at this, staring open mouthed at his butler while considering that things had come to a pretty pickle when a chap's butler began to discuss a chap's personal arrangements without so much as begging a chap's leave.

'If we're going to have a man to man here, Bloss,' he said, lowering his voice, 'then I think we'd best go and have in in the pantry, Bloss.'

Lord Pemberton got up and led the way out.

'Don't mention Bert Ackroyd in the pantry, Bloss,' he warned him en route. 'Don't want her ladyship overhearing. Can't have that. Not that I think she'd mind, as it happens. But you know how it is with the ladies, Bloss. They can kick up very rusty if you let them in on things too early. But there's no two ways about it, it must be done. The cut must be made.'

'So it seems, milord,' Bloss replied dutifully, following his master to the pantry.

'I just can't afford to go on like this.'

'I know, milord. And please note you I am the first to understand. It's just a little hard, after all this time.'

'I know, Bloss. Couldn't have put it better meself. We've been through so much together, Bloss. But it's wartime conditions for the very rich out there now. You just can't hang on to what you have any more, and it has to be faced - six children is twice as many as I had bargained for, quite frankly. But you understand. You're such a good fellow. I can't contemplate life without you.'

Pemberton patted Bloss's arm and was surprised to see tears in his retainer's.

'My dear fellow, don't upset yourself so!' he exclaimed. 'Worse things happen at sea. Far worse things, I do assure you.'

He then preceded Bloss into the pantry where he waited for his much loved butler to pour the usuals.

Georgiana's return home had been, to say the least, fortunate. As soon as she had seen that Gus obviously wanted to be able to go his own way and do what he wanted and when he wanted, she realised she really did not have to sit about feeling too bad about her reunion with Kaminski.

The trouble was that she did feel bad, constantly leading her to wonder quite how she had done what she did do. How could she have done what she did? How she wondered could she have allowed Kaminski to walk back into her life and have his way with her? Sometimes, such as now when she was brushing her hair very slowly in her dressing mirror she would literally blush, just remembering that evening. Other times her shame would wake her in the night and she would just lie there again wondering about the reasons for her bad behaviour before eventually falling back asleep again, only to reawake with a start at dawn when she would finally manage to put things in a better perspective and would lie and remember how special their love had been when she would curl up, clasp her pillow to her and smile, remembering how much there was in fact to smile about when she thought about her and Kaminski.

Finally she would find herself free of guilt and thinking only of how magnificent Kaminski was, how much more powerful, intense, and exciting he was than Gus, remembering how he had watched her in the dark of the bar as she imagined a sultan might sit in his harem while selecting his next concubine. And therein as she realised lay Kaminski's fascination, for since he had rejected her when she was young and beautiful, she knew that he might, all too easily do so again but for very different reasons, from boredom or even from fear of boredom. She found she could even bring herself to bear that thought, too, particularly now that Gus no longer wished to paint her and just her alone, enraptured by the texture of her alabaster skin, enthralled by her large eyes, and mesmerized by her oddly distant and seemingly aloof expression. Now that her lover had found someone else by whom to be artistically enslaved, Georgiana had in her turn a new need to be enthralled herself, or better still have someone in her thrall. For if she were being quite honest Georgiana longed for someone to be her slave, to be mesmerized by her, to be ready to be her slave and to be helpless without her, and already she had sensed even as Kaminski had left her that famous evening to return to his current amour - she knew well enough from the gossip columns all about Kaminski's current amours – she had felt that he was in precisely the frame of mind that she liked best in a man, namely that he was finally ready first to worship her and then to die for her.

She enjoyed her emotional volte face, having decided that nowadays she had no time for women who wanted to be slaves to men but the exact opposite – that men must be slaves to women and that the moment they stopped being so - as had very obviously happened to

Gus – then it was time for an emotional change. Stranragh her husband had brought about the first real sea change in her, altering her too-availing nature to one of subtle resistance, and now it seemed to her Gus might have brought about not only a second change but actually a complete change of attitude.

Georgiana now sat on the edge of her bed slowly buffing one perfect pink finger nail while thinking about Gus and his new *amour*, wondering what he saw in such a buxom type of girl, so different to Georgiana in every way – dark skinned, big bosomed, large boned, eyes that were worrisomely small and untrustworthy with a great mane of long red hair. And it was only now, now that she was beginning to heal and established her own emotional independence, it was only now she could admit to herself how shocked and hurt she had been when she had discovered them both naked in Gus' studio the day she had returned from London. It wasn't just that they had been naked and that Gus had obviously just enjoyed her, it was more to do with the fact that what had happened had taken place in what had once been Georgiana's own precious studio room, the room that she had so sacrificed and lent to Gus to paint in, and which he was now using not only as a place of work but also as a place to debauch himself. Seeing a girl such as Gus' new mistress sprawled naked on a chaise that had been in her family for centuries had actually made Georgiana feel quite ill. Gus may have tried his best to have shaken her down and changed her, but Georgiana now knew he had failed and that come hell or high water she would always be the person she had been born to be, the Lady Georgiana Longborough, just as she knew that now was the right time to move on.

She rose and walked to her window to look out over the gardens, musing as to how much more restful it would be to be with someone who did not criticize her at every turn as Gus did. She knew she had to change her life, and the only way that she could she reasoned would be with and through Kaminski, which would be difficult to say the least for he was the one person in the whole world she knew would never telephone or write to her. Indeed, knowing exactly the sort of man Kaminski was she thought he would even now have forgotten all about her and moved on to some new and infinitely more interesting conquest.

At breakfast which she took by herself, turning to the diary page she found an item about the very man who had just been entertaining in her thoughts. It concerned Kaminski and his new film and his search for strong athletic and nubile young women to play scuba divers in an all-important sequence. For a second Georgiana felt a sense of disappointment at the fact that Kaminski was looking for women the very opposite to her in physical type before suddenly realising that she knew a perfect example of the sort of young woman who would look good close up in scuba diving gear, an amply bosomed someone with long blonde hair who was probably right at this very moment talking her clothes off in what had once been Georgiana's garden studio. If she could interest Gus' model in such an opportunity she could be rid of the wretched girl while re-presenting herself to Kaminski, all in one go. Kaminski, who prided himself so much on his chess playing, would be proud of such a clever move.

The banner on the magazine cover announced an exciting new feature for the delectation of its devoted readers. It seemed the famous florist Annunciata Cauldron was about to reveal all.

Elliott, the person behind the open magazine, sighed with a pleasure. Besides James Beard, Annunciata Cauldron was to him the absolute tops. She was just what he needed to read about on a damp morning in latish May with Twinks was far from well. She had only just taken Elliott through her latest cure for tinia – namely the application of lard in places to Elliott quite unimaginable, a remedy which had apparently been used to great effect on some ailing person in the village. Another sigh escaped Elliott. There were sometimes just a few drawbacks to village life and recommended cures were undoubtedly one. Only last week, the Village Voice Mrs Dupont had written out a cure for Fulton's seasonal hay fever which sounded and in fact turned out to be worse than the affliction, an inhalation of nettles crushed and boiled in dried spinach leaves which Fulton was instructed to apply to the afflicted part. Fulton had complained and really quite vociferously since he was well over the worst of his hay fever that to refer to his nose in such terms was simply too horrible for words, for even if his nose was a part the last thing he wished to do was to think of it as afflicted.

Elliott lay back on the kitchen sofa, and as the rain outside began now to come down in stair rods flicked through the magazine from back to front, because he found that way it made everyone on the pages - even the ghastly potters in very bright jumpers - look better. Finally, he arrived at the article featuring Annunciata and her latest ideas.

He poured over the pages, staring at the photographs of Ms Cauldron and her arrangements. When it came to informal lower arrangements around the home it seemed artichokes were in as firmly as coloured cabbages with their attendant caterpillars were out. Elliott stared at the large central colour photograph with great interest. He so badly needed a shot in his creative arm, what with Twinks having made a hash of the Duchess of Roseberry's wastepaper basket and matching pin tray, and Nanny throwing a moody because Bessie had spilt rose hip syrup all over Beau's newest Swiss cotton angel top. It had been that kind of morning all morning, and it was still only half past nine.

Smoothing out the article on the marble-topped pasta-making surface, Elliott held it carefully down at the corners with two weights to read more about the growing fashion in artichokes, glad that he had brought the magazine in from the stables. It would be hours before Twinks to whom it belonged would find it missing, and by that time the lard might have worked.

Artichokes with radishes and small stiffened marguerites worked in between the leaves would be just the kind of thing that would add the right tone to the double christening of Beau and Daisy-Marguerita at the beginning of September. Having to come to terms with the whole idea of twins had not been easy. At this very moment Elliott knew that Fulton was out getting the best possible price on his metallic bronze Golf convertible with matching alloys and concert quality stereo. Of course ever since Beau's unexpected arrival in their world they had touched on the christening, most especially over the past few days if only as a refreshing change from the ball, and it seemed jointly to both of them that their newest christening should not be an ordinary Wasp sort of christening. They had both agreed that this time round it was not going to be just the Vicar and godparents with long fancy names who once the christening had been announced in *The Times* would spend the rest of their days trying to forget that their spiritual and more importantly financial obligations. For the twins it was going to be something very different, something to celebrate their duality, some sort of statement of fertility - not quite centaurs leaping or a sort of Bacchanalian orgy, but certainly something with a Druidish sort of feel, with everyone retiring to a decorated barn, and people from the village dressed up in robes while they turned spits with deliciously organic produce spiked on them.

'Come and see, won't you?'

Fulton stood by the door. Since Beau's arrival he had already started to affect different types of trousers, and at home in the mornings, horn-rimmed half-moon glasses which really rather suited him. They made him look a little more of the professor and little less of the antiques dealer. Reluctantly Elliott turned from the double page on the artichokes and followed him out into the drive. Even though he would have preferred to have stayed out of the rain and in front of the magazine, in another way he couldn't wait to see what Fulton had exchanged for the metallic bronze Golf.

'Well?'

'Well.'

Elliott stood very still under his very small inflatable paisley umbrella which he knew had been a mistake, but which like all umbrella mistakes just would not go away and get lost the way really nice ones always did.

Fulton breathed in and out.

'It's a Mubishi two-toned metallic Cross-Trekker with bull bars,' he announced, a little pointlessly since they were both standing in front of it and both the type and the model were spelt out on the bodywork in raised gold letters. 'Well?'

'It's certainly different.' Elliott said, staring.

'It's an off-roader.'

'So it says everywhere. Why have the tyres got raised white writing on them?'

'Absolutely no idea,' Fulton replied. 'They're a no cost extra. It's also got twin heavy duty fogs,' he went on, pointing at them. 'Five doors and seven seats counting the two pull down seats on the back in Kiddy-coated velour. And a surround sound stereo system for Nanny to play nursery tapes and – and a no cost extra emergency sand shovel under the spare wheel on the back door.'

'I hope we won't be needing that too often.'

'Now we are six, who knows? Seven including Nanny.'

'I see it won the Paris to Dachau Rally,' Elliott said, reading the information on the rear window from one side to the other before turning to look at Fulton.

'So?' Fulton demanded.

'As I just said - it's certainly different,' Elliott replied. 'Utterly different to anything we've ever had before.'

'That's what I wanted. Something very different from anything we've ever had before.'

'If it's what you wanted, you certainly succeeded. It's just that I rather thought that you might have preferred that maroon Porsche with the thing on the back you saw in the *Sunday Times* last week.'

'Of course I should have preferred the maroon Porsche,' said Fulton shortly. 'But sacrifices must be made. One glimpse at my bull bars and every headmaster in England will be begging us to send Beau to his beastly establishment.'

'I didn't know headmasters looked at your cars.'

'They look at everything.'

'In that case it's obviously the right choice. I mean, it's got so much writing on it no-one could possibly suppose we can't read.'

Even so, following Fulton into the house, Elliott couldn't help feeling that there was still a slight question mark over the whole enterprise.

Over very coffee in their special window overlooking the rain and the garden, Fulton knew immediately.

'You're thinking something.'

'I know,' Elliott was forced to admit.

'You know you're going to have to tell.'

'Yes, I do know I'm going to have to tell.'

'Very well, tell.'

'If you're sure.'

'Well?'

'If you really want to know,' said Elliott, with a deep sigh. 'I'm entirely sure that your new cardigans and your half-moon spectacles go with the heavy duty fogs, the bull bars, and all that writing on the motor car.'

'How do you mean?'

'Well. The cardigan says solidity, dependability, responsibility, and on a grey day, perhaps even disability, but the bull bars and the heavy duty fogs seem to be saying something else.'

Fulton nodded bravely.

'I know what you mean. You think I should perhaps change them for polo-necked cashmeres and shirts with very small collars and surprisingly short sleeves?'

'No-o, I don't think so,' said Elliott, carefully offering Fulton a home-made pistachio biscuit. 'No, I think you need some of those military type jumpers with pieces set in on the shoulders in very plain colours, corduroys trews and shoes with deeply indented soles that cake with mud at very inconvenient times and then spill out later on someone else's floor.'

'You're right. They're much more the thing to go with bull bars and fog lights and slip differentials. Pity. I love my cardies. Still, I suppose I could always give them to Twinks - she's very fond of anything woolly.'

Elliott stood up quickly. He didn't want to discuss Twinks, particularly not just after one of his best homemade biscuits.

'Let's talk artichokes,' he said brightly. 'I've had some nice Druid type thoughts for the christening,' he called to Fulton as he exited towards the kitchen. Then, passing Lady Tizzy in the hall as he went, he said: 'You're going to be a High Priestess at the christening, how about that?'

'Can I have snakes in my hair?'

'If that's what you want - or you could perhaps try a viper at your bosom?'

'Not a real one though,' Patti frowned. 'A papier mâché one. I could get Twinks to make it.'

'Not before she's re-made the Duchess of Roseberry's wastepaper basket and pin tray you won't.'

'Twinks wasn't in a very good mood this morning,' Patti told Fulton as she joined him at the drawing room window. 'So I gave her the christening invitations to do for me. She'll like that of an evening - take her mind off things.'

'I didn't know she had a mind – let alone one on things.'

'Oh yes,' Patti nodded, while expertly running her nail file around her long talons. 'All she can think about is tinia.'

'Probably explains the poor Duchess's waste bin,' Fulton remarked. 'She got the coat of arms right, but the bit at the top was extraordinary.'

'Really? What?'

'It was a hand wielding something. As a matter of fact, now you come to mention it, it did look remarkably like some sort of back scratcher.'

'Fulton?'

'Mmm?' said Fulton, his mind torn between the complications of exchanging his cardies for jumpers in army colours and shoes with complicated patterns on the bottom, and trying to interpret the extraordinary thing that Twinks had put into the hand at the top of the Duchess's coat of arms.

'How are you getting on with the ball, Fulton?'

'Like everything, as well as can be expected, if not less. The Countess has backed out, as you know, so now we're all back to apricot tones, but lumbered with cream and green for the tenting because it was already ordered when she stepped in, and now she has stepped out, nothing to be done.'

'Our christening's after her ball, isn't it?' asked Patti carefully.

'Yes, why?' asked Fulton, surprised suddenly, which he prided himself he very rarely was with Lady Tizzy, because she was after all his wife.

'Nothing.'

'When girls say nothing they always mean something.'

'And when men say it?'

'It means everything. You don't want to have the christening until Nanny and her friend have finished copying the Duc de Berry gown so the babies' are both matching, do you?'

'No, it wasn't that. It's just that I want our christening to be very special, and I wasn't sure it could be if it came after Jennifer Pemberton's ball.'

'They will be different. There will be no comparison. One so formal, pleated, tented, and matching, the other a sort of Wiltshire fertility gathering.'

'Have you told the Vicar?'

'Absolutely no need. The churchy bit will still be in the churchy, and if he doesn't like the Druidy feel to the party afterwards he can always go home.'

'That's all they do though, isn't it, vicars and priests, go home. Every time I feel like a bit of church time, it's either closed or there's a school play, or they've all had an argy-bargy and gone home.'

'They don't pay them enough, darling,' said Fulton, and he patted Lady Tizzy's cheek affectionately. 'If they paid them more they'd get a better class of person, more people in the churches, better sermons, everything. After all, just because it's a vocation doesn't mean it can't be a job too.'

'What do you think about lady priests?'

'I can never tell the difference, quite honestly,' said Fulton, getting up to answer the front door. 'Why?'

'Nothing.'

'Not nothing again, surely?'

'Well, it's just that I was thinking I might as well go in for the priesthood, the way things are going, or not going, and what with one thing and another.'

Fulton stood by the door. He knew it. *Real Man* was raising its ugly head again. Torn between the front door and Patti, he nevertheless hesitated. After all, a certain person's going to *Real Man* affected them all, most of all him and his bank manager.

'Has he still not been?'

'Not according to Bloss.'

'And he should know.'

'Exactly,' sighed Patti. 'He should. Apparently every time he drives up to the clinic, Bert - that's Pember's name at *Real Man* by the way 'cept you don't knows that – Bert gets out, goes in, and then comes straight out again saying there's a queue and he's never queued for anything in his life and he doesn't want to start now.'

The front doorbell was now insisting that it should be answered.

'You're not going to give in, are you, darling?'

'Of course not, I love you far too much.'

Fulton kissed his fingertips.

'And I love you too,' he said. 'In my fashion.'

What a relief. For once he really believed Lady Tizzy. He knew that she really, really wouldn't do anything to hurt or distress him. After all she hadn't meant to have twins, or a boy, and now that she had, they had all three of them come to terms with it and it didn't matter in the least. In fact Fulton decided it was really very nice. Even so, it was most important that the whole episode at *Real Man* must now be closed down firmly.

Just before he opened the front door it occurred to Fulton that perhaps going to *Real Man* was a little like giving up cigarette smoking. A person needed an incentive. What Pemberton needed was an incentive, something with which he could be rewarded after the act of curtailment was over - like a weekend away with the lady of his choice- something that would make him feel brave, and able to queue, Fulton thought. He must mention this to Lady Tizzy the moment he had closed the front door behind whoever it was that was now standing on the other side, and whose face Fulton rather unsurprisingly could not make out, seeing that he was standing with his back to them.

'Now what?' Elliott called from the kitchen, which was fairly cheeky considering he only ever opened the front door in an emergency, and then only if he thought the person on the other side would go away very quickly.

The person the other side of the door turned round, and all at once Fulton realised that it was no wonder he had thought the mackintosh had a slightly familiar look to it since the man inside was none other than Andrew Gillott, and he was holding an unmistakable bunch of flowers all done up with a mauve bow, which didn't suit them at all, since Fulton noted the flowers were obviously the sort of cheap red roses that never opened, even if their stems were put their stems in boiling water and they were liberally dosed with a whole packet of cut flower food.

'I thought you were in China?' said Fulton, taking the flowers from Gillott as if they were for him, although they were both quite aware they were not.

'China's closed,' Andrew told him, while lighting a very strong untipped cigarette and peering anxiously past Fulton as Fulton had noticed other men always did when they were feeling too excited for anyone's good, let alone his.

Lady Tizzy appeared at the drawing room door. Fulton did not need to turn and see this because the light in Andrew's bloodshot eyes face told him quite clearly that it was so, and also because Patti's scent as always announced her presence long before she arrived on any scene.

'Lady Tizzy,' Andrew murmured.

'I thought you were in China?'

'It's closed,' said Andrew again, and his senses reeled before the sight of Patti in her plunging cocktail frock. It was just as if she was expecting him, which they both knew she was.

'I called on the off chance -'

'I always think people who call on the off chance are a bit off,' Fulton murmured, hurrying off with the flowers without telling Patti they were for her.

'What's he doing here?' Elliott hissed, peering through the crack in the kitchen door, and speaking above the sound of his new pasta machine.

'He apparently took it in his head to call because China's closed,' said Fulton, throwing the red roses into the double Belfast sink with single brass reproduction Edwardian tap.

'China may be closed,' said Elliott thoughtfully. 'But by the expression on Lady Tizzy's face she may well not be.'

'What do you mean?'

'You know,' said Elliott, picking up the red roses and ripping off the mauve bow which was useless even for Christmas presents, and running very hot water into the left hand Belfast sink.

'I can't bear it.' Fulton sank down and rested his head on the marble of the kitchen top.

'It'll be all right. After all, she has promised - nothing doing until after *Real Man,*' said Elliott, shaking out the red roses and trying to un-squash their leaves.

'But this is the wrong man!'

Elliott turned and stared at Fulton.

'My heavens - you're right. Of course. This is the wrong man.'

They stared at each other.

'Better do something.'

'What?'

Elliott looked round desperately, and then called for help at the top of his voice.

'Help!' he called again.

'What's wrong with you? I must know what's wrong with you!' Fulton demanded, as he prepared to dash out into the hall.

'I don't know,' said Elliott. 'Think of something, that's all. Just think of something, and call an ambulance. It's the only thing that will stop whatever's going to happen from happening. You know, we both know, when she gets that glazed in aspic look to her, disaster shortly follows.'

Only too anxious to oblige, Fulton ran into the hall.

'Help,' he cried out on Elliott's behalf. 'Help!'

He flung open the drawing room door, and saw at once how right they both were. Lady Tizzy and Andrew were melting together already, and she hadn't even poured him a gin and tonic or herself some of the Emva Cream sherry that Elliott always got in for her.

'Help!' he went on.

They ignored him.

'Help!'

'Something the matter, Fulton?' Lady Tizzy turned towards him at last, and with great reluctance, as the pulse in Andrew Gillott's neck doubled its normal rate.

'Yes! Yes! Come quick. Elliott's hurt himself. We're going to have to call an ambulance.'

Lady Tizzy seemed hardly to hear him.

'And the fire engine,' he then added.

That was it, the bolt of inspiration he so badly needed. He realised the thought that Elliott might be dying of food poisoning from his own pasta would never disturb Lady Tizzy, not in the particular mood she now was in – but she did have an absolute passion for fire engines, and as Fulton happened to know her, very dearest and unfulfilled wish had always been to call one.

'A fire! No, don't you call, I'll do it, I'll do it!' she cried, jumping up and looking at Fulton with sudden excitement. The awful predatory look had gone from her eyes, and her normal day-to-day expression of serene ignorance returned as she grabbed the telephone from Fulton. 'I forgot what you got to dial.'

'Try 999,' Fulton suggested. 'Usually works.'

Slowly, with a pencil so as not to break her long red finger nails, Patti dialled the number nine three times, and the expression on her face quite changed.

When Fulton saw they were out of danger, he half closed his eyes in relief as yet another *crise* was safely negotiated. In the nick of time he had managed to pull the ass's head from off Patti's own pretty one, and she was their own dear Lady Tizzy once more with her silly expression quite gone. He turned back towards the kitchen. Now all they needed was a fire.

8

Jennifer sighed deeply as nowadays she had noticed she was wont to do. She had had a funny feeling about Pember for a few weeks now as if part of him was missing, not just his mind but a whole piece of him. It was a piece that she had once known and very much liked and it now seemed to her that it had been posted off and was living somewhere else, and what was worse, very possibly with someone else.

That was the feeling that she had had up until only a few minutes before, but now it had become quite different because now she was sure she had positive proof that Pember had slipped from the straight and narrow and when she realised it a lump came into her throat at the thought of all the glee that everyone – particularly her mother – would derive from Pember and she getting divorced. It would be a positive deluge of emotional joy for them, and they would enjoy more speculation at the story than all the material that had gone into the beautiful cream and green tents that Fulton and she had had designed and ordered for the ball. Heavenly tents they were, tents that begged to be decorated them with magnificent floral arrangements and that invited guests to come in their best gowns and jewels – but that was to be no more. The ball would have to be cancelled. She knew that now quite definitely. After all how could she dare to throw a private ball when she knew that her husband was obviously being flagrantly unfaithful and going to leave her for someone else, and she and her babies might end up penniless?

No, Jennifer decided, she would have to cancel everything. She would have to pay for the tents, shut up shop and wait for Pember to come and confess. Jennifer dug her rather too short tapestry needle into one of the floribunda roses that made up her new tapestry, and promptly caught her finger. It was nice to watch the blood, and then to suck her finger and taste it mixed up with that curious metallic taste of needle, thinking that both the blood and the pain were appropriate, and moreover - the pain stopped the tears coming.

Bloss stood by the door.

'You rang, milady?'

Jennifer looked up and across at him, and removing her finger from her mouth slowly shook her head.

'No, you know I didn't, Bloss. How could I have rung when I've just pierced my finger?'

'I'm sorry, milady. I was quite sure I had heard a bell. I must be getting like the late very great Sir Henry Irving and hearing bells where there are none.'

Jennifer didn't know what Bloss was babbling on about, so she frowned. She was so fed up with Bloss she could have hurled the cut glass decanter from the mahogany side tray at him. She had positive proof that Bloss was on Pember's side, driving him around to meet this woman whoever she was every afternoon. Bloss was nothing more than an enemy in the camp.

'You know I'm having to cancel the ball, do you, Bloss?'

Bloss stiffened.

'Why is that, milady?' he asked with suitable caution.

'Because, Bloss, with an eye to the future I have simply decided that we cannot afford it. Straightened circumstances are just around the corner, and I happen to know that it will be a complete waste of time.'

Bloss's face remained commendably impassive.

'I'm not a fool, Bloss. I know what is going on, you know. I know that Lord Pemberton is up to something, and it is only a matter of time before he comes and tells me.

Whatever it is, he will have to confess to it, you must know that, and if you don't, I certainly do.'

Jennifer's words had come out in a rush, and she now flung off her embroidery spectacles and jabbed the canvas of her tapestry with abandon. Embroidery was beginning to get her down because it was so small and fiddly. She found tapestry was better – and not only tapestry. She found talking honestly was better. Much better, she thought with a rush, to have everything all out in the open. A clean sweep with a new broom *et voilà!* Suddenly life was an open road with no more worries, with just decisions to be made and taken firmly, fairly and quickly, just as it was when driving. And she had just made and taken one her first firm, fair and quick decision. No ball, and that was that.

'Your ladyship is very kind to confide in me this way,' Bloss told her carefully, choosing his words. 'Most kind.'

Outwardly calm he might be but not inwardly. His mind began to race towards everything and everybody. He knew all too well that upon his next words depended a great deal, most of all his thoroughly cosy life at the Hall. Forget the new Peugeot. If he left the Hall and if there was a scandal, not only would he have been replaced, the whole of life at the Hall would be replaced, and most likely not by a Lady Tizzy with a nursery full of by-blows, but by a modern sort of girl with power shoulders and fancy ideas about employing Filipinos for butlers.

'I very much appreciate your confidences in this. After all, milady, I have been at the Hall a very long time. Since his lordship's bachelor days, as you know, milady.'

Jennifer's eyes that had so recently been threatening tears, now narrowed and fixed Bloss with a stare, as she realized in a rush that he had really funny-shaped ears, a little like one of those new rabbits the children had brought back from Stanton. The tops of his ears turned right down, and quite a way too, but that didn't make him any easier to deal with, unfortunately. Having thoroughly examined the peculiarities of Bloss's listening devices, Jennifer suddenly decided to stay silent, a little technique which she occasionally used.

'As you know, milady,' Bloss continued, 'I am and always will be devoted to both his lordship and yourself, and your continuing happiness is at the very heart of everything I do, even the silver.'

'Really, Bloss.'

There was no question mark to end Jennifer's short sharp exclamation, just a thick custard coating of sarcasm. Not too much, just enough, so that her inability to believe in Bloss's devotion shone through.

'Well, that is something,' she couldn't help adding, returning to her sewing with feigned interest.

'The question of finance, however rich we are, troubles us all, wouldn't you say, milady?'

Bloss sharply changed his tone, adopting one he was all too accustomed to hearing the accountants who so plagued his lordship using on rainy November days in the library.

'Expense is not stretched by small items such as the giving of balls, which after all, as your ladyship and myself are well aware, can be written off as advertising the Market Garden Company we are thinking of starting. No, it is the larger items, such as children, school fees, Nanny and her motor cars.'

Jennifer looked up sharply.

'Nanny's only got one motor car, Bloss,' she said defensively, because they both knew that this was a vulnerable area for both of them. 'Quite a small motor car.'

'Quite a small motor car with the newest registration,' said Bloss crisply and quickly. 'It also has traction control, a locking petrol cap, and foot mats finished in non-stain rubber neutralizer.'

'She needs those for her special shoes,' Jennifer put in quickly. 'They're inclined to pick up the mud.'

'Nanny's motor, unlike the ball, cannot be put down to the Market Garden Company,' Bloss intoned.

'Yes, but it is necessary,' Jennifer exclaimed, just managing to avoid jabbing her needle into a new finger. 'And by the by I had no idea we were starting a Market Garden Company.'

'That the reason why his lordship and I have been spending so much time together,' Bloss continued smoothly, while in direct contrast his mind continued in a ferment of activity. 'We have been doing business on behalf of the new projected company - talking to local farmers, discussing produce etcetera. We want all our produce to be local rather than organic, which is a little too advanced for us, we thought. That sort of thing, milady. It was to be a surprise, I understand.'

Jennifer shook her head.

'His lordship knows I don't like surprises. In fact I hate surprises – like people springing out of cupboards and singing happy birthday and everyone wearing funny expressions as if they've just sat on a whoopee cushion.'

'This surprise was intended to be a better class of surprise, milady - a business surprise, something to tell you about in the winter when thoughts are turning to the cost of the central heating.'

But try as he might Bloss could see that her ladyship was not in a mood to be mollified.

'Well, if we're having to humble ourselves and go into trade, Bloss, we most definitely can't afford a ball, which is precisely my point, or one of them,' she told him crisply. 'And now here comes my mother. I suppose you'd better let her in.'

Bloss and Mrs Parker-Jones were old allies, although no-one would have known it as he opened the door to her. Normally they exchanged smiles, and little facial grimaces that expressed their mutual understanding, but today Clarissa was somewhat surprised when Bloss, who had among other things perfected his butler's nod over the years - curt, gracious, and the depth of the nod depending on whom he was opening to - now delivered her one very curt nod indeed, before stalking ahead of her to the library door.

If Clarissa had had a clear conscience Bloss's nod would not have worried her, but the truth was she did not have a clear conscience, so Bloss's nod made her overly tight Rose Bruton hand-made ladies' cross-over all-in-one corset seem even tighter than when she had first struggled into it and done it up with difficulty that morning. From his nod Clarissa suspected that Bloss had heard that she and the Countess had spent the previous week spreading the rumour that the Pemberton ball was going to be a somewhat cheap affair, with just local County as guests and absolutely no media stars, pop singers, or even minor royalty – and that the two ladies were actively encouraging Lady Mary Stranragh, the Countess's daughter, to give a rival ball in Sussex, the Countess's old stamping ground, and with every chance of success, since it had to be faced Sussex was far easier to reach than Wiltshire if you were driving from London which after all was the only place that really mattered.

Bloss had his faults as he was only too well aware when going to bed at night and saw his many sins floating in front of him, iniquities that included such things as watering down Nanny's sherry that he knew finally would have to be paid for - but disloyalty was not one of his immoralities. His first priority at the Hall was the Hall, its continuance and happy survival, and if the ball at the Hall's was going to be to flop he knew that was not going to add to the common good. It was by this point and this point alone that his curt nod to Mrs Parker-Jones was validated. He knew what he knew from Maria, the Countess's maid, his ally and friend whom he kept so liberally supplied with fresh young vegetables and fragrant and rare herbs, for precisely the same reasons that she kept him supplied with the latest up-to-date bulletins on the Countess's domestic plans and politics.

'Bloss seems out of sorts this morning,' Mrs Parker-Jones remarked to Jennifer after he had closed the library door a little louder than normal.

'And so he should be,' said Jennifer, not rising to greet her mother and sucking on her piece of wool before re-threading her needle. 'He's been conniving with Pember which I now know but he does not as yet. And not only that, but it seems we are having to go into trade like everyone else. No doubt it will not be too long before there are hippos below the ha-ha.'

'But the Hall isn't anywhere big enough for hippos in the ha-ha.'

'The Hall isn't big enough for most things, let alone at is happening at this moment,' Jennifer stated, and having successfully loaded her needle she now stared stony-eyed at her mother.

'How do you mean, Jennifer?'

Clarissa looked at her daughter uneasily. Her only child had a steely side to her that definitely came from her father Aidan's side of the family and it had always surprised and discomfited her mother. It was the kind of obstinate determination that was so often displayed to such a frightening degree by thoroughly virtuous persons.

'How do you mean?' she enquired once more, having been met with silence.

Jennifer jabbed her tapestry, successfully stabbing the centre of a pink rose and making her mother start while at the same time glancing longingly at the sherry bottle on a nearby mahogany tray.

'I mean that there are things happening at the Hall that should not be happening,' Jennifer finally replied, doing her best to keep her voice as calm as possible. 'Things that I am about to make stop happening, including the ball.'

Mrs Parker-Jones' mouth, carefully coated in two layers of Esther Lantern's Peach Perfect lipstick dropped open, and stayed open until she remembered herself and quickly shut it. If she smoked she would have had a cigarette, but since she didn't and since she never had, she opened and closed the clasp on her handbag instead.

'I am about to cancel a lot of things,' Jennifer confirmed. 'And as I said, I am starting with the ball.'

'Why on earth should you do that?'

'Because, Mother dear, I am not in the mood to be made a fool of, that's why.'

Mrs Parker-Jones opened and shut her handbag once more, such was the fright she had received. She hadn't felt so set back since her husband had dropped dead on the hearthrug on the day of Jennifer's coming-out dance. It was all very well for her to be scheming with the Countess to make Jennifer's ball a flop, but it was something quite other when Jennifer took it upon herself to cancel the whole shooting match. If Jennifer cancelled her ball it would make the Countess and herself look terribly foolish, found to be scheming and plotting against something that didn't exist.

'You mustn't cancel the ball, Jennifer. Think of the dismay it will cause the people who were so looking forward to it. Think of the disappointment.'

'I have, and there will be very little or none,' Jennifer replied. 'No-one really wants to come to these things anyway. They all pretend they do, but then on the night they'll all cry off and the whole thing will be a disaster - so it's much, much better if it doesn't go ahead. And anyway I shall probably be immersed in divorce proceedings by then, which will mean I will have to keep an eye on every penny, if only for my little nursery brood's sake.'

'This is ridiculous, Jennifer. I mean to say, Pemberton – John is worth millions. And you have no proof he has done anything wrong.'

'He was worth millions, but he won't be soon, and I don't need proof of infidelity. A woman knows.'

This last was uttered with such grim certainty that utter panic seized Clarissa. Normally she hated the fact that her daughter was richer and took social precedence over her, but now that Jennifer seemed intent on smashing her own position and committing social suicide it was altogether a different matter. To be the Marchioness of Pemberton living at the Hall was after all not nothing; to be an ex-Marchioness living in some village house would be really nothing. Mrs Parker-Jones caught her finger in the catch of her handbag as she snapped it shut yet again but the pain was nothing compared to the internal agony she was feeling. She knew that Jennifer must be stopped at all costs. She must be stopped from divorcing Pemberton, and whatever happened the ball must go on. The ball particularly must go on, which it quite evidently would not, not, not if Jennifer was thinking seriously in terms of divorce. And apart from anything else the ball simply had to go on, Clarissa realized in a renewed rush of emotion, because the Countess and herself had already set Lady Mary's ball if not rolling and there would be no point to it at all if it wasn't given in competition with Jennifer's ball at the Hall. It would lose its whole point, its veritable cutting edge.

'No-one in our family has ever got divorced -' Clarissa began, deciding to take a different and more wholesome approach.

'Until you.'

'Until me,' she agreed. 'Yes, yes but that is different. Besides, my divorce from Andrew has not come through yet, and another thing - Andrew came into my life when I was on the rebound from the grief of losing your dear father. I should certainly never have made that particular mistake had I not just been sadly widowed.'

'How is Andrew?' asked Jennifer, not really wanting to know.

'Still being a walker to the Countess. She takes care of him most of the time. But to get back to this business of the ball -'

'No ball, Mother dear. No point in arguing.'

'But why?'

'Because I say so.'

Mrs Parker-Jones felt close to tears. Things were going dreadfully. Her whole world seemed to be shrinking and fast disappearing.

'And talk of the devil,' Jennifer said suddenly, having seen a car coming up the drive. 'Here's Pember. I wonder where he's been *this* time?'

She watched him climbing out of his car and found herself thinking how handsome he still was and what a shame she had to divorce him. Then she noticed Bloss hurrying down the front steps and making a beeline for his master. Jennifer watched intently and saw the two men having a brief exchange. She had no doubt as to what they were talking about, most certainly not the Market Garden Company, she determined. Then all of a sudden she saw Pember put out a hand and leaning forward seemingly collapse against Bloss. With a rush of guilt Jennifer gave a low moan, dropped her sewing and rushed out of the room, leaving her mother to leap to the drinks tray and help herself to two large glasses of sherry in swift succession.

As Clarissa downed the second sherry she realized she wasn't in the least bit interested in what was wrong with Pember because she was far more fascinated by what was wrong with Jennifer. The Marchioness of Pemberton was quite obviously out of sorts, as a girl who is about to cancel a ball and divorce her husband must be expected to be, but that didn't mean she should throw out the baby with the bath water, or in this case the husband with the ball. She had to persuade Jennifer to go ahead or the Countess and she would fast become the laughing stock of Society. Clarissa had to move and she had to move quickly.

For Jennifer's friend Georgiana life was no easier. Having decided that she would put Gus' latest model cum-girl friend up for selection by Kaminski's casting agent, she now had to manoeuvre events so that they appeared quite normal which wasn't always easy, because Gus had a strange and almost unnatural way of knowing the very moment anything went out of kilter; if for one moment he felt Georgiana was distracted for even a single second from running life as he wanted it run, he seemed to sense it and would come after her. Happily in return Georgiana knew this as instinctively as Gus seemed to know it, the way she had always known how her first husband Stranragh would hide outside her bedroom door while watching her undressing through the keyhole before tip-toeing away and leaving her quite alone and untouched.

'I thought I would take a day off to go to London,' Georgiana suddenly announced to Gus, knowing these were two of the most emotive words that she could ever pronounce in front of Gus. They had the kind of effect on him that the announcement of an infidelity might have on someone else. But happily this evening she had chosen her moment right, a moment when Gus, having spent a very long hot afternoon pursuing considerably more than the muse with his model, was now downing his second California Dreaming cocktail, a drink to which Georgiana had had no hesitation in introducing him, knowing precisely how light his head was, and how especially helpless it would render him.

'That's a good idea, George,' he agreed happily. 'Very good idea. Go to London with Cynthia. You can bring me back some more little presents. Okay? You bet.'

Georgiana didn't reply, because she had a feeling there was a limit to how many more little nice presents she wanted Gus to enjoy.

'But you've only just been to London, Georgie,' Nan complained the next day at breakfast as she sat feeding little George on her knee.

'That's the whole point, Nan,' Georgiana agreed, happy that she did not have to cross her fingers, 'I have to keep going to London at the moment, because there's someone there who I have to see. It's about my future - and little George's future as well.'

It couldn't have been truer, so Georgiana was well able to smile and nod at Nan and Nanny over their cornflakes and Weetabix, and clip her small crocodile overnight case smartly together. 'I'm taking Gus's model with me – what's her name?' she added artlessly. 'Cynthia. That's it. Cynthia – or rather Cynth as Gus likes to call her – Cynth is up for a part in a film directed by an old friend of mine. She's terribly excited, as you can imagine.'

'It doesn't take much to excite that one,' said Nan, feeding George another mouthful of egg. 'I hope you're not going to London on that motor bike of hers.'

'Course not,' Georgiana agreed. 'We're going by train. I told her to pack some overnight things, just in case things. You know how it is in London.'

Even if she did Nan said nothing in return. She was too busily occupied wiping George's eggy chin with one corner of her napkin.

Georgiana liked second-class travel on the train much the best. She liked the people knitting bright-coloured baby clothes, gossiping and playing cards, and the general sense of camaraderie that was so absent in the First Class half empty carriages. Furthermore today she had company of her own in the shape of Cynthia whom she now watched lighting a cigarette which she then smoked while holding her right elbow with her left. Georgiana wondered at this, as to why and how she had adopted such a peculiar habit before she found herself becoming drowsy and finally dropping off completely. When she awoke she found the train was already pulling into Paddington station.

With Cynthia trailing along beside her, her eyes and her mouth both wide open in astonishment, Georgiana wondered to herself what Gus would think of his latest paramour now, so visibly bothered and bewildered by the sights of the busy city. Back at Longborough where pretty girls were thin on the ground Cynthia's appeal to Gus could be seen as understandable, but in London where beautiful, long legged and elegant girls were to be seen everywhere, Cynthia looked positively unexceptional and sadly provincial – which brought Georgiana up with a jolt as she suddenly realised that the girl at her side was probably going to be far too ordinary even to get as far as the interview stage that Georgiana had already arranged with the casting director on Kaminski's film.

'I expect you're dying to work in London like everyone round Longborough?' Georgiana asked Cynthia over a coffee and Danish pastry, talking to her companion for about the first time since they had boarded train at Longborough some two and a half hours previously.

'Yes I would as it happens,' Cynthia replied. 'Who wouldn't?'

'What would you like to do?'

'I dunno. Work in a shop maybe. A pub. I dunno.'

'You don't mind?'

'Why should I mind?'

'Because most people when they come to London think of instant stardom, I suppose,' Georgiana replied.

'That's just stupid,' Cynthia returned. 'That can always come later.'

'So you wouldn't mind say – say working in a shop say?'

'Why?' Cynthia eyed Georgiana over the top of the cigarette she was now lighting up.

'Only because I think I know a place that's looking for people like you, and you might feel quite at home there too,' Georgiana replied.

It was to a new shop in Pimlico called *Sunday Painters* that Georgiana took Cynthia, who within only a few minutes of Georgiana talking to the friend of the friend who owned and ran the shop found herself in employment. There was even a room for her to rent in the flat above the premises, sharing with two Australians who were working as barmen in a local pub. Best of all, Cynthia could start straight away since the shop was not yet fully staffed.

'Cynthia has modelling experience too,' Georgiana told her friend over coffee while Cynthia was on the phone to her mother to tell her she had got a job in London and asking her mother if she wouldn't mind posting her some of her things until she had time to come back home and collect them. 'She's quite the all-rounder our Cynthia,' Georgiana concluded.

Leaving Cynthia in the hands of her friend, Georgiana then headed for Knightsbridge, feeling a little as if she had just sent an unwanted horse to the sales. As she approached the house that contained Kaminski's apartment, Georgiana examined her emotions. She knew what she had just done was not a particularly nice thing to have done, but she felt she hadn't really been able to help herself. Having discovered a little late in the day quite how stupid Cynthia was, she had felt rightly or wrongly that she was too stupid even to go up for a part of a scuba diver in the film, despite having a suitable enough sort of figure, and so she had taken advantage of a ready alternative. It wasn't very moral of her to have lured Gus's model and mistress from him but as Georgiana reckoned the way the two of them had behaved wasn't exactly moral either. Her only problem was wondering what Gus might do if and when he ever discovered what Georgiana had exactly done.

E.F. stared at Kaminski. He did not know what the great man would do to him if he found out that E.F. was knocking off Kaminski's mistress Sofia. Nor did he know how he had been able to do so for so long now and with such regularity without Kaminski finding out. For her part Sofia had constantly reassured E.F. with equal regularity that she was not two-timing Kaminski, since Kaminski was currently not one-timing her.

'He's in his run-up phase, darling,' she explained to E.F. 'It seems you might as well be his best friend, of whatever sex, when he is in his run-up to a movie,' she continued with the total assurance of someone who had hardly known Kaminski at all before he cast her in her non-speaking, non-acting role.

E.F., who had known Kaminski for many a long and sometimes quite a short year, remembered concentrating only on Sofia's magnificent if somewhat swamping prow while she talked such rubbish. The only problem was that when she continued, with the same authority to talk about Kaminski's attitude to his work with the sort of confidence that E.F. noticed seemed to come so naturally to all graduates of the American Warehouse School of Acting, E F found that despite himself - or more precisely because of himself - he suddenly and quite quickly no longer felt in the least bit aroused by her.

'This is so often the trouble with actresses,' he told himself as he waited for Kaminski at his newly leased apartment. 'They have everything – the looks, figures, legs, the tits, teeth, hair, everything except the one thing that could make the whole thing motor sweetly – the right engine.'

Beautiful figures, beautiful legs, beautiful bosoms, beautiful teeth, beautiful hair, they were all as nothing without the personality to make them anything except cuties and bimbos, and Sofia was altogether typical of her breed. In fact when Sofia was lecturing E.F. on some new acting technique or about something about which she knew less than nothing, E.F. came to the ready conclusion that by saying Sofia knew less than nothing was in fact to give her credit for knowing far too much.

Kaminski was on the telephone in the next door room, which was why E.F. had fallen to thinking. Now bored with his introspection he got up and peered through the crack in the door. He saw Kaminski was still on the phone where he had been now for quite some time, something that was most unlike the great man who generally hated holding conversations of any length on an instrument he called the *Great Interrupter*.

'I'll call for you,' he was now saying repeatedly. 'I said I'll call for you. Stay at the hotel, and I will call for you.'

E.F. knew that he couldn't be talking to Sofia, because Sofia had moved out of the hotel and in with Kaminski, which was where she and E.F had been holding their get-togethers, as Sofia liked to call them, sometimes early in the morning just after Kaminski had left on some location hunt which was of absolutely no interest to E.F. or sometimes they would conjoin at midday when the great Director was out lunching with one of their producers. It was one of the greater perils of being a film director, having to be seen lunching and re-lunching your producers. Happily as the scriptwriter E.F. had no obligation to attend such lunches so he normally used the time to occupy himself more creatively.

Sadly he had found out and very quickly too what a boring, uninteresting and untalented girl Sofia really was and had just as quickly found himself wishing that he had not taken up with the wretched women in the first place. He was bored and he hated being bored – not quite as much as Kaminski hated being bored, but almost.

'In that case change hotels,' he now overheard Kaminski saying and now when he took a closer look at the expression on the Director's normally expressionless face E.F.'s eyes widened when he realised this was no business call.

'What's it with you and her?' he asked when he finally entered as Kaminski finished his call. 'I mean – *still?*'

E.F. stared at Kaminski as the great man stood regarding the telephone as if it were still alive and talking and as he did for just a few seconds he remembered what it was like to feel the way Kaminski was so obviously feeling, to be in the grips of that kind of a love, of that kind of a passion. The only time E.F. had ever really been in love he had felt and no doubt looked as his friend Kaminski was now looking, his one and only true love, his very first love, the girl his own father had stolen from him.

And that - if he ever let it - was another question that could spring to mind, as to how much hate could a son have for his father. Sometimes it seemed to E.F. that even the depth of the most bottomless sea in the world could not match the feeling of hate that he had for his own father for stealing his first and his only love from him, because his father felt he was growing old and the young man's sun was rising as his own was beginning to set. The girl stood no chance, none whatsoever. Dazzled by the older man's sophistication, his charm and his worldliness, she had been seduced, and then as if in some ancient tragedy had become almost instantly and then died giving birth.

Of course, since it was indeed such a good tragedy E.F. himself had not been slow to make use of it. His first love became the basis of his first play, his first screenplay, his first novel, his first poem, his whole life in fact. It would be fair to say he had reaped not just a good living from that first agonizing and heartbreaking experience, but had also made a small fortune. He had lived off it, out of it and from it; it had been the central force of his life. But, nevertheless and notwithstanding, he had made quite sure never to fall in love again. This was something that he shared with Kaminski; in fact it was the very basis of their friendship, their mutuality, their partnership. They both abhorred and scorned love and its endless and to then mindless repercussions. Lust they recognised and were eager to indulge and enjoy. Dalliance was a high art to them both, but love - that which forces a man or a woman to forsake sanity and walk to spend the rest of their lives looking over their shoulders was not for either of them. Except that now as E.F. looked at Kaminski in the clear bright light of a spring morning, heard him hum a little snatch of *Violets for Her Fur* and saw the misty look in his eyes and pause a little too long before turning back to E.F., it occurred to E.F. that maybe the two of them weren't going to have quite so much in common in this matter in the very near future after all.

'It's time to talk,' Kaminski said, nodding towards a chair into which E.F. then lowered himself as he did indeed most every morning preparatory to starting to write, something which at present was difficult for not just E.F. but for both of them since they were both involved in working on a film which neither one of them would have chosen to write or direct. However, judging from Kaminski's serious eyes and the way he had his hands in their customary praying position with the tips of the fingers touching the top of his nose, and the fact that coffee was now being poured, E.F. got the impression that this morning there were serious matters at hand.

'Look - I'm bored with Sofia, E.F.,' Kaminski confessed suddenly.

It was E.F.'s turn to stare.

'I know. I know you told me I shouldn't bring her over here, and you were right. And now this other thing has come around once more. I realize it was a very big mistake.'

Kaminski shrugged expressively. On a good day his shrugs could express more than a great actor's eyes.

'Even so, it doesn't have to be the worst mistake anyone ever made,' Kaminski continued. 'She's beautiful and now that she has lines in the film she seems very willing to work hard. She goes to the actors' studio every morning. You know that?'

E.F. knew and only too well, and frankly if he heard Sofia mention it once more he thought he'd scream.

'I know you find her attractive, E.F.'

There was a long pause, as Kaminski dropped his hands down from his face on to his lap and looked sadly at his friend.

'Even so -' he said at last. 'I want you to take Sofia off my hands.'

E.F. stared.

'You can't be serious,' a near dumb-struck E.F. replied. 'Kaminski you cannot be *serious.*'

'Never more so, E.F.,' Kaminski replied. 'You can do it. You can do most things. You can sure in hell do this.'

'What do you mean by taking her off your hands?' E.F. asked, trying to keep the rising panic he felt out of his voice. 'I mean Sofia is beautiful, sure – she's a real looker but she does nothing for me *here*.'

E.F. put his hands somewhat dramatically near a most tender part of his person and then stared at Kaminski quite foolishly.

'How do you know? You haven't even thought about it, E.F. How can you say that? You can't possibly know that.'

Given the circumstances, E.F. said nothing, deciding to lie low on this one.

'Just give it a go, E.F. – for my sake, will you? I have to go out so why not you take her out to lunch? She won't be down for a while, but once she's up and about - take her out to lunch. Take her shopping – spend what you like - I'll put it down to the movie, and then take her to some hotel. Maybe Lexingham Gardens? Go have a good time. Okay?'

'I can't, Kaminski,' E.F. said sheepishly. 'I really can't.'

'Sure you can,' Kaminski assured him. 'I've seen the way you look at her.'

'Maybe you have – but I'm getting too old for this sort of caper – lunch, shopping, sex in the afternoon. It's of less and less interest to me, you bet.'

'I don't buy that.'

'What don't you buy? You surely must have noticed, Kaminski? I gotten quieter. I'm older. A lot older and a lot more – a lot more sensitive.'

'In this game no-one is ever too old for a caper, E.F. That's just a fact.'

'I have, Kaminski. I've changed. It's all this time I been spending in Vermont with my new wife -'

'You're not in Vermont now, E.F. And it doesn't count in war, on tour or on location, right?'

'Since I remarried I really have changed, Kaminski,' E.F. protested. 'You might not have noticed it but it's a fact. I changed about all sorts of things – small detail, the finer points of life. They used to escape me but not anymore. Every time I go to a city I think I'm going to enjoy myself, but I can't because I keep noticing the things too much, like how scuffed the waiters' shoes are, how grubby the table napkins are, the hairs in the shower – the dirty glasses in the bar. Same goes for the women I meet. Take Sofia. A good looking broad. A stunner one might say. But what do I see? I see the small hairs at the back of her legs that she's forgotten to shave, and the way her lipstick comes off after a glass of wine, how close her eyebrows are together - that kind of thing. I don't mean to, but that's what I see, and I'm telling you - it has a limiting effect on my hormonal activity.'

But Kaminski was no longer listening. He just turned to E.F. and squeezed one of his arms.

'You'll be fine,' he said. 'Don't worry about it - you'll be *fine*. When it comes to the moment you'll be fine. You'll have some champagne, she'll give her deep throaty laugh, and you'll be away. Trust me. You'll forget about the little hairs on the backs of her legs and her smudged lipstick and how she keeps talking about herself – because you will be having *fun*. Just keep her amused until well after five. I have business back here.'

Kaminski snatched up the keys of his rented car and headed for the door. E.F. watched him walk outside into the street before crashing his head against the suede-covered walls of their rented study, cursing Kaminski but knowing there was no way he could disobey him, not if he wanted to get paid. But he really had no idea what to do, how to go about this wretched sexual errand. The last time he had voluntarily made love to Sofia had been tough enough, but now that he absolutely had to keep her occupied all afternoon he wondered desperately what he could do. The only thing he could come up with was an idea from a draft of one of his recent screenplays where when stuck with a woman he simply doesn't fancy the desperate hero ties her to the bed and then pretends to have a minor heart attack and passes out – but since he had been quite unable to make it work on the page E.F. had serious doubts about making it work in reality. Finally he sat with his head in his hands, regretting that such a day should come to him, a time that he should be trying desperately to think of some way not to have to make love to a beautiful girl.

Kaminski had mixed feelings about meeting Georgiana. He was too sophisticated and too well versed in the art of seduction not only not to have mixed feelings but also not to be aware of them. He might feel charged with adrenalin at the sound of her voice, thrilled with the anticipation of meeting her for lunch, and quite helpless with desire when he finally saw her - but the one thing he was not was fooled.

Georgiana was no longer the helpless kitten who had never had a love affair. The slender young girl whom he could pick up and put down at his will was gone forever. Kaminski knew that. She was a woman now, a young woman who knew the frisson that real sexual power bestows on her sex. She had eaten of the true tree of knowledge and now she was only too aware of the effect that she was having on men and on Kaminski in particular. Now she was cool where before she was uncertain. Before she had been shy but now she was confident. Moreover and just like himself, now she had a past.

And yet, as he watched her sipping her glass of champagne, her long legs so artfully arranged and her slender fingers holding her fluted glass, he also realized that self-confident though she might be she was still not so self-assured that she had lost her charm. Charm after all was based on not knowing you had it, an inner uncertainty that asked, indeed demanded, that the person you were with reach out to you so that two people could become one. People who were charmless were like the very rich, desperately dull because they knew what they had. Georgiana's eyes still told Kaminski that she needed his presence to reassure her that she was as alluring as she undoubtedly wanted to be.

Looking at her in her full-skirted suit with a nipped-in waisted jacket, and the dull turquoise blue silk shirt which they both knew showed up the colour of her eyes to perfection, Kaminski was only too happy to remain where he was. Soon he hoped he would be a great deal nearer. Perhaps the only question in both their minds was how long would it last this time around.

9

The Countess was feeling greatly by Colonel Bentley, her co-patron of the Field Mouse Rescue and Rehabilitation Centre. It wasn't that she wasn't used to feeling irked because being irked was quite a normal state for her; what she wasn't used to feeling was being irked with Colonel Bentley. He had started off as a rather pleasant sideline in her new life, telephoning her on rainy afternoons when her knees were feeling far from good, posting little cards to her to remind her of their mutual duties to the dear little field mice, cracking the whip behind the out-workers who were making Dormouse Units out of recycled winter woollies and old plywood boxes, not to mention working on the design of their charity card, three dormice bringing their gifts to the Infant which the Countess found utterly charming.

Just lately, however, things had begun to change. Colonel Bentley had started to call frequently and mostly somewhat inconveniently. His last visit on the previous evening had seen him blustering up to her house and knocking on the drawing room window at the very moment when the Countess was doing the one thing in the country to which no-one but no-one admitted - namely watching television.

By the time he was finally admitted the television set was once more back and out of sight in its cabinet, only for the Colonel to wonder quite readily and to the Countess' way of thinking extremely impertinently as to what she might have been watching. Naturally the Countess feigned complete innocence and in turn wondered what he could possibly mean by such a remark.

'I heard the distinct sound of the box,' Colonel Bentley replied. 'Just couldn't hear what it was exactly.'

'The box?' the Countess wondered in her best Lady Bracknell manner. 'The *box?*'

'The idiot's lantern,' the Colonel laughed. 'The tele-welly.'

'Never watch it meself,' Colonel Bentley continued. 'Housekeeper's got the only set.'

'I have absolutely no idea what you are talking about,' the Countess continued to lie. 'If you heard what you claim to be the sound of a *television set* then it can only have been Maria's. My maid's.'

'She watches it with you then, does she?' the Colonel asked, setting down a large box he had brought with him on a table. 'Most democratic I must say. Most democratic.'

'Maria – if she watches television at all – which I very much doubt, her being a foreigner – then she would watch it in her own room, Colonel.'

'Saw the flickering light, Countess,' the Colonel insisted. 'Saw the dreaded old flickering blue light.'

'You should not have been outside the window, Colonel. What pray is wrong with the front door?'

'What's wrong with the front door, old girl,' the Colonel chuckled, 'is there's no on one answering it.'

At this very moment the person who should have been on duty downstairs – namely Maria herself – entered backwards through the door carrying a large tea tray and then seeing the Colonel standing beside in front of the fire place she all but dropped the whole tray.

''Ere,' she hissed. ''Ere 'ow you get h'in please? I no hear you.'

'Obviously not,' the Countess agreed, sensing a chance to deflect the pressure of herself. 'It seems no one did.'

'I no hear 'im h'over my televishon,' Maria continued to hiss, before turning back to the Countess. 'You no hear 'im h'over yours neether.'

'My what?' the Countess demanded.

'Your televishon,' Maria replied. 'He's very loud.'

The Colonel smiled at Maria then beamed at the Countess.

'Thank you, Maria,' she said as regally as she could manage. 'That will be all.'

'I theenk it is the man in the h'orange whig what does it,' Maria informed the Countess, placing a table and the tray beside her employer. ''E shoot 'is wife then say the swim pool boy 'e do eet.'

'*Thank you*, Maria,' the Countess repeated. 'I said thank you.'

'Now we nevaire knows,' Maria muttered as she went to the door. ''Cept if you know, madams, you maybe tell me manyana.'

'I have not the faintest idea what she was talking about,' the Countess said after Maria had gone. 'But then I very rarely do. What is this you have brought with you, Colonel? Is it what I hope it may be?'

'That all depends, my dear,' the Colonel aid, with another beaming smile. 'That all depends on your expectations.'

'Mrs Parker-Hone!' Maria announced, reappearing at the door. 'Mrs Parker-Hone h'is 'ere, madams!'

'Thank you, Maria,' a surprised Countess replied. 'Kindly show her in, please.'

But it was too late for Clarissa Parker-Jones was already upon them.

'I had to see you!' she announced, taking off her hat in a dramatic sweep. 'Forgive me for not telephoning but as I was passing I thought you should be among the first to know.'

After effecting an introduction to Colonel Bentley who was busy helping himself to tea and cake, the Countess indicated for Clarissa Parker-Jones sit.

'I should be among the first to know what?' she wondered.

'What has happened, Countess,' Clarissa replied, sitting down opposite the Countess, crossing her nylon-tighted legs and feeling doubly self-important the way bearers of bad tidings generally do. 'Just wait till you hear. Jennifer has cancelled the ball.'

The Countess stared at her visibly aghast.

'But she can't have!' she cried. 'Such a thing is quite impossible!'

'Nevertheless she has cancelled the ball and is now talking about divorcing Pember.'

'This just cannot be true!'

'Perhaps I should go,' the Colonel said through a mouthful of cake. 'This seems to be women's palaver.'

'Yes perhaps you should, Colonel,' the Countess agreed. 'This could become quite delicate.'

'Let me know what you think of the little houses!' he called from the door as he made to leave. 'That's what in the old box there. The little mousey houseys! Jolly good!'

Clarissa stared after him in silence then back at the box at the table.

'Shelters for the field mice,' the Countess explained. 'Just one of my charities. Do go on.'

'Of course,' Clarissa replied. 'Where was I? Yes – yes all this is true. I have only just come from the Hall and I assure you every word is true. Pember collapsed in the drive, and Jennifer lost her rag and accused him of rank infidelity, maintaining that the reason he fell over in the drive was that he was too tired to walk. She had some insane idea that he had come straight from his love nest, would you believe? I mean Pember of all people. He is so utterly reliable. Why on earth should Jennifer possibly think that he was maintaining a love nest? Do you know, sometimes I despair of my daughter. She seems to find it so difficult just to maintain the status quo – and as for cancelling the ball. I mean what does she think she is *doing?*'

'I agree,' the Countess replied, for once almost at a loss for words. 'What indeed?'

'Apparently, at least according to Jennifer,' Clarissa continued slowly.' She says if they have to halve everything she'll need the ball money to clothe and feed the children because men always get very tight-fisted once they decide to ditch you. Unfortunately that was something I told her apparently.'

'And quite right, too,' the Countess chipped in. 'Men do, but not men as rich as Pember. Judges always take a very dim view of very rich men divorcing their wives. Just jealousy really, they know rich men can afford to do what they can't. She'll get a very good settlement so she mustn't worry.'

Now Mrs Parker-Jones knew true panic. Suddenly Jennifer's divorce was real. The Countess was making it real, so real that for one brief second Clarissa saw herself following Jennifer out of the court, holding her arm sympathetically as they both posed for the photographers, pausing to smile in a dignified way for the television cameras before politely declining to say more. She even saw a headline in the *Daily Mail* - *Marchioness Uncovered Love Nest* - and then a sub-headline *Peer's Collapse In Drive Told All*, at the same time wondering whether to wear her navy blue Terylene two-piece with the knife pleats or the grey and mauve mottled coat-dress with dove grey hat and matching hat ribbon. It was difficult choice but not an impossible one, she decided.

'Since you're getting divorced too, you may well both feel like making it a double,' the Countess observed tartly. 'This is a pretty kettle of fish,' she added, half to herself, because not only did it place her in an awkward position as far as her daughter's ball in Sussex was concerned – although she saw no point to Mary now holding a ball if there was no competition since everything would be very flat and unexciting – but since she knew that Pember undoubtedly had not just a love nest but also a nest full of babies at Flint House, the fat had quite obviously hit the fire and it looked to the Countess as though everyone was going to get it in the eye.

There was a long pause as both women saw the end to their cosy chats together. No more planning and plotting. The two balls, all those people they had spent hours listing into tidy columns, *Very Important, Less Important, Even Less Important* and so on, had suddenly come to nothing and all because of Jennifer.

'Of course she does realise that once she divorces Pember, although technically she will remain a Marchioness, she will no longer live at the Hall, no longer command the same respect, the same service from others – that she will in fact be a back number,' the Countess said. 'It's something that girls forget, you know, in their sudden flurry of self-righteousness when they find out that their husbands have been doing what all husbands do, namely having a little enjoyment without them. After all, it's always gorn on, you know, always. Never been any different. Never known a naturally faithful man. It simply doesn't mean the same to them, wouldn't you say?'

Clarissa leaned forward and placed her coffee cup in front of her. Lately she and the Countess had grown, if not together, at least less apart. They had a cautious if enjoyable alliance, which was a new and fascinating hobby for both of them.

'I do so agree with you, although I will say for Aidan,' she told the Countess. 'I will say that he never did stray, you know.' She felt a little rush of unaccustomedly genuine tears flood into her eyes. 'Not once.'

'Was he very fat?' asked the Countess with interest.

'Yes, as a matter of fact he was,' said Mrs Parker-Jones, surprised, and the tears stayed at the front of her eyes, not attempting to flow down her cheeks 'He was very fat indeed. Why?'

'Very fat men aren't unfaithful very often. They have too many meals to think about, and while of course they dance very well – and so they're usually very romantic - Freddie, my husband for instance, Freddie was quite fat, a Master of the Greys and Greens, all that sort of thing, wonderful dancer, but he never strayed, despite all the temptations thrown at him in the field and at hunt balls. Not enough energy finally, that's the thing. It's all very well having the idea and all that, but one has to have the energy,' the Countess concluded. 'But he was very special and I still miss him. Always will, always have.'

The two women looked across the years at each other and smiled. There was a short pause, and then the Countess reopened proceedings.

'So, what to do about this pretty kettle of *poisson,* then?'

'Must just bring Jennifer to her senses. Tell her to start interesting dear Pember more,' said Clarissa firmly. 'She can be terribly boring, Jennifer, and not at all attractive. Time to pull up her socks and put on her suspenders and do her stuff -'

She stopped, realizing too late that a little too much of her original background had popped out before midday. She looked at the Countess, waiting for immediate censorship, or at the very least sarcasm, only to find none was forthcoming.

'Quite right,' the Countess agreed warmly. 'No I quite agree.'

'She has taken long enough to settle into the Hall and its ways,' Clarissa continued.

'I do so agree,' the Countess said. 'Although perhaps you might not be the person to tell her all this. You know how it is, daughters and mothers. I have only to tell Mary that she looks lovely in mauve for her to burn everything mauve, or give it away to Juanita. It's always the same. Might it not be better if the advice, whatever it may be, came from another source?'

Clarissa looked sharply at her new ally. She was right, of course. One word from her and Jennifer would get divorced straight away, if only to spite her mother. And that was something that Mrs Parker-Jones wanted about as much as she wanted bunions.

'Would you . . . could you perhaps say something?' she wondered.

'If you think it's a good idea, I certainly will. I have known Pember since he was quite a little boy, you know, so perhaps it might be a good idea if I explained the birds and the bees as they undoubtedly are to the Marchioness. Girls take infidelities, even a hint of them, quite badly. And really, as I say, they needn't. Most of the time men are only interested in seeing if their bodies are in working order. They just can't help being curious, it doesn't mean a thing, and of course women take it so very badly when they needn't at all. I always say the difference between men and women is that men will do anything for a new lover, and women will do anything for a good one. By the way, I must mention Andrew.'

'Andrew.'

Clarissa felt dull at the very idea of her soon to be former husband.

'Just must, I'm afraid. You see, I think he may have found another interest. Has he given you that impression at all?'

Clarissa's bosom, size thirty-eight on a warm day, now grew to forty plus as she swelled in indignation. The very idea of Andrew being unfaithful to her, and before they were even divorced, was appalling.

'Do you want me to have a word with him too?' asked the Countess delicately. 'After all we don't want him to rock the boat before the decree comes through. You don't want to find him back on your hands, and if some other woman's husband names him in his divorce, that could well happen.'

'I shall be most grateful.'

'Good. Well then, that's that. Only thing we have to do now is get the Ball rolling again, and if I do my work, that should take care of itself.'

The Countess smiled and then sighed as she realised how much she now had to do with so it seemed the whole of Wiltshire in turmoil. There was no doubt about it - she was going to be kept very busy.

'Needs must when whatever it is,' she said vaguely, smiling at Clarissa. 'Only thing to do is kick on.'

If Elliott was in doomy form, peering out of the kitchen window he could see quite, quite clearly that Lady Tizzy was in far worse than doomy, she was in private hell. He knew this from the general un-made-up pallor which she was presently disporting round the garden, not to mention the over-natural bushy look of her hair. It was impossible to ignore Lady Tizzy when she was experiencing the mean reds. Even from outside her mood, like the currently cloudy weather, seemed to penetrate every corner of Flint House.

'You're right, Elliott, I am feeling decidedly iffy.'

As Elliott stared sympathetically at Lady Tizzy he noticed that her lips seemed to be protruding even further than normal. The idea suddenly crossed his mind that she might once have been a trumpeter.

'Feeling iffy's beastly.'

'Yes, well, just now iffy's exactly what I am feeling. I mean, I'm sure I know just how Kipling felt when he had looked on his twin thingies and found them just the same'

'I've always found that a bit hard to believe, that *If* business. Try reciting *If* to a starving man.'

Elliott's eyes narrowed with vague indignation and then he let them roam at random round the garden which Twinks was meant to be helping maintain and very obviously wasn't. It seemed to him that the garden at Flint House was reflecting their life more than somewhat. Tidy lawns perhaps, but the flower borders were just a mass of confusion, with some things going in one direction that should be going in another, other things going too far up when they should be going sideways, and among it all the wild outside creeping in stealthily through the undergrowth.

'*Real Man* has been a flop, Ely-ot.'

Elliott looked sideways at Lady Tizzy now. If it wasn't for the babies, Beau and the girls, he really would feel like flinging her out on her ear even though she wasn't even married to him. Her love life was chaos, first with Pemberton, and then the policeman she had a crush on, and then Pemberton again, and now Andrew Gillott who was anyway meant to be being the Countess's walker, not Lady Tizpots' lover.

'How d'you know *Real Man's* a flop, anyway?'

'Bloss rang me in a flurry.'

Patti dropped her voice, and removed a finger, the nail of which she had just bitten in a particularly tense manner, from the side of her mouth.

'Yes.'

Elliott had noticed that Lady Tizzy always used the word yes as punctuation when she had managed to grasp a very uncomfortable idea and was just about to explain it at length for Elliott's discomfiture.

'Yes Bloss rang me and told me. We have an arrangement. I wait for him to ring at midday and then he calls me and pretends to give me the fodder order for the week.'

'So that's why you keep disappearing into the great outdoors in the mornings. I must say I had wondered.'

Patti nodded sadly. Matters had come to a pretty pass, they both knew, when she was missing the re-runs of *Wiltons and Company - an everyday story set in a shopping mall* - in order to take a morning call.

'Bloss is really very clever really,' she went on in a thoughtful voice that hinted a little that he might not, even so, be currently being quite clever enough. 'You see, what happens is he puts in an order for more fodder for the horses, oats and bran and so on, and I take it down, and then when he's quite happy no-one has picked up the other receiver he quickly tells me the latest about *Real Man.*'

'Which is?'

Patti burst into tears quickly.

'Terrible. Poor Pember. Bloss finally got him to go off to the agency, and he was quite fine, it seems - you know, chatting and joking and everything - until he actually got there disguised as Bert Ackroyd, you know, all old clothing and everything, not at all Pember. Even so, nothing bad happened until he got to the door of the building when there was a man coming out looking terrible, all green around his gills because he was quite obviously all blue elsewhere.'

'Well, he would be,' Elliott agreed, feeling really quite faint himself.

'And Pember saw him, and it was just too much. He began to - you know, pass out, and only just managed to drive himself home where he actually did pass out in the drive which was worse than anything because he was still disguised as Bert Ackroyd, you see.'

Elliott frowned.

'I don't understand,' he said, continuing to frown. 'Why was - why was how he was dressed anything to do with anything?'

'Because Jennifer saw him!'

Patti nudged Elliott hard. Really, he was being so thick He needed a good dig in the ribs to wake him up and make him see just how awful everything was.

'I still don't understand. I wear funny clothes sometimes but that doesn't mean anyone thinks I've been especially naughty.'

'Oh, Elliott, really, that's just how you are - that doesn't count at all,' Lady Tizzy insisted. 'Anyway, it's different. You're not naughty like Pember. So there was poor Pember dressed as Bert Ackroyd, and even though Bloss saw him first, it wasn't enough, because Jennifer soon joined them, and there was Pember all in a heap wearing funny clothes, so Jennifer immediately took it that he had been being a very naughty boy with someone else instead of trying to be a good boy and all responsible as a father and everything, and now she's going to divorce him and not give a ball. Bloss told me this morning, just now. And that Pember told Bloss it was all my fault for making him go to *Real Man* in the first place, and that he felt like never seeing me again, even though he hasn't been seeing me anyway. So you can see why I feel I've looked on Rudyard Kipling's twin whatevers and found them both the same.'

'Yes. Sort of.'

There was a long silence while Elliott stared straight ahead. It could be reasonably admitted that Lady Tizzy was right to feel that she had looked on Kipling's twin whatevers and found them just the same. Things having been sort of the same at one point, now could hardly be worse.

If Jennifer divorced Pember, Pember might well marry Lady Tizzy, and if he married Lady Tizzy she would have to divorce Fulton, and they would both live at the Hall, and Fulton and he and the babies would be parted forever, particularly Elliott, because he wouldn't even have visiting rights and be able to talk smocking with Nanny and potting with Bessie.

'This is just like something that happens in Monday's paper - in somewhere like Penge,' Elliott remarked.

'Where is Penge?' Patti wondered.

'Just a little to the north east of everywhere else,' said Elliott, giving the sort of deep sigh that only a man stretched to the end of his tether could bring to a situation.

'Oh, Elliott, what shall we do?'

Tears were brimming and about to make a watery trail down Patti's cheeks. Elliott removed a handkerchief from his pocket with a sigh. The sigh came first of all because he knew if he gave his handkerchief to Lady Tizzy he would never see it again, and it was one of his best, and second because he knew that giving her his handkerchief would never stop her crying, and there was something about girls crying that made him want to shout at them, because when they cried they made him feel so especially helpless.

'We had better go in now,' he finally said after Patti's sobs had died away a little and he had given them both a Polo mint to suck. 'And we had better tell Fulton everything, and find out if he has a solution.'

'God do you think he might have, Elliott?' Patti wanted to know, pushing his handkerchief deep into her top pocket.

'Certainly. I mean, he has just finished reading *Wisdom and its Consequences*, so you never know. He could have found out something useful.'

Patti gave a dry and racking sob. On hearing it Elliott felt a vague sort of lump of terror come into his throat as he thought of their babies who would just now, at that very minute, be coming back from their walks, two in the pram, and one toddling. It didn't take much imagination to picture how pretty and adorable they would be looking. Nevertheless, if Fulton had managed to learn anything from *Wisdom and its Consequences* their bacon might not be altogether cooked - just a little too crispy maybe, but not burnt to a frazzle. He took Patti's hand and walked into the house with her praying hard all the while, which despite his deep belief in an all-seeing all-hearing Great Central Force, he nevertheless feared might be just a trifle optimistic, because it seemed the all-seeing all-hearing Great Central Force did seem to have been a tiny bit deaf of late. *Please, please God, help things get sorted out,* he prayed to himself. *And sort out Jennifer and Pember and Lady Tizzy particularly, and soon, please. Very soon if not immediately.*

Georgiana stared around her, uncertain if she were in a house or an apartment. She didn't feel like asking, principally because she had a feeling she was going to find out anyway, so that asking might be just a little *de trop*. She felt safe despite being quite on her own with only Kaminski and a secretary in another room, as a girl could feel who has a very good nanny looking after her young son, a common-law husband far away in the country, and a set of wonderful excuses to visit London. She imagined that she must after all be in a house, because she couldn't sense a bedroom anywhere near by, and she knew there was an upstairs because she had seen one when she jumped out of the taxi on arrival. She had always loved being alone in a house. Sometimes at Longborough, when she was a little girl, she had seemed to be alone for days and days on end while her parents went away on a visit for more, and still more different hunting with more, and still more, different friends.

While the servants listened to very loud radio comedy shows in a kind of religious rejoicing at the absence of the master and mistress, Georgiana would wander round the many rooms, hiding in cupboards from no-one at all, talking to her dog and encouraging him to jump over obstacles in the attics. Reading alone in her pony's stable while it slept, and the comforting sound of rain outside made their two presences together inside a poem of cosiness. Being alone had been, and perhaps still was, in her mind anyway, one of life's great luxuries.

She stared at what she could see of Kaminski's presence in the brown suede-lined room. There were many, many books but they were not paperbacks; they were all hardcovers with nice bindings, many of them old, some of them she saw from the London library, and they were she supposed all for the film. There were flowers arranged by someone else which extravagant and beautiful, crowded into square-cut vases in the approved fashionable manner.

Then there was a paper knife with a strangely foreign-looking cypher, which she decided must belong to someone with Russian blood, a leather folder with the initial K beautifully engraved and inside the folder the first correctly and perfectly typed pages of a script.

Georgiana sat down behind the partners' desk but instead of opening the folder she closed it, not bothering even for a second to read what was written on the expensively typed pages. She was not a reader of other people's letters or diaries, or scripts for that matter, any more than she could ever have brought herself to look in someone else's bathroom cabinet. It would have upset her to think that she had ever even known someone who did things like that, although knowing that Nanny did it, and Nan for that matter, didn't bother her at all, because they were old and allowed to be different. And anyway that was all they had, things like that, letters to steam open, other people's lives upon which to speculate now that their own were just a little still. So she closed the folder without giving its contents even a first glance before the leather slipped back over Kaminski and E.F.'s latest work. Only the K for Kaminski remained for her to read.

This, in contrast to the script inside the folder, she did scrutinize, picking it up and turning it towards the light to see how deeply the K was etched on the leather. She traced the letter with her finger, just a little sensuously, thinking from the chicness of it that it must be French, before putting the folder back down and carefully reading the listings on the telephone beside the numbers. From these, since they were many and varied, she was at last able to ascertain that she was actually in a house and not an apartment.

She yawned, carefully putting her hand in front of her mouth, and then because Kaminski appeared still to be busy despite having been told that she had arrived by the secretary in the other room, she picked up the internal telephone and rang 4 for the housekeeper and asked her to bring her up a glass of Evian water.

From the spyhole inset on the other side of the suede-covered door Kaminski had been watching Georgiana all the time she had imagined she was quite alone and unobserved, reluctantly allowing himself to be enthralled. She looked so detached from everything she was doing, not bored just detached, as if she knew time was passing, time had passed, and time would continue to pass and really what she did or did not do would make not the slightest difference to everything happening around her, now or ever.

His hidden eye was Kaminski's camera, and he was self-conscious enough to know it. He knew he could not have directed Georgiana better in the scene, moving around, touching everything and yet not really looking. If she had been Garbo in *Queen Christina* she could not have performed a scene without words so well. But now she had rung for her Evian water he would have to go through to her, and become part of the same scene he had been so silently and excitedly witnessing. Becoming part of a scene meant that it at once ceased to be beyond his direction. After all it was the number one rule that direction went out of the window once emotions became too heavily involved, and as he walked into the library-study and smelt Georgiana's curiously lemon-tinged perfume, and saw her long fingers wrapped around a leather-covered book, and her eyes with their new detached expression look up as she heard him make his entrance into the room, Kaminski felt himself sinking into a quicksand of emotion that he really didn't want, and yet he could not and would not resist.

The truth was he longed for the Georgiana whose first lover he had been, who hadn't known her power over him, and whom he had therefore been able to leave behind as he was able to leave a canister of film, or an old script, quickly moving on to some newer, and therefore more interesting project, or in the young Georgiana's case, some newer and more interesting affair. Certainly once he had flown back to Los Angeles Kaminski doubted whether he had cast his mind back to Georgiana more than a few times, and then only to celebrate her contribution to his film, and the fact that their affair had proved to be the inspiration that he had so needed for his re-make of the Bolst classic. But that was all. Really, nothing more, nothing less than a mental comparison had been made, while watching rushes, or talking to his faithful editor, which was why when he saw her sipping her cocktail at the bar of that hotel he had been so astounded at his own emotions. Right then and there he had wanted to make love to her, and without a doubt he saw that she felt the same, yet the person whom he saw, whom he had once made love to, who had enchanted him with her indoor picnics was quite gone, replaced by someone quite different, someone more powerful, someone now seemingly detached - someone capable of dominating him where he had once dominated her. How he longed for the person he had once known, and yet he could not but stay to become enthralled with the person who had come to replace her.

'I see you have a new prison.'

She looked at him smiling, but the look in her eyes was just a little mocking.

'You're staying.'

There was no question mark as far as Kaminski was concerned, but he was all too well aware that there might be a considerable one from her point of view.

'This is very different from your last prison, Governor Kaminski,' she continued, ignoring him 'Actually, I think I rather liked the last one a little better. Charles Street. More chic, the interior more faded, the neighbours a great deal more prestigious for having always been there.'

Kaminski felt that odd sense of panic that comes to everyone when someone with whom they are currently impassioned makes a reference to something in their mutual past, however brief, which they are meant to remember and can't. She was obviously caught up with this analogy of prisons, but he couldn't remember why.

'You used to lock me up in Charles Street and throw away the key, remember? Only the maid was allowed in and out while you and E.F. went away filming and came back with things for me to wear. My prison clothing I used to call it.'

He couldn't remember so he gave up, not bothering to hide the fact that he was not even going to try to.

'Here - look, Kaminski - there isn't even a fireplace where you can smash your drinking glass for luck, for instance.'

Georgiana turned a full-circle, indicating the whole room with one long graceful gesture as she did so, all suede, no fireplaces, nothing but the chicest and newest of everything, steel, glass, leather. Only the desk was old, but even that had new handles, she noticed with amusement, and was all polished up and vulgar in a way that would have made her mother wrinkle her nose and say *Why they always insist on doing that one will never know.*

'I'll have someone smash a hole in the wall and make a fireplace, if you wish.'

Georgiana smiled, but this time only slightly, because they both knew that Kaminski was perfectly capable of not only ordering but carrying out such a thing. He was after all a director, and once they had the go-ahead directors could order anything, more than generals really, which Georgiana found rather funny when she came to think of it.

'It would look strange though, wouldn't it, with suede on the walls? Besides, it would have to be a log-effect fire, and that kind of fireplace is hopeless for smashing glasses.'

'Can you stay the night?'

Too soon – he knew he had said it too soon, but it was too late. He couldn't stand another afternoon like the last one, when they had made love brilliantly and passionately, and then she had left him rather too promptly to catch the train back to Wiltshire and her painter.

Georgiana could stay the night, as a matter of fact she wanted to stay the night, but she wasn't going to tell Kaminski that, and nor would she for some time to come, if at all. She preferred both to keep him strung along, and to keep an avenue of escape open. After all they might not even love each other by the end of the afternoon. She knew now that these things happened, and quite often. People met and made love, were passionate about each other, ready to die each for the other, or commit murder, or suicide, and then just as quickly they were dying of boredom at the very thought of each other. Allowances had to be made for this. No, she couldn't tell Kaminski that she was able to stay the night, she couldn't, and what was more she wouldn't.

Besides, she liked seeing the dying hope in his eyes, and the way he turned away from her aware only of her power over him, not of his over her. She would never let him be aware of that again, not ever. He must always be at her feet, quite crushed, begging for mercy, squirming and wriggling with anxiety as to whether or not she loved him. Anything else, anything less than that and a man became bored. That at least she had learnt, not just from Kaminski who had left her, but from Gus who might as well have.

Indeed it might be preferable to be left - the clean break, the sudden change of existence - rather than suffer the dull little wearing away, the little pieces taken out of you, like the birds that robbed the scarecrows around the fields at Longborough, taking pieces of their bodies to build up their nests. Nothing would ever be the same again between her and Gus, so that being so, she thought, as she saw Kaminski walking towards her with a certain look in his eyes, that being so she might as well change everything in her life.

'You rang for an Evian water, ma'am?'

The maid at Charles Street when they had last been lovers, had been small and dark and foreign, and eager to be on Georgiana's side, approving always of her affair with this famous director. A very young girl with an older man was after all to be approved of, providing the older man was rich. To continental eyes it was a perfect match, and the maid had cried when Kaminski had left Georgiana, perhaps because after Kaminski had left her Georgiana had found it impossible to cry for herself.

Now as Kaminski advanced towards her, so full of purpose, Georgiana could only remember that time of growing up. The pain of the ending of that first affair, and how afterwards she had walked and so often past that house in Charles Street in the months that followed, wondering to herself over and over again why she had meant so little to someone who had meant so much to her. The memory made her turn away from Kaminski towards the window that overlooked the outside street, a street that held no memories, only passing people, people hurrying, people strolling, people standing waiting for someone, none of them knowing that she was watching them, to distract herself, to take her mind away from the past, away from the pain.

Kaminski watched her, her back turned towards him, the long dark hair on her shoulders moving slightly as she sipped the Evian water, and he wondered, as he so often did with women, whether he would be in love with her if he understood her? Probably not was his usual answer to this most unanswerable of questions, and yet with this one, he then thought perhaps he would. Suddenly he found his heart literally sinking at the thought of how much power she could have over him. If he came to understand her, if she came to possess that kind of power over him, he would never be able to leave her, not for a second. It was a terrifying thought. He could never allow such a woman out of his thoughts, or indeed out of his sight. He would want her with him all the time, beside him when he filmed, beside him when he walked, ate, or slept, he would talk to her for the rest of his days, and that would still be too little.

'A lifetime's talking will be over.'

That was a line of his and E.F.'s in a film they had written, or was it E.F.'s? What did it matter? It was true of so few relationships. To be with most people was to be alone and shivering with loneliness. *Huis Clos* was the greatest film ever made about hell. Hell was indeed other people, as was heaven. Heaven was looking across a luncheon table at someone and laughing and laughing, and knowing that they saw the same colour in that laughter-making thought, the same exact vision, and when the laughter stopped the silence that followed did not have to be filled, because the relationship was perfection.

Still watching Georgiana sipping her water Kaminski challenged himself to walk out of the room and leave her. It would be so easy, and make life so easy for him. He could leave E.F. to Sofia, make the movie, go back to the US and forget about this grown-up version of what he had once just played around with. It was easy. He could just leave her. It was easier than easy, he only had to walk across the room, put his hand on the door, and slip out into the hall, walk to the outer door, let himself into the street, and it would all be over. Outside there would be cars and streets full of people and restaurants and trees every now and then, and dogs on leads, and umbrellas that were about to be put up, and taxis waiting to be caught, and shops with models facing outwards so people would look inwards. It was all so easy, but then she turned and he saw the look in her eyes, and it was very grown-up and very tender, and he realized that for that moment she was feeling older than him, and the idea made him giddy. She knew better than he did that he was caught, and that the look in his eyes was no more the look of a man who could walk out of the room, across the hall, and let himself out into the street than it was of a successful man of great fame. It was the look of a dog in a pound, and only one person in the world at that moment was capable of paying to get poor dog Kaminski out. But would she? Or would she leave him caged up, his nose against the bar, longing always for that one voice that would say 'Yes - I'll take him'?

'Shall we go upstairs now?'

Before it had been hotels, first hers, and then another that he rather liked, but now it was his room, and yet she walked up into it as if it were already hers, as if she had already redecorated it, made it over as the Americans said, and as women always did when they moved into your life, changing everything except the man, and sometimes they changed him too.

Kaminski pulled down the blinds. They were strangely old-fashioned and made of stiffened cream Holland with insets of old-fashioned cream lace. They reminded him of Russian trains, of his grandmother, of samovars, of the old days when he was a little boy and wore silk suits, before Paris, and then America.

'I want to take you to Paris,' he told her before they started to make love, and he found himself wrapped up in the mystery that was passion.

'When?' she murmured between kisses.

'Tonight,' he told her casually. 'We'll take a train. It will be wonderful.'

Georgiana said nothing. There was, after all, very little to say. It was a long time since she had been in Paris. She couldn't remember how long, but as Kaminski drew her towards the great draped four-poster that dominated the room she sighed with pleasure at the idea of the beautiful streets, the women in their smart clothes, the pavement cafés, the restaurants, and as they began to make love it seemed to her that she could even hear an accordion playing and Edith Piaf singing. So great was her desire to escape from Gus and her life with Nanny and Nan at Longborough, the voice of the famous Parisian sparrow could have been that of a siren.

10

It had been a fine morning all over Wiltshire, and it was continuing to be so, so fine that even Clarissa Parker-Jones had been forced to pause and reflect about how strange it was that no-one had ever become used to calling her Mrs Gillott. They had all, to a person, had to be reminded that she had changed her name, and now she had, pending the divorce, quickly changed back to Parker-Jones once more, no-one had really noticed at all.

Of course, having been through so much with Andrew, marriage, and putting up with him, and so on, it seemed only fair and reasonable that she should, even after her divorce came through, retain the Honourable bit of his name. It wasn't that she mentioned it very often herself - indeed hardly at all unless it was to do with the cup she presented in the village and they wanted to know what to put on the posters - that sort of thing. No, she didn't fling her handle around, or insist on it or anything, but now she was faced with the decision as to whether or not to give it up, she realized she couldn't. It wasn't that he was a snob, far from it; with a great-grandmother who had been known as the Belle of Bishopstrow, how could she be? No, it was that she had come to realize how much other people enjoyed titles and handles and things. Shops loved it, even quite big ones, and then of course there was a certain satisfaction to be had from people taking the Honourable to mean that she was an M.P., as in the Right Honourable, and asking her advice about their rates and things, which she was naturally quite happy to give whenever she could, and it was pleasant to see how grateful they were for even a little crumb of comfort.

All of which thoughts, as she sat on under her old apple tree with an approved clematis climbing through it, led her to contemplate the ghastliness of life if Jennifer, her only and fairly beloved daughter, divorced and became the ex-Lady Pemberton, the former Marchioness of Pemberton.

Clarissa sipped an indifferent cup of coffee as she freely imagined Jennifer living in the village, squatting in some little eight-bedroomed house of the kind that people frequently turned into antique shops, bringing her children up to go to the village school. Heavens, how sordid it would all be, even before Clarissa's friends started ringing her up and commiser-ating with her.

'Ghastly for you, Clarissa, and on top of your own divorce, so public always. You haven't been having much luck, have you?'

She could just hear the voices, and the hidden delight that would be behind them, and imagining them made her foot swing up and down, and her hands grasp her coffee cup until the knuckles showed a little white. She had to stop Jennifer being headstrong and doing whatever she wanted when she wanted. It all came from being an only child, but with her father being so over-weight what possible chance had Clarissa to have had more?

She cleared her throat loudly several times, and allowed her imagination full rein. Christmas would be so different, for instance. Spending Christmas in a village house would hardly be the same as spending it at the Hall with the security of a butler and staff. Clarissa took out a handkerchief and blew her nose very hard. Jennifer was impossible. Why couldn't she just turn a blind eye like every other decent wife? Why not forget about finding Pember in the drive dressed in funny clothes? Why not accept his story that he had merely been going around disguised as someone called 'Bert' in order to find out how many people would be interested in his new scheme for marketing local rather than organic produce? But no, that would be too easy for Jennifer, she had to plump for the big one, for disgust and divorce instead.

The telephone, small and plastic, rang from under a nearby philadelphus. Clarissa hurried to it. She hated to admit that she couldn't do without a telephone within a few yards of her, even in the garden, so she always took the trouble to hide it beneath the freshly planted philadelphus.

'Are you in the garden?'

It was the Countess, vibrantly alive and full of news, Clarissa could tell because she could hear her smoking on the other end of the telephone line, one of her small gold-tipped Turkish cigarettes that came in different colours, no doubt.

'No - I'm not.'

Clarissa hated to admit that she was in case the Countess didn't want her to be and rang off, or made one of her little remarks that could, at times, be so cutting.

'That's funny. You sound as if you're in the garden. Telephones are so sensitive, I find, I thought I could hear little leaves and things rustling, but perhaps you're flower arranging?'

'Yes, flowers and leaves, something special,' Clarissa lied.

'Things are going from bad to worse,' the Countess related with relish. Clarissa had often noticed that the dear Countess seemed to enjoy bad news almost as much as she didn't enjoy good. 'Jennifer has been to see a lawyer, but only one, and in Stanton, and they don't count. Mary, my daughter -'

'Yes, yes.'

Clarissa knew only too well that Lady Mary Stranragh was the Countess's daughter, and had no need to be told.

'Mary has apparently decided to cancel her ball! How she found out about Jennifer's scandal -'

'Pember's scandal -'

'Exactly, how she found out I wouldn't know. I have to take the train to London straight away and sort things out. She can't cancel, not now Jennifer's cancelling. I just don't understand the young now, really I don't. Nor, as I say, can I understand how she found out about Pember in the drive in funny clothes. It's too awful.'

There was a sudden and very long pause as at either end of the Wiltshire line both ladies came suddenly to realize that perhaps after all they did know how the London-based Mary could have found out. Bloss.

Lady Mary stared fixedly in the mirror at her hairdresser. He was being boring, dull and egotistical, and if he had been doing anything except her hair she thought she might have had the greatest pleasure in kicking him in the shins, but since to do so meant turning round and getting her hair in even more of a muddle, most unfortunately she couldn't even attempt such a thing.

On and on he was going about doing many and varied, if not various, other boring people's hairstyles for 'your dance'. She had corrected him two or three times with 'ball' when he said 'dance', and then had finally given up and lit a cigarette instead, which she knew he couldn't stand.

The trouble was Lady Mary could not bring herself, at any point, to tell him that she was about to cancel the stupid ball and go to Scotland for a very long sabbatical instead. For heaven's sake, she hadn't even told her wretched husband yet, and just as well since he was in New York handing out invitations to every other friend on Wall Street, as far as she could gather.

There was no getting out of it, however, none at all. She had to cancel. The whole point of giving a ball had been to put Jennifer and her mother's noses out of joint for the first and last time, and now that Jennifer was getting divorced instead, the whole thing had to be wrapped up, and as soon as possible.

Lucius, her one-time lover, had tried to persuade her otherwise last night over supper, but of course he had been quite unable to do so, because in the end even he could see that if the whole point of a social occasion had been taken away, then that was blasted well that.

'Couldn't you just give the ball for some new reason? For the sake of enjoyment, say?' he had asked a little plaintively at one point.

'Really, Lucius.'

That's all she had said, and that was all she'd had to say. After all, who had ever heard of giving a social arrangement for enjoyment, of all things? It was like being asked to give a wedding and have the guests not bring any presents, just themselves, because you were fond of them and liked them, and that sort of thing. It was perfectly laughable, and perfectly ridiculous at the same time, and she only hoped that she had made it plain both to Lucius and to Juanita who was listening at the door that it was probably the silliest idea that she had ever heard mooted, if that was the right word.

Anyway, enough of that, except that even thinking about cancelling things was almost more work than getting them up, so it was really no good pretending that the subject would go away by saying to yourself 'enough of that'. So instead she thought to herself 'besides that'. Besides that, and besides wanting to scream at the hairdresser and murder Jennifer, and her mother, and so on and so on, besides all that, and if that wasn't enough, she knew that when she arrived home for luncheon she would, be in the unenviable position of finding her mother waiting for her, something that neither of them would enjoy at all, but which had to be endured.

The Countess was indeed waiting. She stared uneasily at Mary's freshly coiffured hair. It had a funny bit at the top which looked rather silly. She had obviously said yes to the funny bit at the top when she had meant to say no, always absolutely fatal with hairdressers. Happily Mary was not someone to say 'How do you think I look?' because if her mother had been forced to answer that she would have had to say 'a bit silly' and there would have been all hell to pay, no doubt of it.

'I don't see why you have to cancel your ball, just because Jennifer's getting divorced and everyone will want to come to yours after all,' the Countess said, almost as plaintively as Lucius had the previous evening. 'After all, it was not the whole point, was it, to give one on the same night as Jennifer? That was just part of the point, not the whole point.'

'If you can't see the point then there's absolutely no point in going on talking about it. Besides, there's another reason why I have to cancel, which is another point,' said Mary with grim determination.

'Which is?'

Mary sat down opposite her mother. Her one oddly coloured eye and her other more normally coloured one stared with vengeful fervour at her mother.

'John is not paying for the ball. He is refusing to help out, and today I have had a letter which makes it quite plain that I can't manage to pay for it on my own.'

The Countess stared at her daughter, and then lit one of her small Turkish cigarettes, and took a leisurely puff. Stranragh, Mary's second husband, was notoriously mean, but not so mean surely that he wouldn't pick up the tab for a ball that could do them both nothing but good?

'How are you to cope, then?'

'How I was going to cope,' Mary told the Countess, and she put her head on one side as her tone turned to one of heavily light sarcasm, 'how I was going to cope was with the insurance money from the Chi-Chi china dog, which Juanita stole. That was what the letter was about this morning. They won't pay out, even though I'm covered for theft.'

Juanita stole! The Countess's puff of smoke, she didn't know how, slipped smoothly out towards the perfumed air of Mary's drawing room without pause, a miracle of self-control in the circumstances.

'She denied it, of course, but I sacked her anyway. You might have noticed, I have a Filipino cousin of that butler I sometimes use instead. Quite nice, except she does smile a little too much for my taste, but then one can't have everything, or indeed sometimes anything, I find, when it comes to maids.'

The Countess's mind raced towards the sacked Juanita, and then turned back and raced towards Mary and her insurance money.

'That, Chi-Chi china dog was very valuable, as you probably know, and the insurance company had agreed a figure, a very substantial figure as it happens.'

The Countess leaned forward in expectation of finding out how substantially valuable that ghastly ornament had actually been. Quite a few thousand perhaps, if Mary had felt able to give a ball all on her own without Stranragh kicking anything into the kitty. Several few thousand pounds perhaps; more than several few thousand even, perhaps?

'It was valued at over fifty thousand pounds in the current market. Well worth Juanita stealing, as it happens.'

The Countess gasped, choked, and eventually, overcome with emotion, stubbed out her cigarette. Fifty thousand pounds! That ghastly relation of Freddie's ploughing her way through all those catalogues and peering at everything with her eyeglass had been more than a dull and boring expert, she had obviously been a dull and boring genius.

'Things Chinese are very valuable nowadays, not just because China's shut, but because they have lost the will to create things for the people they killed off years ago, you know, a bit like the English. That red Chinese box of yours must be quite valuable now, I should think.'

If the Countess could have blushed she would have done. The red Chinese box was currently sitting in an upstairs room filled with old buttons and pieces of lace.

'If it has a phoenix in flight on the side I should pop it straight in to somewhere and have it looked at for the insurance, if nothing else.'

The Countess sipped her perfectly horrid glass of sherry and tried to conjure up the decoration on the side of the red Chinese box now filled with buttons. Did the wretched box have a bird in flight on the side? The sherry began to burn her insides as she suddenly couldn't remember whether or not the box, full of buttons or not, was still in place in the little sewing and ironing room in her house. She thought it was, but then, on the other hand, she had been in a bit of a tearing hurry on her way to the races the other day when a wretched woman from the village in a faded green quilted coat had called asking for bric-à-brac.

Being in a flurry and the drawing room being full of an impatient Andrew puffing and panting and waiting for the off, the Countess had instructed Maria to find something, anything, to give the silly woman. That being so, it was perfectly possible that Maria, who had first been directed towards the attic and found the ladder too giddy-making, and then towards what she would insist on calling the 'utility room', had snatched up this perfectly boring box, emptied it of its buttons, and given it to the equally boring do-gooder Mrs Dupont - always it seemed and ever known to the surrounding countryside as the Village Voice.

'Why is a phoenix in flight a good thing?' she managed to ask Mary eventually, in a low, quiet, controlled voice.

'Because it means it was made for an empress,' Mary replied in the ever-patient way she now adopted towards her mother, and which her mother thought was nasty and made her feel old, but about which she could do nothing whatsoever at all. 'Anything made for a Chinese empress is very rare and special.'

'Well, it would be,' the Countess agreed, her mind now completely made up. She must return to Wiltshire immediately, and find the red box. She could ring Maria, of course, but Mary would be sure to overhear, and to admit that she didn't know where the red box was, or whether it was still in the so-called 'utility room', would not only make her feel terribly old, it would make her seem terribly old, and that would be twin evils of the most hellish kind.

Watching her mother leaving, and climbing with just a little difficulty into a taxi cab, Mary sighed and wondered. 'Do nothing to cancel until you've heard from me,' her mother had said. Fair enough, she would do nothing, particularly since the invitations were still sitting in their boxes, their engraving shining with lovely glossy black, the words 'Lady Mary Stranragh' set in beautiful flowing type, their left-hand corners without any names of friends, acquaintances, enemies, or other bodies. Not that she was going to tell the Countess that, by any means, for this was her revenge on her mother for breaking the Chi-Chi dog and not telling her, and for letting her sack Juanita, who would now have to be enticed back from the beastly new family who had taken her on and re-installed, and a very large and handsome endowment deposited in her Post Office account to make up for the whole unfortunate incident.

Happily her mother had no real knowledge of things like insurance. She would never know that it would be impossible to claim on the Chi-Chi dog, since most claims were impossible anyway, but particularly when it had been broken beyond repair. Now the silly old bag would be sent back to Wiltshire on a wild-goose chase, and serve her right too. It had seemed like such a perfectly lovely idea, to give a ball in opposition to that frightful Jennifer Pemberton's, but then everything had got so out of hand. The final straw coming when she had had to do her own house-work while waiting for the new maid to arrive, had found the Chi-Chi dog, and putting one and one together had realized that it was Mamma who had broken the dog and hidden it, the day she had thought to arrive and depart from Mary's study without trace. (She forgot small things like leaving the butt of a Turkish cigarette in the ashtray, and the bill from lunch screwed up in the wastepaper basket.)

How could Mary know it was her mother and no-one else who had broken the dog, Stranragh had wanted to know when he called from New York at five o'clock that evening? Simple, she was able to tell him, very simple, dreadfully simple, because Juanita never dusted!

'You know I always have to get in the Belgravian Dusty Company to do heavy housework, every other Thursday and all the months with an 'r' in them, darling,' she was forced to gently remind him. 'Juanita only does and opens doors, she doesn't actually *do*, and one doesn't and can't expect her to.'

'Ah yes, of course, darling. But if you get her back what will you do with the Filipino?'

'I will keep her to iron. She's very good at ironing.'

'But do we have that much ironing?'

'Really darling! With Scotland! Of course we have that much ironing.'

'Do we send laundry south?'

'My sweet, how on earth do you think one gets the napkins so stiff? Have a nice day, bless you.'

Mary replaced the receiver. Really. Imagine Stranragh even suggesting leaving the napkins in Scotland to be done. What were things coming to when he thought that even a possibility? And where he thought they found peppercorns, Bath Olivers and Belgian choccies in the Highlands she wouldn't know. But that was men for you, completely impractical, which was why they had to be sent off to offices to run governments and businesses and so on.

When they were first married, (both on their seconds of course) Stranragh had not gone to an office, but Mary had pretty soon altered that. A husband at home was one thing to which she could never get used, and was never going to either. She picked up the telephone once again. Lucius. The dear darling, he must come round at once. Now that he had left Hugo they had so much to talk about. As she dialled she smiled at the thought of the discomfiture she had put her mother through. She didn't even really care whether or not she had a Chinese box, she just liked to think of her beetling back to Wiltshire to find one.

'As it happens I shall keep the invitations,' she told Lucius later when they were cosily dining together. 'They will come in useful for my 'at homes' for the next fifty years.'

'You were going off the ball anyway, weren't you?'

'Mmm, absolutely. You know how it is, you order the invitations to be engraved and while you're waiting for them to be engraved you draw up the lists of guests. You study the lists of guests, you mark them 'a' and 'b' and so on, and it all seems very nice. You imagine your dress, your friends, the orchestra, the band, the food and the flowers, and when the blessed things finally arrive you've enjoyed it all so much in your head -'

'You might as well not give it at all?'

Mary nodded.

'Oh dear. We always did feel dreadfully the same about everything, didn't we?'

Lucius nodded. It was true. They had.

'Love is such a pill, isn't it?'

Without exactly meaning to Lucius leant over the table and kissed Mary briefly on the lips, and Mary quite suddenly remembered a great many things that she had previously forgotten about Lucius, about herself, about all three of them, Hugo and her and Lucius. Very nice things. Very beautiful things. Very good things. It was Capri where everything had gone so wrong. But now it was no longer Capri, it was Knightsbridge, and they were alone, just the two of them. How heavenly.

The Countess's journey home was more of an odyssey than a journey really. Thanks to the train service which wasn't she spent three hours waiting for a connection which never transpired, and was forced to hire a taxi, which also wasn't, just one of those broken down cars that are always pretending to be taxis in the country and which might as well be pump-kins for all the comfort they afford. She didn't arrive home until near enough midnight to make it nothing but selfish to wake Maria, so she had to let herself into the hall, quite alone, having paid a fortune to the cabman. When she was finally able to sit down in her own dear home, it was hardly surprising that she found it quite easy to burst into tears.

It was pathetic and dreadfully old-ladyish, but she hadn't been able to resist it. The tears were from relief mostly, and frustration a lot, but she had felt a great deal better after them, and having poured herself a really lovely stiffy she nipped straight upstairs (although nipping was a little out of her range nowadays) to the wretched utility room to retrieve the button box.

Except it wasn't there. No box, only a great many buttons, and all piled in neat stacks. Shirt buttons in one stack, brown coat buttons in another stack, navy blue coat buttons in another, and so on. The ironing table upon which clean clothes were placed after starching had now assumed the rakish look of a casino.

The Countess looked desperately round, wondering as she did why she was doing so, because she knew now, and for certain, that the red Chinese box had gone to the village bazaar to be sold for a few pence in aid of the Vicar's Watercolour Classes and the Annual Wildflower Award.

The thing to keep was calm, she told herself, as she wobbled slowly downstairs to the hall again, and back to the drinks table for another stiffy. She must keep calm. Except she couldn't, and for a very good reason, perhaps even fifty thousand pounds' worth of reasons. Having given up any attempt at calm, she tried to assemble her thoughts. Just because the box had been given to Mrs Dupont for the bazaar didn't mean that the bazaar had taken place and the box been sold. The Countess eyed the telephone on the kitchen wall as she paced up and down and through all her many rooms. It was both too late and too early to telephone the Village Voice.

She sat down at the kitchen table. Sitting at the kitchen table gave her an odd feeling, the feeling that she used to have when she was a child. She thought she could almost smell the fine flour that her mother's cook would use, and feel the sides of the rust-coloured bin in which the flour was stored. Everything was home-made in those dim, dear, long gone, past and gone, days. Nothing bought at all. What a wondrous thought that was. And also very nice too. Nice that one had known those things, even if they were gone now; they were there in her mind, whenever she wanted them. Now she put them away and allowed her eye to fall upon Maria's little notice board. So many little reminders. Maria was a good maid. Faithful and loyal, despite everything really.

Suddenly there it was. The notice of the bazaar. On Maria's board as large as life, and when she read the notice, twice as horrible.

CHURCH BAZAAR it said in very, very faded home-done misprinting, on very, very funny thin yellow paper of the kind usually only used by firms who wanted to wash your cars for you and added ANYTHING ATTEMPTED - NO JOB TOO SMALL, which if you ever had the misfortune to brush with them made you want to alter it to EVERY JOB TOO SMALL.

CHURCH BAZAAR IN AID OF WATERCOLO/R CLASSES AND GRAND WILD
FOWERR COMPETITION!!!!!!
SATURDAY TWENTY SECOND MAY. ALL WELCOME.
DOGS NOT admittedED EXCEPT BY REQUEST TO BE
GRANTED BY THE REV!!!

The Countess sank back on to the kitchen sofa. Saturday twenty-second of May had been and gone two days ago, and so too doubtless had the Chinese box. She put her hands up to her face but because she'd had two stiffies she felt no inclination to cry whatsoever. There was nothing like a touch of the Laphraoig for drying up the tear ducts. She had no intention of crying, so she bit her lip instead.

'Countess.' Fulton nodded importantly into the receiver of his old black Bakelite phone as if he was greeting his old friend in person.

'You've got to help me.'

'Naturally.'

'I knew you would.'

'Naturally.'

'It's Maria. She's given my Chinese box to the bazaar, and she shouldn't have.'

'Of course she shouldn't.'

'She should have given - something else. At any rate, you know that dreadful woman, Mrs Dupont. Can you get it back off her for me? If I try she'll only smell a rat.'

'It's valuable?'

How grateful she felt towards Fulton for saying that in that way, the Countess thought. He knew at once.

'Very.'

'Leave it to me,' said Fulton smartly.

'By the way, how are the babies?'

'Valuable.'

They both rang off understanding each other completely. How refreshing, and how *comforting* true understanding was. No need to say words, or be or do anything, no cheapness, no crowing at another's discomfort. Fulton was there in one, and of how many people could she say that? The Countess continued to wonder as she staggered off to put herself to bed in broad daylight. She'd had no sleep whatsoever since the late-night discovery of the disappearance of the Empress's Box, as it was now known in her mind.

As she sank between her sandalwood-smelling linen sheets, grateful for the heaviness of her Colefax and Fowler curtains keeping the bright morning at bay, the Countess put all thoughts from her mind except that which would best induce sleep.

Fulton was a miracle worker. If he did succeed in retrieving the Empress's Box, then she would reward him heavily. A dozen of those ghastly papier mâché trays of his with matching wastepaper baskets and ink trays, spill boxes, or whatever he wanted. She would order dozens and dozens of them. She fell asleep contentedly designing and counting them as Fulton at last found Elliott in the kitchen where he had been all the time.

'Have we got a knotty one here.'

'Not another really knotty one, I can't bear it,' Elliott moaned, slapping his Grant loaf hard so it hurt both him and it. 'Oh-dear-I-shouldn't-have-done-that, now it won't do a thing. Will nothing go straight for us at the moment?'

'I'm not answering that without my lawyer.'

'The ball, Patti and the fearful Gillott, Pember, *Real Man,* Bloss and Jennifer, Mrs Parker-Jones, the divorce, Mary's cancelling — is there anything more that Wiltshire can throw at us?'

'Mmm, 'fraid so.'

Elliott stooped, banged the hateful Grant loaf into the oven, banged the oven door shut, and then straightened up feeling much better.

'Very well, tell me, but if it's something too knotty I shall tell you something you won't want to know either.'

'Really? What about?' asked Fulton, momentarily distracted.

'About Twinks and lard?'

'Not before midday, thank you. In brief. The village bazaar has been given, and during the proceedings a person or persons unknown has sold to another person or persons unknown, whom we don't as yet know, the Countess's invaluable Empress's Box.'

'How do you know it's invaluable?'

'Because she would only say it was valuable.'

'Oh my heavens. So what now?'

'We must get it back.'

'We must get it back? And get Pember to *Real Man,* and Lazy Tizzy out of bed and wanting to live life to the full again? And rid of Twinks's tinia? And the ball in or out on time, whatever balls are meant to be?'

'Fraid so.'

'You're afraid? I'm scared stiff. Does our little Countess know what Mrs Dupont's like? Does she know that the world is round? Once Mrs Dupont knows we want something from her, or indeed from someone else, she will do her level best to make sure that we never ever, ever get near it ever, ever again.'

'I don't think she knows exactly, but I think she might have guessed or she wouldn't have asked, would she?'

Elliott shook his head slowly.

'Do you know, Fulton, if life goes on at quite this pace for quite this amount of time again, I think I shall probably quite give up.'

'I can quite understand your feelings.'

'A plan must be made.'

'Not *another* plan!'

'Mmm.'

They stared at each other, and Elliott, noticing that Fulton's eye was flickering first in one direction, and then in another, knew without being told that Fulton already had a plan in mind. What it was he couldn't guess, but the tell-tale flicker was all it needed. Mrs Dupont, the Empress's Box - the game was on and would be fought for all it was worth, even if it meant chucking the Grant loaf at the Village Voice and knocking her for six and stealing the wretched box back while she lay prone on the floor.

'I think I might just have an idea - dot, dot, dot.'

11

As soon as Georgiana was boarding the train to Paris with the night outside the windows dim and black around her and she had a glass of champagne on one side of her and Kaminski reading on the other, all she wanted was to go back to Longborough and her son. Stars shone ahead in a night sky, an oddly quiet London was being left behind them as the train started to move out, and all she could wonder was not at the delight of it all, the private apartment, the new luggage, the beautiful shoes that Kaminski had just bought her and fitted himself, but how her little boy was, and if perhaps he was asleep.

She knew that her sudden concern came was because all at once she was feeling helpless and trapped. It was also a direct result of her usual helplessness in the face of happiness. Happiness was not something with which Georgiana knew how to cope, any more than she knew how to cope with her small son. The fact that he would not miss her for a second, that his face lit up not only when he saw her but just as much for his Nan or his Nanny - or even for Gus – none of this diminished the misery she was now feeling because she had left him behind her if only for a few days.

Kaminski and she had made love. That was all that had happened, and for the first time in her life Georgiana realized she had known serenity and been completely happy - not a transient sort of happiness, a small pause in the difficult game of life, but total bliss. For an age it seemed while the sounds from the street outside enveloped her and as she watched Kaminski move quietly around the bedroom nothing could disturb her tranquility, and it had taken some time for her to search and find some reason to be unhappy. Having found it in her absent child, she lay back and allowed it to hurt her. After which she found she could be happy again, even though her previous serenity had now disintegrated.

'Don't you want to read?'

Georgiana shook her head and allowed herself another sip of champagne. Ahead of her lay Paris and all its delights and behind her the endless and dreary days spent with Gus, and with his moods and his dreadfully domineering ways. It seemed nothing she had ever done for him had been right, not ever - not even when he had decided to be unfaithful, not even then had she been able to be right, because when she had discovered his infidelity the fault was made hers because it seemed she had disturbed his painting and by so doing had very probably deprived the world of a great work. It was therefore small wonder she was going to Paris with Kaminski and was being unfaithful to Gus, who in the end hadn't even bothered to marry her and make her little boy legitimate. When she thought about it she considered the whole thing ridiculous, and wondered why she had gone on as long as she had in putting up with Gus and his selfish demanding ways.

She decided it had all started with Jennifer's invitation to the ball and the fact that Gus had not even bothered sending her as much as a postcard when he had been away painting in Israel because that was when she knew what kind of person he must really be, the kind of person that could travel halfway round the world and not bother to think of the people he had left behind. It was all his mother's fault spoiling him the way she had, and now if Georgiana was not careful while he was in his Nan's care George was going to be another only little boy, growing up to be as domineering and selfish as Gus.

'Are you sure you don't want to read?'

'Quite sure, thank you.'

Georgiana sipped some more of her champagne and swung one beautiful silk clad leg sideways on to the next seat so that she was posed carelessly, and beautifully, but not exactly opposite Kaminski any more. She did this in the hope that he would stop looking up at her every five minutes and asking her if she didn't want to read.

'Why don't you want to read?'

She stared at him, but only after a small dissatisfied pause during which she stared first out at the dark night and the lights of the small towns the train was speeding through, and then eventually back at this tall distinguished man with his new look of besotted gentleness.

'Probably because I don't really like reading.'

Kaminski stared at her.

'That's not true,' he said.

'Yes it is,' Georgiana insisted. 'I only really like magazines. I hate reading long books and waiting for the end to come, which usually is rather disappointing anyway. I like films,' she added, as a sort of token gesture, since she was sitting opposite one of the world's greatest directors, after which brief exchange she turned and stared out of the window at the darkness and the lights once more, as if the scene beyond the carriage was a movie which Kaminski had interrupted her watching.

Kaminski put down his book, picked up one of her hands and kissed it.

'You win,' he told her. 'You have my complete attention.'

Looking at the seriousness of his complete attention Georgiana smiled mischievously, and promptly forgot George and remembered once more that she was in love, while Kaminski tried to forget the warnings of his partner.

'Going to Paris with Georgiana? Are you crazy?' E.F. had cried. 'She'll bury you. And what am I meant to tell our esteemed producers in your absence? That you have taken temporary leave of all senses and run off with the one who will wreck your entire life?'

'Tell them I have gone location hunting, okay?' Kaminski had replied.

'The movie is set in America and England, not in goddam Paris France!'

'You do not have to mention Paris, E.F.'

'If you just want sex stay right here and have it off in London!'

'London is not Paris, E.F., and it is not a matter of having sex, as you so poetically put it. You might be able to fall in love in London, but if you want to become lovers you must go to Paris.'

Kaminski knew every yard of the old quarter of the sixième arrondissement where he used to live with his grandmother and her samovar, his mother and her perpetual sacrifices, and the large émigré community that always found its way to their apartment on Sundays.

'First you cross the Pont des Arts,' he instructed Georgiana the following morning, after they had arrived at the Georges Cinq and had dined, made love, ordered breakfast in the middle of the night, made love again, slept, ordered breakfast once more, made love once more, and finally drawn the curtains to admire Paris outside the windows of their sumptuous suite. 'But you must wait until about twenty to six in the evening, or like this morning until about twenty to eleven in the morning when the air is very clear, and you can lean on the bridge and wonder at the beauty of the Seine – with its *bateaux mouches,* with the painters setting up their easels, the old men with their medals pinned to their mackintoshes walking their wives' poodles, the smell of coffee being brewed all over the city, of glasses being polished in expectation of lunch, and finally of lunch itself. That is the warmth, the excitement of Paris, and you can feel that, you can sense that, just by standing on the Pont des Arts at the right time of day.'

Georgiana stared at herself in the mirror. She was looking wonderful in a new coat of a brilliant yellow with a matching dress beneath. She knew that yellow made her dark hair shine and so she smiled at herself and to herself with her eyes half-closed, before turning back to Kaminski who was waiting to put on her hat for her.

'Women always wear their hats too far back, particularly English women,' he said, holding the prettiest little confection poised on the tips of his long fingers. He stared very seriously down at Georgiana, and she knew it must be the look that he had when he was staring at his actresses, famous as he was for never using a viewfinder or staring for hours through the camera. He lowered the hat on to Georgiana's head, and she stared at him as seriously through the half veil while remaining perfectly still, one leg poised in front of the other as a model will stand, as he stepped backwards to judge the effect.

'That is as near to perfection as we will arrive at this morning,' he announced.

He stared at her and thought how vulnerable she suddenly looked – not as young and as vulnerable as she had looked when he had first fallen in love with her, but vulnerable and uncertain none the less. Knowing that she was no longer the girl he had first taken made the now wretched Kaminski love her more, realising that the magical sprite who was never going to grow up had in fact grown up and she had grown up all because of him.

'We never got near you, you know,' he told her as they left the hotel. 'In the movie.'

'I never saw it,' Georgiana replied. 'So I wouldn't really know.'

'You never saw it?'

'I didn't see the point.'

Kaminski smiled as he realised this was one of the many things he had grown to love about the young woman at his side, her strange and absolute honesty. She never dissembled. She told it exactly as it was and that he just loved.

'Okay,' he said, warming to his subject. 'The actress looked right, she did everything right - but E.F. and me she just didn't happen. You know when you trace a drawing, and then you lift it up, and then you try to put it back on top of the drawing again, it never quite matches? That's what happened, right? You were there as the original drawing, and we drew round you really pretty deftly, but when we lifted it up and took away the image we lost you. Not in our heads. We still had the memory of you. I did most certainly. And once I got to the edit the more I remembered and of course I was never free of you. Same went for old E.F. Consequently we were neither of us ever happy with the movie – but no matter. It was a pretty big success and everyone said so, critics included. But E.F. and I knew it wasn't what it should have been, and now I at least know that it was never ever going to have been possible.'

He stopped, smiled down at her and then kissed her briefly but tenderly on the lips.

They walked on. Paris was already well ahead of London and was already wearing her early summer finery.

'This is a city made for walking,' Kaminski told her. 'In London you take cabs, in Paris you walk. Or perhaps stroll is even better, particularly for lovers.'

He slipped a hand through her arm and they walk on now linked together like all the other lovers they passed, couples apparently out for a walk to see the sights of this one of the most beautiful cities in the world, while really only having eyes for each other.

After about half an hour they stopped for a coffee, sitting in the sunshine outside the café.

'Can I have a patisserie as well?' Georgiana wondered.

'Before lunch, and so soon after breakfast?' Kaminski laughed.

'You've quite forgotten how greedy I am,' Georgiana replied but she did not seem in the least apologetic because it was so obviously not true, and anyway she knew she was too slim to be deemed greedy. And that was another thing that Kaminski loved in her – her particularly English habit of exaggerating matters in order to forestall any criticism she feared might be about to come her way. Kaminski knew Georgiana wasn't greedy in the same way that Georgiana did, but well understood her reasons for claiming to be so – just in case anyone might think she was.

The coffee arrived, and a patisserie was chosen by Kaminski for her, one with apricot which was the kind he liked and therefore wanted her to enjoy. Georgiana began at once, delicately cutting at the pastry with a fork, but eating quickly and appreciatively, but for once Kaminski did not watch her. Instead he turned his attention to the avenues and the boulevards, to watch the women so chic and so savvy. To him only Paris could sport such women and as always he wondered how irritating it must be for women who were not French to see what French girls could do with simple pleated skirts, a silk scarf and a plain cardigan. It was fascinating to Kaminski but it was also irritating for he knew in truth that however beautifully he dressed Georgiana he would never be able to give her that particular sense of French chic and that nor could she acquire it.

But then when he turned his attention back to her and saw her smiling at him from underneath her little veiled hat perched so perfectly over one beautiful eye he thought that perhaps after all style and le chic was not everything.

'Come here,' he ordered her as they left the café.

Obediently Georgiana stood in front of him as Kaminski tilted her hat a little more forward, arranging the precise angle with such finesse that the two gentlemen seated at the table behind them applauded. Kaminski turned and acknowledging their appreciation made a conductor's bow as if from a podium. It was a moment they would both remember and treasure, a moment from a painting perhaps by Renoir, with the bright yellow of Georgiana's hat and coat, the gentlemen seated at their table behind, the reflections on the windows of the café, the film director in his collarless silk shirt, his French-cut jacket, his Italian trousers and his hand-made English Lobb shoes, but most of all there was the girl – there was Georgiana, glossy-haired, large-eyed Georgiana. She did not bow as Kaminski had done. She had no need. She knew the applause was for her. Kaminski might be the conductor, but she was the music.

Again they walked and now they drew near the Pont des Arts. Always at this point when Kaminski crossed the Place de la Concorde and started the walk towards the river as well as what he felt - like everyone who has visited Paris and lived near it – to be his own bridge, he would start to feel as if he was once more a little boy, not as he had felt then all those years before when he had been bewildered by the newness of it all, not understanding much of the language and not realizing that the city would be forever his home, but as if he was a little boy in spirit now - as if the whole of his idyllically successful life only made sense if he returned to this most beloved spot in the guise of a small boy, seeing it for the first time, remembering it, treasuring it. And so at last as he walked towards his beloved Pont des Arts, just as a painter might wish to become the colours on his palette, or perhaps even the picture on, Kaminski wished that he could become part of his bridge.

He was grateful for Georgiana's silence. It would have been quite terrible if, having arrived at what she knew was beloved for him, she had at once demanded to know something or had tried to talk. But she seemed too interested even to attempt to talk to him, too busy watching a painter at work, looking down the river at the boats, across to the steps where brightly clothed children were playing, their piping voices carrying on the warm summer morning to the pedestrians on the bridge. While she watched Kaminski turned towards the familiar nearby archway behind which lay all his boyhood.

He knew there was no avoiding a flashback, a device for which Kaminski himself had once upon a time had a particular fondness, but which just recently he had of necessity religiously avoided.

It had always seemed to him that his grandmother had been the great beauty of the family. Somehow she had managed to escape Moscow, bringing with her a maid, a samovar and a daughter who was healthy and could work, and had set up house in the ancient unfashionable rue de Seine in the bohemian quarter of Paris, where she had carried on as if she were still in Moscow. She commanded and people came and brought, dancing attendance on her as if there were not just the three of them but fifty three living in the apartment.

Whenever he came homer and he pushed open the door the apartment had always smelt the same, of the strong cigars and cigarettes of other émigré visitors, of the musk used in the oil put on the lamps, and of his grandmother's perfume - *ma patchouli*, he thought she called it, but her usage of some words was always so difficult to understand it made little difference what it was called, only that its scent seemed to be more overpowering and have greater force than any of the other scents that mingled in the air, which is how his grandmother had been – more overpowering and more present than either his mother or any of their visiting relatives.

She had always thought that Sashie, as she called her grandson, would grow into a great man, yet she never said any such a thing to him, but like a great actress she simply thought it, and young Sashie perhaps had even managed to read her thoughts and perhaps from his ability to do so grew his talent to direct. *Don't speak the dialogue, look it,* he would later tell his actresses. *Then the words will be there in your eyes.* His grandmother had never commanded. All she had done was look. One look towards her daughter, Sashie's beautiful mother, and she ran. One look towards the long-suffering maid, and she was back to her work. One look towards Sasha and he climbed on her knee.

She had told him stories when his mother was out - stories about the old days, about troikas, and about lovers who ran away, and about parents who ran after lovers, and about fortunes lost and brains blown about, but because he had been only seven he had not really understood a word. But he had *remembered* all the stories though and saved them up in his mind without exactly realising it, the way young children can. They listen, they don't seem to understand, but they remember. Then as he grew older he gradually realised that they were poor when they shouldn't be, and that all dressed up in her finery his mother did not go out to a business like other women but went to hotels like the Georges Cinq where she lunched or had tea with gentlemen who were staying over in Paris, gentlemen who enjoyed conversation and erudition, and sophistication, as well as making love. Once he had sensed that what his mother had to do to keep them was not what other mothers in less beautiful clothes did, who shopped in the neighbourhood market on Sunday mornings and bemoaned the lack of good cheese and wore black clothes for most of the year, young Sasha determined that one day his mother would never have to lunch or have tea with some total stranger ever again.

As he gazed in to the courtyard of his old family home he realised how old he had been when he was young. Because life was so hard he had grown up perhaps too quickly, and now the memories were almost too hard to bear – memories of his mother quietly weeping through the night, and sometimes well into the morning too, and not even his climbing on her knee and bringing her flowers stolen from the side altar at the great church of St Germain brought a halt to the tears.

'Oh Sashie, Sashie,' was all she ever said, and he put his arms up to kiss her and found only the salty tears of despair.

His grandmother ignored the tears even though she must have known why they were shed. She looked only into the future, to a time when their fortunes and their style of life might be restored. She knew Sasha was to be their saviour, that he was the one to rebuild their lives and her eyes told him this – and so powerful was her determination that young Sashie knew his destiny by the time he had reached his teenage. He was going to be famous because he knew being famous and important was very important when his family was as unimportant as it was then.

Yet to the other people in the neighbourhood, the concierge, the shopkeepers, the café owners, they must have seemed quite affluent. His grandmother always wore the finest lace clothes in summer, and fur-lined cloaks in winter. His mother who never wore anything but the most fashionable and expensive that could be arranged, and as a child he was never allowed to wear anything less so, if she was to continue to take tea or lunch with rich and successful men. Sasha was always in something silk - silk shirts and trousers, silk vests even, all made by Katya nicknamed Pompom, their devoted maid. He realised now how exotic they must have seemed to their neighbours and yet how deprived they felt to themselves.

As soon as his reading of French became tolerable Sasha read from the newspaper to his grandmother. Everything was to do with fame. People had to be famous to be anything at all. It wasn't enough to be what they were, they had to be seen to be what they were. So if a writer was to be read, he must be read about. If a director's film was to be seen, he too must be seen. Even then young Sasha knew that it was a fraud, that it was all a pretence, that it was only what you did, not what you were seen to be doing, that really mattered. The end was Art, but the path that led to it was - littered and often dangerous - was fame.

Paris had been meant to be just a temporary resting place for the family before they sailed to New York as planned, but they never got to save enough for their trip let alone the tickets. The longer they stayed in Paris the more they seemed to spend, supporting a lifestyle which was quite unsupportable on what Sasha's poor mother earned. Somewhat absurdly but very typically in their French exile they became ever more Russian, all except for Sasha who began to learn from and absorb the wonderful city in which he was being brought up. He fast became fluent in French as well as English and of course Russian and soon the neighbour-hood was his neighbourhood and he an intrinsic part of it, so much so that any pastries that remained unsold at the end of the day, any flowers that were discarded by the flower buckets, any chestnuts that had been cooked and then not bought, they were became his at the end of the day, and to each and every person who gave to Sasha he gave back, because in the future he was to entertain them all with stories that had begun with them all.

He learned the art of his story telling in his teenage, regaling Madame at the patisserie with tales of the flower seller's infidelities, the flower seller with the story of how Madame at the patisserie had been left by her husband for a woman who made lighter profiteroles and the chestnut seller with accounts of money spent by Americans in the left bank bookshop on novels of a kind that would cook the seller's chestnuts without his needing to light a fire. And as he did so instinctively Sasha came to realise that so long as he entertained people, he could not only get his own way but he could also greatly improve the quality of his life.

'Basically every artist is a whore at heart, anxious to please, but much more anxious to be paid,' he would later joke with E.F.

Eventually one particular bookshop on the left bank became his second home, much more so than any student cafés, sometimes more of a home even than the apartment where his grandmother still held sway and from where his mother still set out to work the hotels, for at this bookshop American was the spoken language and constantly so. American businessmen would cross the river to buy from the owner, always returning to exchange their volumes when read, because all of the books that they chose were not of the kind that their wives would like to find them reading, and were certainly banned in America. In the bookshop coffee was served at all times by the owner of the shop, and at first Sasha helped to hand it round as well as plates of small biscuits. When things were quiet he would just as quietly read and whenever he had some spare change he would buy some well-read copy of a book on which he had long had his eye. Soon he became a permanent assistant, developing a wry and apparently distant personality which was in fact in homage to the actual owner of the bookshop, a man who became his father figure, the man whose personality through adolescence and into early manhood he started subconsciously at first but later quite blatantly to assume. This personality was later to become the man who was to be Kaminski, for Kaminski was not the surname of Sasha's family but a name he assumed, the very name of the best customer at the shop, a Monsieur Kaminski who arrived every Wednesday afternoon with a small leather briefcase which he would empty of last week's volumes, beautifully unmarked but assiduously read, and promptly fill again with new books with which he would return the following week.

'Monsieur Kaminski read more dirty books than anyone I have ever met or hope to meet,' Kaminski told Georgiana as they stood outside the shop, which now no longer sold books but instead towelling and sheets which could be monogrammed to the customer's own preference, objects that the French liked very much because they thought of such linen as being very English.

'Very occasionally there are English things which please Parisians very much,' Kaminski observed. 'Things which they imitate, while always stressing how *très* Anglais they are while happily staying très Français themselves.'

To recommend any book to the customer Sasha knew it was necessary first to read it. And so he read Sartre and Camus, James Joyce, Tolstoy and Dostoevsky, as well as all the new, young American avant-garde writers. He read much that was bad but more that was good, but what really began to obsess him was the idea of turning the sort of thing he liked to read into film. Film had become his secret and unapproved vice, for it seemed none of his family or his family's relatives had ever attended a movie house. Instead for entertainment Sasha would be expected to read Russian classics such as Pushkin out aloud to his grandmother, while all the time his secret vices was gradually taking over his whole life. When his mother finally discovered his predilection she took him out to lunch. Sasha wore a suit that had been altered or him. The restaurant was fashionable. To their table came many and interesting people, and because Sasha was eighteen he noted that they all, to a man, greeted is mother with that affectionate but possessive manner at men are wont to use towards women whom they have known intimately, and feel they might know again at some future date.

His mother had always been a beauty but now as they sat to lunch the eighteen year old Sasha for the first time saw she was getting older; there was a slight sagging under her once perfect chin and lines were appearing under her eyes and around her mouth. But she still spoke to him as gently as ever, her Russian accent giving her French a charm and an originality which the mature son could appreciate in the elegant surroundings of *Le Vefour*, and although he was only eighteen he deferred to him, nodding to the *sommelier* to give him the wine list, and letting him talk to the avuncular figure with his riband and his spoon about the perfect accompaniment to each of their courses without interruption, before turning her full attentions to him.

'You are not, of course, to go into the film business,' she said. 'But then I think you already must know this.'

'Let us lunch here.'

Kaminski stopped in front of the door of the place that was now a discreetly fashionable restaurant, although no longer bearing the name it did when he was a young man. Because it was early they were found a table in the best corner, and because in Paris Kaminski was justly famous, they were treated with immediate deference.

Classical French food and wine remains classical while tastes of course change. As Kaminski examined the menu he thought the mussel soup that had so delighted him before would doubtless now seem coarse to his cosmopolitan palate. Even so, he found there was enough on the menu to bring back strong memories of the lunch that day so long ago, the day when his mother had made her feelings about his future so clear, although as she had talked to him all Sasha could hear was his grandmother speaking.

He had still loved his mother, but then as he sat listening to her forbidding him his future he found himself freed from her and from his grandmother, and while he knew he still loved them both it was with the sort of love about which he might read in one of his precious books, dutiful, faithful, attentive but almost dispassionate, and while he felt no feelings of resentment towards her either for her way of life or for the way she was trying to deny him his, the one that he so passionately wanted he knew all obligations were now at an end and he was free to do as he chose to do. And so at the age of eighteen he defied her and her own mother and his courage set him free.

As Kaminski regarded Georgiana across the restaurant table he wondered how he had managed to be so brave and to act with such maturity all those years ago, and how it was that now all these years on he felt so weak and immature as sitting opposite this beautiful girl in her yellow coat and her small veiled hat he found himself feeling the way he imagined he should have felt when confronting his mother – who coincidentally on that day had also been dressed in yellow.

He hadn't realised how much he had been talking. He hadn't realised that he had in fact been talking but from Georgiana's animation and from the questions she was now asking him he saw he must have been talking all the time that he had been thinking and that he had been talking about exactly what he had been thinking about. For herself, Georgiana was both intrigued and astounded for Kaminski had never ever talked to her for so long and in such personal detail. He even looked at her differently now, with infinite more affection and perhaps even with a certain regard, as if at last she was a human being with a soul and not just a good looking girl with a great pair of legs, and for that Georgiana knew she would be eternally grateful.

Yet now she wished he would stop talking, because the more he talked about his youth and his family the more he became Sasha and not Kaminski the great director - *auteur*, the man who commanded all and was respected by all. The more he became childlike and vulnerable she feared that in a way he might become more ordinary which would not do at all since she knew what it meant to him to be rich and famous and not poor and vulnerable the way he once had been, and if that was who he truly was Georgiana was frightened in case he would also cease being so fascinating. She wanted to tell him to stop, to stop filling in the gaps for her, to stop looking back into the past, to stop searching in places for things that might never have even existed and to go back to being the person who had taken her back into his arms in his apartment the previous afternoon. She thought he had wanted him at her feet but now she saw that was exactly where he might be headed she no longer wanted any such a thing. Georgiana didn't want him to be ordinary and sorry - she wanted him to be arrogant, hard, and forceful. She had no interest in little *Sashie* who poached old chestnuts when he was hungry and sold discarded flowers to passersby to help pay his way. She wanted him extraordinary and unapologetic, dominant and arrogant. She didn't want to be loved by Sashie. She wanted to be taken by Kaminski.

After lunch as they made their way back almost in silence to their hotel Georgiana walked on the other side of him and held his hand quite differently, as if this might help to change things, praying as she went that by the time they had crossed the river on to the opposite bank of the river the man by her side would have left Sashie behind them and would once more become the great Kaminski.

12

In order to enter the sitting room of number two Cheap Street, it was necessary for Fulton to duck his head. He was feeling pretty fed up with the world in general and Wiltshire in particular, so it would not have surprised him if he had knocked his head on the wretched lintel and knocked himself to the floor. Try his best as he had he could not find a single person other than Nanny, Twinks, Bessie, and the babies who would speak to him at that moment. The Hall was on non-speakies after the proposed cancellation of the ball and not only were Pemberton and Jennifer not speaking to each other, they weren't even speaking to Bloss, which Fulton found strange since he could not see how a person could get their butler to bring them what they wanted if they weren't to him.

Jennifer in particular had been acting most strangely towards Fulton of late, so much so that he had been forced to put on his thinking cap and worry as to what he could possibly have done to make her behave towards him as she had been behaving, insinuating things at one moment and then suddenly becoming overly possessive the next. Try as he might Fulton could not find out what he had done to deserve such a change in manner, but something must have happened for her now to treat him as if they had once had a raging affair. The worst of it was that Jennifer having convinced herself that either she or Fulton or perhaps even the both of them had somehow behaved badly, it now seemed that even Pember was convinced something had happened, hence the non-speaking to status to which Fulton had been raised. It was all desperate. There was no other word for it, since for the life of him Fulton had simply no idea of what he might have done. All he could admit to doing was helping to arrange a perfectly private ball, and now he was supposed to talk this ninety-year-old woman covered from top to toe in Honiton lace out of the Empress's Box. What more, he asked himself, as he shifted his position in a thoroughly over-polished and absurdly uncomfortable Windsor chair, what more could life in Wiltshire throw at him?

'She's attached to it summat dreadful,' the old lady's granddaughter informed Fulton primly after the first twenty minutes had passed in appreciating the Honiton lace on her grandmother's blouse, and the horse brasses around the fireplace. Fulton would have loved to have contradicted her by saying she couldn't possibly be attached to it summat dreadful since she had only had the box a week but didn't because these were farming folk, and as everyone knew that when it came to farming folk you were always walking on egg shells.

'Of course she must be,' he agreed instead. 'Of course she's become attached.''

''Tis up to you, course, Gran,' the girl shouted now at her grandmother. 'Don't let me 'fluence you, know-what-I-mean? You wanna sell your box to the gennelman for more than I paid for it, t'is up to you. Just 'cos I gave it to you for yer ninetieth don't mean you have to hold back on selling it to him. You could buy yerself summore horse brasses and all, if you have it in yer mind, but 'sup to you. 'Course it is. I'm sure the gennelman means no harm, Gran, no matter what you first thought.'

Fulton took this afterthought to refer to him calling on her the previous afternoon when she, with the natural old world courtesy of many Wiltshire folk, the old woman had slammed the chained front door in his face.

'She's been watchin' too much telly on the box,' the daughter had informed him. 'Nothin' but endless robberies and such like and all local. T's not nice at all nor good for her, that's what the Health lady keeps tellin' her. Better off gettin' stuck into her lace and she would and all the Health lady says, but she keeps gettin' her lacing hook caught up in her hearin' aid, see.'

Fulton eyed the Empress's Box resting contentedly on Granny Moore's knee. She had not one but both hands on it.

'I'll open the box,' Granny Moore said suddenly.

'See?' the granddaughter cried. 'See she likes her box, see! Bless her! Bless you, Gran! Bless you! You keep your box!'

'I'll open the box!'

'Bless her!'

'No, no I won't, I'll take the money!'

The old lady nodded towards the telly. Fulton straightened up, but only for a second before sliding down once more to subnormal height thanks to the over-polished Windsor chair.

'Very well, Granny Moore, if that's what you want.' As quick as lightning, Fulton counted out ten very clean and ironed ten pound notes and put them on the small three and a half-legged oak table to the side of him.

'There we are,' he said in the forced jolly tone that he always found himself using towards people named Granny.

'She dunno what she's sayin', thinks she's on the telly. Open the box, take the money, that's the one she thinks she's on. You want to keep the box, Gran, could be worth a great deal of money to you, that could be. Our mam says that could be an investment for yer, that could. What's money when it comes down to it except rotten money?'

The old lady leaned forward and gave Fulton the box.

'No, I'll take the money,' she said happily. 'You open the box,' she told Fulton.

Fulton could hardly believe it. Luck was coming his way at last. An all too rare feeling of serenity and happiness pervaded his whole being as he took the box from the old lady and she took the money, promptly counting it out while licking her fingers tenderly between each note.

'I tell you, you done better to keep the box, Gran. Could be an investment for you, like I told you. Never mind.'

She leant forward to her grandmother.

'I'll have summa that then, seein's you're not keeping the box, and seem' as how I paid for it in the first place. T'is only fair.'

It was only when Fulton reached his car and slung the wretched box on the seat beside him that he remembered to look for the bird, the phoenix in flight on the side of the immaculate red lacquer. The sight of that alone would make it worth all his while, both for the Countess and himself.

13

Jennifer stared at Pemberton her husband who as far as she was concerned was pretty soon to be her ex-husband with something very close to hatred, appalled to think that he seriously expected her to accept his absurd story that the reason he had been caught going round dressed as a sort of tramp person because he was doing market research for his and Bloss's newest money-maker, *The Local Rather Than Organic Garden Produce Company*, rather than doing research of a more intimate kind that gentlemen of his age were somewhat inclined to do if not watched.

'Really, I am no longer the innocent person that you once knew,' she hissed, and then hesitated, shooting a look towards the drawing room door, but since the handle was not moving and she couldn't hear Bloss snuffling she presumed they must be more or less alone and she could go on regardless.

'I am no longer the innocent person you first met and married,' she repeated. 'I have actually read magazines. *Cosmo*. That sort of thing. In the hairdresser's. I do know to what people, men, especially middle-aged men, I do know what they get up to. There are certain habits which once a marriage is well under way they can resort to unless either caught or actively discouraged.'

Pember had his back turned to her which she took to be a sure sign of guilt.

'You can no longer expect to treat me like a fool, Pember.'

'Don't suppose I can, old thing,' Pemberton admitted with his usual candour. 'Even so, I don't think you want to know the truth - too damn' painful for both of us. You know how it is. If you tell someone how things are, it never goes down very well. Always ends up all ends to the bottom and nothing to do but chuck the whole thing in. The truth is never really a good idea, you know, it never has been. Quite apart from anything else, d'you see, it changes so from day to day, one day it's the truth and the next day it's altogether something different. Last year's notion is never this year's fashion, besides there are other things more important than the truth.'

'Oh, really? And what, may I ask?' demanded Jennifer bristling. 'And if you think this sort of eyewash is going to stem the tide of my indignation I do assure you it is not. Oh no, by no means. I demand to know the truth, Pember. Why in God's name were you dressed up as a tramp and driving Nanny's car at the time of day when most gentlemen are to be found reading *Sporting Life* and putting on bets with their butlers?'

'Very well, Jennifer,' Pember said, breathing in and out quite slowly because he had an idea that too much oxygen at too early an hour might be harmful and cause a sudden rush to the brain. 'Very well, you have as they say in popular newspapers asked for it, I'm afraid, and I only hope you don't get what you don't deserve. The reason as you have undoubtedly guessed was not the furtherance of *The Local Rather Than Organic Garden Produce Company*, the reason was -' He paused and gave another slow breath in and out as an opera singer might if he was given the time. 'The reason was because I have too many children.'

'What! Do you expect me to believe that? A man of your wealth? You count three children as too many? What kind of turpitude is this?'

Pember frowned, puzzled. He wasn't quite sure of what turpitude was exactly, but even so he had the feeling that accuse him of what she might Jennifer could well be barking up the wrong tree.

'My father used to say that economics and women don't mix, but I'm not so sure. Sit down, Jennifer, and let me tell you about money.'

'Do I have to listen?'

'As a matter of fact you do if you wish to find out why I was dressed up as Bert Ackroyd and driving Nanny's car at ten o'clock in the morning.'

Jennifer sat down very suddenly and spread out her dog skirt evenly around her as if it were a crinoline, and then by way of comfort she took one of her dogs on her knee just in case the news was so hideous she might need to bury her face in its fur.

'Money is a very difficult thing to understand, Jennifer. You are an intelligent girl, which was one of the reasons why I married you, so I know you can bring yourself to understand modern economics, probably as well as any Chancellor.'

'Pember? Is this going to take long?'

'Possibly as long as the Chancellor on Budget Day if you don't pipe down, old girl,' her husband told her evenly as with quiet triumph he saw her eyes sliding off towards the rose garden outside the window. With a bit of luck he considered he might already have lost her interest. 'Do you know how much money it takes to run this place?'

'Lots,' said Jennifer shortly.

'Precisely. Lots.'

Once again Jennifer's eyes were drifting like petals on the water of his eighteenth-century raised goldfish pond towards the garden and then back towards the top of her dog's head, and then out towards the garden again, and then down to her tapestry where they stayed fixed with an expression of increasing longing as Pemberton proceeded with his economic lecture in such a measured tone that the dog had started to nod off before he was halfway through.

'So you see, if one child's education in ten years' time, given the steady growth of the cost of living, is going to cost me a hundred thousand pounds and that's before he decides to go to university, three children will therefore cost me three hundred thousand which on tax paid at my level is a million pounds. And then there's Bloss. Bloss we know we can't do without, most definitely. Bloss is paid ten thousand pounds a year which is nothing by today's standards, and he has kept his salary down for the past fifteen years which is more than can be said for Nanny.'

Jennifer's gaze transferred itself to Pember for the first time now for some minutes.

'Well, but, Pember, if you think we have too many children you must expect to pay Nanny a decent wage.'

'Bloss is on ten thousand a year, Nanny on six thousand a year, which at present tax levels makes it necessary to bring home forty thousand, and then there is the garden which at present tax levels needs to generate an income of more than fifty thousand which over a period of the same ten years given the same spiralling costs will mean at least half a million pounds, and that's before we put any petrol in Nanny's car or the lawn mowers or indeed, Jennifer, before we come to the horses. We maintain a stable of ten to fifteen horses in training which at present costs more than the garden.'

Having defended the need for Nanny Jennifer's mind switched itself back to her tapestry. She was glad she had abandoned her embroidery for the minute, because her tapestry was nearing completion in not one corner but three. Soon she would be on to the hare and the flowers which would be much, much more interesting.

'So all in all, without taking into account our other houses, and their upkeep, it is necessary to think of the household of the Hall as needing four million pounds over the next ten years, and that's with only three children.'

Even Jennifer had to sit up at that.

'Four million pounds. Goodness, Pember, that does sound rather a lot,' she said a little faintly.

'Sound rather a lot?' said Pember, dropping a small stub of pencil with his bookmaker's name in gold on to the table beside him. 'Sound rather a lot? It is more than a lot, Jennifer. It is a very great deal.'

He stared ahead of him, wishing that he hadn't decided to make any calculations, wishing that he had never taken it upon himself to instruct Jennifer in the art of what everything cost.

'Pember darling, you look quite white.'

'I feel quite white.'

'That's the worst of all possible worlds - to look quite white and to feel quite white.'

Jennifer leaned forward to her husband and touched his arm. He didn't appear to have seen what she had just done, or indeed even noticed. She had not touched him for some few weeks, not even when she nearly kissed him good night.

'We'll manage. You mustn't worry.'

Pember turned his now dulled gaze towards his wife, appalled by what he had just calculated.

'So Jennifer, Jennifer I have suddenly realised that there's nothing left to us except prayer. We must pray that Bloss and I somehow or another can make a go of *The Local Rather Than Organic Garden Produce Company*, or else we'll just have to move out, camp in the grounds and generally live off cheese parings if we can get any, which I very much doubt thanks to the decline in cheese-making in these parts.'

With some difficulty Pemberton struggled to his feet and stood swaying a little. His mind was made up. The sacrifice must be made. He would have to go under the knife, and that afternoon, chop, chop. He needed a stiffy to strengthen his purpose, but it wouldn't make any difference. Whatever happened, he would have to go over the top at *Real Man* and cut the caper, that was all there was to it.

Even so he agonized on secretly to himself. If Jennifer knew that that was only the half of it, which he thanked the heavens above she did not, heaven knows what she would think. If she knew what and whom he had to support at not just the Hall, but at Flint House, if she knew that it was not just four million pounds that he most likely needed, but more properly six million pounds, then she would probably strangle him with her dog skirt.

'Pember, what is it? You look quite ghastly.' Jennifer ran in front of her husband to attract his attention. 'You look as if you want to faint.'

'I do want to faint, but I can't, not until this afternoon, and then I shall have good reason to faint.'

'What's happening this afternoon, Pember?'

'What's happening this afternoon, Jennifer, is I am going to go to that place which I was going to go to when I was all dressed up and calling myself Bert Ackroyd. You wanted the truth, now you have it. I am going to go to *Real Man* where I was going before, but now I am not going to bother to go as Bert Ackroyd. Thanks to your demands for the truth I don't mind if I am seen or it is discovered that the seventh Marquis of Pemberton was spotted going to *Real Man* in his normal clothes, far from it. Now I know, now I have done my sums, now I understand just how hard it is for common man to make ends meet I am going under the knife, and in doing so I shall be setting an example not just to all of Wiltshire, Jennifer, but the Third World, Catholics everywhere and Fulton Montrose-Benedict-Cavanagh in particular.'

'Is that what you were really doing, dressed up as a tramp?'

'It certainly was. I wanted to keep this hidden from you, to protect you from the cruelties of life, but you insisted on the truth and here it is, millions of pounds' worth of the truth, unvarnished and painful. |And particularly painful it is I must say .'

'Really? Fulton says it's not at all painful.'

'He's been? Why has Fulton been?'

'Because, Pember, he and Lady Tizzy have been procreating too much, just as we seem to have done.'

'I see. Right you be. I see.'

'As a matter of fact I gave him the cutting from *The Parishioner.* You know how it was, with twins and everything,' Jennifer added. 'Things were certainly hotting up a little for them, weren't they?'

'They certainly were,' Pember agreed. 'They certainly were. So there you are, you see what I mean? The need for *Real Man.'*

'But I never realized that's, well, that's where you were going, Pember darling. I wish you'd told me, I should never have been so worried.'

Pemberton turned and stared at his wife, his hand on the eighteenth-century door handle, eyes on his wife's face. 'Whatever happens this afternoon, Jennifer, I want you to know that I loved you.'

Jennifer flew forward, her dog skirt billowing out behind her.

'Oh, Pember!' she cried. 'Pember and I do love you, too.'

Pemberton stared down at her.

'No, you don't, Jennifer,' he said suddenly 'You love another, you love Fulton. I've known it for some time and now I have proof. Why else would you have been so worried about him going to *Real Man?* You can't expect me to believe you were worrying about the cost of things at Flint House. Why should you? You never worry about the cost of things here, so why should you worry about the cost of things at Flint House? No, you were thinking about the dangers to yourself and your lover – that's what you've been thinking about, Jennifer.'

Jennifer screamed. There was no other word for it, Pemberton realized as the terrible sound reverberated around the room. It was a scream, a long, hard scream, and it was as full of menace as anything he was likely to hear.

'That is not true!'

Jennifer stamped her foot. Pemberton had hoped to put her off the scent, to call the hounds off, but all it seemed he'd done was reveal something he had only half believed, namely that his wife's interest was elsewhere. Never mind his own interest elsewhere, a chap's wife was a chap's wife.

He put out his hand and pulled Jennifer to him.

'There's a little time before the place opens after lunch,' he said suddenly. 'Time that I could profitably spend with you, Jennifer. Yes, just time enough to take you upstairs,' he said with sudden determination and relish.

'No, really, Pember, I don't think -'

But what Jennifer had been about to think was something that neither of them would ever find out.

Only Bloss was witness to the spectacle of his lordship dragging her ladyship up the great staircase to their boudoir. He gazed after them with interest. It was not often his lordship felt like anything like that before lunch nowadays, he observed. Things must be looking up.

He turned back to his snug underneath the stairs. Luckily enough for all of them *The Local Rather Than Organic Garden Produce Company,* having been invented for amatory rather than serious business reasons, had now turned into a positive fact. The accountant had become quite excited which Bloss considered never to be exactly a very edifying sight at the best of times and it seemed that Bloss had come up with a winning idea, since it seemed if *The Local Rather Than Organic Garden Produce* was really going to take off, with all the local gardens, the Hall included, coming together to sell off those vegetables and fruit that local people normally only gave away to reluctant visitors. Now instead of heaping weekend guests with old cabbages and chrysanthemums they would heap up Bloss's smart new van and his driver would take them to a central point where local people would buy them, which would make a refreshing change from Londoners putting them in their dustbins on Monday mornings.

There is a hand that guides us all, Bloss told his new bottle of Madeira, as he put back the time for lunch thirty-four minutes - a hand that guides, a path that makes itself clear, a purpose that we can know not of.

He paused, wondering where exactly he had memorized this charming thought, but couldn't quite place it. It was either the *Golden Treasury of Positive Thoughts,* or the mini-Bible translated by the Cantering Cleric, a sometime television personality who had had a short success as a wine snob on an early evening programme which Bloss had been in the habit of watching while his lordship changed for dinner, and her ladyship fussed over the children. He'd liked that programme, but of course they'd taken it off as they took off everything with nothing offensive in it nowadays. Ridiculous now he came to think of it. After all, there surely must have been enough people prepared to be offended by recipes and interviews with wine experts for it to run and run, but no; it seemed it had offended no-one so off it had come.

The first glass of Madeira had gone down so well he followed it with a second, which he sipped. Life had been so tense lately, so very tense, that he had taken to drinking Madeira which he found immensely soothing. With his lordship finally off to *Real Man* - from what he could gather from outside the door - and her ladyship and he not only speaking to each other but enjoying each other too which didn't after all always go together, he decided that everything in the garden was becoming just a little more rosy even though as yet the goose could not be said to be hanging high.

The telephone in the snug rang. Bloss picked it up. It was her ladyship's mother, Mrs Parker-Jones. He had actually found her a house, quite near the Hall, something with which he knew she would fall instantly in love, but he was not in the mood to convey this to her, since her ladyship's mother had not been in a very kind mood with him lately. He knew of what she suspected him, and it shocked him to think that she could even imagine him as capable of deception. Even so he was generous and warm enough, thanks to the Madeira, to forgive her for being so suspicious, and worst of all, for getting it wrong. He would never give away his or anyone else's secrets to anyone. It was not in his interests. Besides, his way was to get his own way, no matter what, even if it meant flying by the seat of his striped butler's pants, he proposed to get it, and get it with the newest registration as well. If Mrs Parker-Jones had suspected him of telling the world her secrets, fair enough, but no, she had suspected him of trading in them, and dealing, and taking advantage, which was something else.

'Hallo, Bloss.'

She sounded positively guilt-ridden, like the father in the last act of *La Traviata.*
'Yes.'

There was enough of the wounded butler in his voice to make Bloss stand back and gaze in admiration at himself in the cracked mirror that stood behind the silver cleaning materials.

'I wonder if I could speak to Lady Pemberton?'

'I'm afraid her ladyship is otherwise occupied.'

'Perhaps you could tell her it is her mother?'

'I'm afraid not, Mrs Parker-Jones. But I could leave her a message.'

'Is she somewhere special?'

'Her ladyship is on the nest.'

It must have been the second glass of Madeira, Bloss decided a little too late, but there it was all the same. The truth was out and – Bloss wondered – who cared? Mrs Parker-Jones had after all asked for it, and to give Mrs Parker-Jones her due, she called back again an hour later without a word.

Fulton and the Countess stared and stared. It would be no exaggeration to say that they could not believe their eyes. There it was on the side of the box, the phoenix in flight, just as Fulton knew it had to be if it was to be at all valuable.

'That's what Mary said, a bird on the side,' the Countess mouthed into the heavy silence that followed both of them putting on their glasses and staring at the side of their treasure.

'That makes it worth fifty thousand pounds.'

'So Mary said.'

'Now what,' said Fulton, but not as a question and quickly removing his specs before Maria came in with the coffee.

'What do you think Fulton?' The Countess was misty-eyed. 'The nicest thing about this is, I don't need the money,' she said, sighing.

Fulton agreed silently while his finger traced the outline of the bird against the red lacquer of the box. He knew exactly what the dear thing meant. It was the nicest thing known to have an unexpected source of money and just when you didn't need it. It made you feel as if life was just a piece of cherry pie with fresh cream from the dairy, after all.

'You can take it to one of those ghastly firms that advertises, Fulton,' the Countess told him. 'You know, auction houses - quite horrible places. Full of people telling you what is valuable isn't and what isn't valuable is, all depending on whether you're buying or selling to them or from them. We'll sell it to them knowing it is what it is, and so we'll get more gold for it than the Empress ever wore round her neck. And then I – I shall give the ball.'

Fulton stared at her. 'You will?'

'Why not? After all it was my idea in the first place.'

It hadn't been, but that was beside the point really, Fulton thought quickly.

'Yes, I shall give the ball and Mary and Jennifer can pass me both their guest lists and everyone can come. I shall give the ball at the Hall, and we can pretend it wasn't ever going to be anything but mine in the first place.'

'What about all the invitations?'

'What about them? As long as I am the first to receive everyone the world will get the picture. I will be Wiltshire's fairy godmother. We'll have tents and fireworks and everything will be as it was going to be in the first place full of zest and fun, just like the old days when people entertained each other for no better reason than that they wanted to see each other. No charity organizers, no causes, just fun. What a change that would be. On one condition only, though.'

Fulton stopped smiling and his heart sank as he saw all too clearly that familiar look of relish come over the Countess's face.

'One condition only.'

'You have a slip put in the invitations?' Fulton guessed, delaying the dreaded announcement as long as possible.

'Not even warm, but put in one anyway.'

'You want Lavinia to do the flowers?'

'Cold. So cold you must have frostbite.'

'Don't know.'

'Yes, you do.'

'No, I don't.'

Fulton knew he did, but he couldn't bring himself to say the words. The Countess stared.

'Provided we change the colours back to cream and green, not peach, Fulton, cream and green.'

Fulton could have said - *but Twinks has just dyed all the tablecloths and napkins in a rainwater butt-* but he didn't. After all, the main thing was to get on with the ball.

'You know what I think? I think cream and green is most tasteful, I just thought peach was more summery. If you want cream and green, who am I to stop you?'

'No-one,' the Countess agreed cheerfully. 'Now come along, you wizard of the Empress's Box, let's go quickly out to dinner before Andrew gets back from China and decides to come with us.'

'I thought China was shut.'

'It is,' the Countess agreed as she pulled on her small gold-embroidered jacket. 'It's what I call the pub he goes to because like China it always seems to be shut when he wants to go there.'

With which she took Fulton's arm and they both headed out towards her motor car and a thoroughly convivial evening.

'Tally whack and tandem again?'

Elliott looked across at Fulton and was only too glad that it was he who was bending down to get the Grant loaf out of the Aga. Fulton did not look as if he could bend down if he tried, or rather he looked as if should he try to bend down for anything at all, he would just keep on going and end up in a heap on the floor.

'Just don't speak to me.'

'I wasn't going to.'

Elliott nodded and put some highly organic muesli in front of Fulton.

'Twinks has already heard, if that's what you're worried about,' he told him. 'Actually as soon as you told me about the box, as a matter of fact, we both guessed the Countess would take over. In spite of only just finishing the cloths and napkins she's perfectly prepared to return to the butt from whence she came and plunge the peach-toned cloths in green. As for the rest - cream's easy.'

'How's Lady Tizzy?'

'Deeply boring.'

Fulton carefully removed a rather strangely shaped nut from his bowl and put it on his side plate.

'You sound like the Countess.'

Elliott sat down opposite him.

'Lady Tizzy is not at her best when she's being deprived of what she calls her curranty bun, or what you and I call her *'raison d'être'*. You know Pemberton's gone at last to you know where?'

'The whole of Wiltshire knows he went.'

'And now of course he can't. Before he couldn't, because he couldn't *in case*, and now he can't because he *can't*. If you see what I mean?'

Fulton nodded. He knew only too well. He had also seen Lady Tizzy's wastepaper basket full of old Del Monte tins. When Lady Tizzy got into one of her pets and felt neglected no-one could get her out of her bed, and when she wasn't lying in her bed feeling neglected then they couldn't keep her out of other people's beds. Let's face it, they couldn't win.

'At least he's been,' said Fulton at last, after a long pause during which he tried, as was his wont, to see the best in everything, including Wiltshire. 'I mean at least Pemberton has been to *Real Man*, and now therefore there are going to be no more school fees to lose yet another night's sleep over. I mean at least there's that.'

'Oh, there's that all right,' Elliott agreed, slicing a hot piece of loaf and buttering it quickly. 'There's that. I just hope it works, that's all. It doesn't always.'

'That we can't think about. We must just cross our fingers.'

'That is not a method that would have worked with Pemberton and Lady Tizzy.'

'Oh really? I believe they're trying it in Africa with tremendous results.'

There was so much to do. The flowers, the napkins, the matching tents which mercifully were still cream and green - Fulton's mind ran over all the details. The lighting, the staff, the candles, the floor, the fruit, the garlands for the poles, the help from all the surrounding villages. People to park the cars and bring the guests to the door or back from the doors - and then there was what to wear - a beautiful dress for Lady Tizzy, a green frock for Twinks, so much to do, so many places to go, so many places they had been, but it would all be worthwhile providing the weather was clement, the food didn't melt or stayed hot, the staff the same, the guests ditto and all to keep a handful of the upper hundreds happy for a few hours in Wiltshire. Except, as Fulton soon realised, that wasn't all it was about at all. People would come and go away again and after only a few hours nothing would be the same, no person would remain unchanged, someone would have fallen in love with someone they shouldn't, someone else with someone they should, at the very least new paths would be sought, and old paths, sometimes of righteousness, fallen from, but whatever happened nothing stayed unchanged, and nothing ever remained the same.

'Do you think if we buy Lady Tizzy a stunning frock she will climb out of her sulking bed and come and join in the game of living once more?' Elliott wondered.

'Yes I do, but first I say you and I visit Nanny and Bessie and the girls and Beau in the nursery. That at least is all safe for the moment. No nasty divorces, Jennifer back with Pemberton again. Lady Tizzy not where she shouldn't be, the ball going ahead after all, and with both the *crème* and the *crème fraiche*. So to the nursery we must go to watch our babies grow and grow. Ignore that. My mind's gone.'

'Are you sure you're up to it?'

'Of course I'm not.'

'You look just a little cream and green still.'

'It's only to be expected.'

Fulton smiled as a quite irrational feeling of serenity crept over him. He would take Victoria up in his arms and swing her round and Nanny would cluck. He would give Beau and Daisy-Marguerita a finger to hold, and they would hold on to them terrifically tight which babies always did, and all would be well. Everything, endless worries, making papier mâché spill boxes and trays by the dozen, keeping their mother somewhere near the straight and narrow, their father from making more babies, keeping everyone from everyone except when they were meant to be with each other, it would all be worth it.

'Just must re-paint those finger plates,' Elliott murmured, as they passed into the nursery and the door closed behind them.

But Fulton never even heard him. He was too busy holding out his arms for little Victoria.

14

Kaminski stared at E.F. He was quite sure he'd heard him right, which was why he was staring at him.

'When did they cancel it?' he asked in his quietest voice.

'Last night, just after you didn't get back for the third time,' E.F. said, and he unwrapped a large bon-bon from the nearest bon-bon dish which was very near since they were seated in the kitchen of the apartment. The previous evening Sofia had given a ghastly gathering that she fondly imagined was a dinner party.

'I doubt that it's anything to do with when I got back,' Kaminski said eventually. E.F.'s fist crashed down on the table. 'You should have come back when I told you. Jumby Island has just had the H bomb dropped on it. All our work over the last months gone. Do you realize what this means? We are without a film!'

Kaminski stared at E.F. He was right. In fact he was very right, and yet somehow it didn't matter in the least either that he was or that they were without a film. The situation they were in was serious. It meant they would have to go back to Los Angeles and begin trading again.

'It's nothing to do with my not coming back, E.F. It's all to do with that romantic little sleeper taking sixty-three million in the past week. That's what it has to do with, E.F.'

'Look, what is this sleeper anyway?' E.F. said more to himself than his director. 'Man, woman, woman. We can rework our script. Forget Jumby Island, the fact that he's a marine biologist, increase the women to two not one, make the island an apartment in Manhattan's East Side, and *voilá,* we have ourselves a nice little *me-too*. We can get back to Los Angeles by Monday with a rough-out, give it to Pan to type - that takes all of two minutes - and sell it by Thursday.'

Kaminski looked across at E.F. He could see all the advantages from his partner's point of view, but only from his partner's point of view, not his own. Kaminski gave a private sigh and thought back to Paris and then forward again to Georgiana who would now be back in Wiltshire with her son and his father. He had no wish to stay in England anymore; he knew that he must leave at once, but he knew also that wherever he went from now on it would have to be with Georgiana who had become his talisman, his good luck charm, his icon. Supposing she forgot him once she got back with the painter, he wondered. Supposing she wanted to stay with her son? Supposing she didn't come through with the invitation to the ball? Perhaps she had merely suggested that they meet in Wiltshire at this oh-so-social occasion so that she could have time to think of how to be rid of him?

He'd panicked when she'd left him, waving one graceful hand out of the train window. It had seemed to him that her gesture had in it all of *adieu* and very little of *au revoir.* It seemed to him that graceful though it was it had only been a perfunctory gesture, a gesture she had made out of *politesse,* and having made it she couldn't wait to get on with her old life once more, as a bored actor at the end of a long day's shoot will run back to his dressing room unable to wait to put on his own clothes again and be himself. It seemed to Kaminski that the object of his passion had settled herself into her first class seat and kissed her hand to him as if to say goodbye forever.

Georgiana stared at Gus. They had been away from each other five days, but he seemed now not merely a stranger but quite definitely an ex. Ex-lover, ex-common law husband, whatever it was that in the present complications of her life she should call him.

He had not been happy at having Cynthia taken from him, so with his usual ruthless egoism he had found out from her mother where exactly she was working in London, gone up to town and talked her into returning to Longborough, where she was now it seemed being put up in the stables and being called upon to model for him when-ever or however he wished. It was all true, Georgiana realised - everything they had ever said about painters was true.

'You'll marry the Earl and we'll see about the painter later.'

That was a line from a book Georgiana had read, although which book she couldn't at that moment quite remember. It was just that the truth of it kept running around her head as if it was a jingle she'd heard on Nanny's television. 'You'll marry the Earl, and we'll see about the painter later.' There it went again, and again, and again. Had she married an earl, any earl, would she not just be hunting her horses and going to the Bahamas in the winter and generally being herself instead of being as she was the ex of a painter and the why of a cinema director? Why she wondered had she gone to Paris with him? Why had she thought him so fascinating? Why had he seemed so changed away from London, away from all her familiar haunts, hotels and shops? Most of all, why had she let him tell her all about himself? Not even his name was his own. It made him seem unreal, as if he himself were just some fictional character in a film and not the great man he really was.

'Gus?'

Gus looked up from the morning newspaper that he only ever read at night with the particular frown that he always conjured whenever someone else took the initiative and he was forced to stop doing whatever he was doing and realize that there was someone else on the planet beside himself.

'I hope what I am going to say is not going to make you unhappy,' she said.

His eyes had returned to the paper now, and a beer was being lifted to his mouth behind a freshly grown beard. Georgiana thought how strange it was that men mocked women for changing their hairstyles, when they themselves didn't just change their hair, but their whole faces and almost as frequently. The beard had obviously been grown in tune with the rekindled affair with Cynthia.

'We're not making enough money, Gus.'

Nowadays his work on *The Lady Loves* series was always late, and the quality was not what it was as even Georgiana had noticed. She had also been the first to notice that the company who had paid him was not keen on increasing his money to keep up with the cost of living, but neither of these facts seemed to matter to dear Gus. Only Cynthia, his studio, his paintings and George – albeit for five minutes in the morning and five minutes at night - that was the scope of things that were of any interest to Gus.

'Gus, we are not making enough money, not to keep all of us - you, me, Nan, Nanny, the gardeners, George, and all the other costs. A place like this eats up money, Gus, and we're eating it up, but not enough of it is coming in. You know the dried flowers? Well, they haven't really taken off at all. There are far too many people doing dried flowers.'

Gus looked up at Georgiana once more and then down again. She might as well have never spoken. For one unnerving moment Georgiana faced the fact that Gus was not very nice, that the father of George was a selfish, egotistical person whom she would have done well to avoid, and by whom she should certainly not have had a baby, not even one.

'I have been offered a temporary job, helping out in Los Angeles for that film director I was doing the reccy in Paris for, remember? He's offered me a job as personal assistant just for three months and it's well paid. I think I should take it.'

Gus still said nothing, but turned the paper over. How old the news looked by evening, Georgiana observed to herself. It all seemed like something from the day before the day before, nothing fresh about it at all – so yesterday - a bit like herself and Gus. Maybe

Even a bit like Kaminski and herself too. They might soon be just yesterday, but that was something about which she still could not think.

'Right, George,' Gus finally said, with no interest. 'Okay - you do what you want,'

'I brought you back something from London,' Georgiana told him, not waiting for him to pick up on his lack of interest, which would be disastrous.

'What?' Gus said looking up, just slightly.

'Open it and you'll see.'

Gus opened it. It was a silk vest from Jobbit and Taylor, the very best that they could possibly produce, of the kind that gentlemen who had gentlemen of their own to lay out their undergarments currently and always had favoured. Smooth and silky next to their moneyed skins, it was so far from a hair shirt to render guilt, about money or anything else, a foreign word.

Georgiana knew that Gus would not wear it as the assistant in Jobbit and Taylor would have fondly imagined as he was stuffing the short sleeves with bright white tissue paper and boxing it up with tightly pulled string. Gus would wear it as a tee shirt. She could see straight away that the colour she had chosen had found favour. A particularly soft blue that would make Gus look harder, leaner, and browner, certainly to Cynthia at any rate. But as he stroked the expensive item Georgiana could see that it was not himself that Gus was visualizing in it, but the newest occupant of the flat over the stables. It would go beautifully with her hair and eyes, he was rather obviously thinking, from the look in his eyes. Georgiana smiled at the top of Gus's head. He was so obvious, totally and dreadfully obvious that she found it really quite amusing.

'What's so funny?'

'Nothing.'

Georgiana turned away quickly. Jennifer's ball was now going ahead as arranged; everything was falling into place. She had time to make arrangements, to talk Nanny into following her out to Los Angeles with George. Kaminski would meet her at the ball, and then they would leave discreetly together, and in the aftermath, the days that followed, few people would notice or even care where she was or how she was or with whom. She thought of her ball gown. When he had taken her to Manuel Manona's for a fitting then at least Kaminski had seemed to be himself again. There had been no nonsense about being Sasha any more, and he had chosen for her the most beautiful ball dress, a piece of perfection in the palest of pink taffetas, another copy of a Winterhalter painting, something it seemed which was so popular for balls at the moment. With it she was going to wear the family tiara and her hair up for the first time for years, not scooped up but folded into her neck in the manner of a prima ballerina dancing *Swan Lake*. The shoes to go with the dress were out of this world, all tiny straps which made her slender ankles look even slimmer.

She moved away from Gus, her head filled with the secret thoughts that she so liked to preoccupy her and as she did so, her soon-to-be-ex-lover Gus looked up from his newspaper and stared after her. Georgiana did not see the look on his face as she left the room, leaving behind her a slight aroma of *à la Recherché,* which was probably just as well.

15

She had arrived. Bloss's new love was sitting gleaming outside the staff entrance at the Hall, as near to the door as Bloss could park her. He liked to think he had easy access to her, so that in between his other duties he could nip out and run a duster over her, the love of his life, a bright red gleaming Peugeot *Starduster* complete with limited slip diff, sporting steering wheel, stay-put mats and upholstery in with pale grey velour. Bloss thought she really couldn't look lovelier if she tried, stepping back to admire her for perhaps the forty-ninth time.

It had been a heaven sent joy the day he went and ordered her up – and now she had arrived there had been so much unalloyed joy his old heart felt near to bursting, especially when he allowed his eye to travel down to that glory of all glories, that plum of all plums, the latest registration - and he hadn't even driven her down to the King's Arms yet. But then there hadn't been time; the Hall had been in a positive whirl for the past weeks, whirling ever faster towards the great day, and now the great day was here along with his new car. Bloss's cup was full to overflowing, and having run a duster over his beautiful new motor car he now strolled round to the side of the Hall to admire the tents which had been put in place the previous day. He found it amusing to see how his old friend the Countess had won the day. The tents were a most tasteful cream and green, and Bloss had to admit the dear lady had a point. Their palely tasteful colour went quite exquisitely with the faded stone against which they were set.

Bloss folded his arms. When you looked at a fine sight like that it was hard not to agree that England was still England for all that people had tried to spend the last few years trying to turn her into Mesopotamia. No, he thought, no there were tents on a lawn set against a background of faded bricks with roses rambling and the pink of the dawn being followed by a sky coloured the palest of blue, when you saw no garish colours and heard no guns killing songbirds in order to eat them, you knew you were in England and that it was the best place to be. From Land's End to John o'Groat's some may have done their best to make life perfectly hideous, Bloss considered, but when all was said and done they had not quite succeeded everywhere. Wiltshire was still Wiltshire, and would remain so, at least if people like himself and the Countess had anything to do with it. They stood for walks on Sunday afternoons, tea on the lawn, a retriever at the heel and tent of pleated silk. They would not let Wiltshire go under. Tax might come and go, but there would still be an English heaven if he and the Countess had any say in the matter.

And now tonight to the Hall would come the cream of London Society. As soon as the Countess had taken over the organization of the ball there had been two lists put into operation. One she had entitled *The Cream* and the other *The Cream Fraiche*, in other words, old money and new. Thanks to one thing and another, and politicians in particular, the first was a slimmer volume than the second. Nevertheless, the fact that it existed at all was heartening to those like Bloss who preferred the older wines. On the other hand the second list wasn't as bad as it might be. It was far thicker, but it was of interest, and the two could mix, and would always mix, to the benefit of each other.

'Bloss!'

Jennifer stared at him in fury.

'I've been calling you for hours, where have you been? Not polishing that wretched car of yours again?'

'Just checking the stanchions on the tent pegging, milady,' said Bloss quickly.

'The slightest weakness and they can come down and cause you and your guests endless entanglements, let alone the insurance. You can imagine.'

Jennifer might have been able to imagine. She probably would have imagined if at that moment she was not intent on hoping against hope instead of imagining.

'Are you all right, your ladyship?'

'Perfectly not so, Bloss.' Jennifer turned quickly and ran out of the room, helter skelter towards the downstairs gents cloakroom, all polished mahogany, wooden trees for riding boots, and flower paintings done by Pember's grandmother. Also cool marble washstands, thank goodness, against which she could lean her face after she had been heartily sick.

Bloss stared after her. In his experience her ladyship only ran from the room to be sick for one particular reason. Of all the luck, he thought. Poor woman. It just wasn't possible - except unfortunately it was all too possible – and it was just too awful for her. It could only mean that there was yet another Melbury on the way – and it must have happened just before his lordship went to *Real Man*. Although come to think of it, Bloss realised, it didn't really matter when it had happened, only that it had. He took a quick nip from the cooking sherry bottle while he had time, because he could see the temporary staff pouring through the back gates even as he drank. He was just so glad that his lordship had let him order his car when he had. If he had waited a few more weeks he would have had as much chance of being given it as he had of becoming an officer in the Guards. As Bloss well knew, if his master knew who or what was on its way the *Starduster* would have remained just a twinkle in his lordship's eye.

'Where's her ladyship?' his lordship enquired, when he had tracked Bloss down to the kitchen.

Bloss was glad to see how much brighter his master was looking. There had been a bit of sitting about in faded leather armchairs after he had flung himself over the top at *Real Man*, not to mention a great many stiffies. But now Bloss could see Lord Pemberton was quite himself again, positively kittenish in fact, ringing up Lady Tizzy on the staff telephone from the snug, and giggling away the happy hour with her. It was quite like old times, so it seemed. They were planning a reunion in the old summerhouse after the ball, which was how it should be. Lord Pemberton had the spring back in his step, a spring that Bloss had been very sad to see go absent for so long. He only hoped that her ladyship's newest malaise would not manifest itself to his lordship until after the ball. It might spoil everything for him, and just when doubtless he was ripening up and looking forward to some frolics.

'Ah, there you are, Jennifer,' he called affably to her ladyship who looked across at Bloss with something more than just a look that quite clearly said *one peep out of you and your new car will be out on the verge with a For Sale sign in its back window.*.

'Here I am, Pember,' she agreed, turning her attention back to her husband with a sweet but false brightness.

'Everything all right?'

'Couldn't be more perfect.'

'Are you sure? You look a trifle pale around the gills.'

'Just nerves before the ball, wanting everything to be perfect, that's all. You know how it is.'

Pemberton nodded. He was only too aware that a great social gathering from London would take it out of most girls, particularly Jennifer who was inordinately shy and usually only liked to sit about in her dog skirt doing her tatting. But there you are, it had been her idea to give the thing and now it was going ahead he was very grateful to her, Pember decided, especially since it was now the Countess who was paying for it, not himself. He eased himself back into the hail with a view to going across to Bloss's snug and having a bevvy. In his opinion it was the nicest part of having a party or helping to give a ball, all the bevvies under the stairs beforehand and one's friends arriving and chucking themselves under the stairs with you and everyone enjoying themselves no end.

'Good heavens, you're at it a bit early, aren't you, Gillott old boy?'

Andrew turned back from the silver cleaning basket where Bloss always obligingly kept a half bottle of his favourite kind of whisky, and nodded.

'Not at it yet; just about to be, though. Like you I like to enjoy myself a bit before the tumbrils roll, and the orchestra arrives, and the hostess faints, and that sort of thing.'

'Something happen to China?'

'It had, but it's stopped now. No I'm going to China all right, the Countess insists. Must go, nothing for it. Got to go now it's open again. But before I go I intend to make an honest woman of Lady Tisbury, I'll tell you that. That's why I'm here, you see. I'm stocking up in order to get together the courage to get down on one knee and demand her hand in holy deadlock.'

Pemberton stared at Andrew.

'You can't make an honest woman of Lady Tizzy, you jackanapes,' he protested. 'You ain't divorced yet, and she's married anyway!'

As he spoke he thought with fury of how much he himself had been looking forward to making a dishonest woman of her in the summerhouse once the ball was well under way.

'She's only officially married,' Andrew 'protested. 'Unofficially she can be anyone's. Want to see the ring I've bought her?'

Pemberton averted his eyes as from a traffic accident.

'No. Can't stand that sort of thing,' he muttered. 'All that will you be - take me for. Thou wilt and such like.'

'Pity. It's rather fine. Used to belong to my mother. That's how much she means to me, Lady Tisbury. That's how much.'

'Shouldn't you be giving that to Mrs Andrew Gillott, on account or something?'

'No, don't think so, not now I'm divorcing her. That's the whole point of divorcing someone, so you don't have to give them anything.'

'What about the Countess? She's been very kind to you.'

'She's got rings enough of her own. No, this is for Lady Tisbury, God bless her. And with it will go my love for ever.'

'Supposing she won't accept?' asked Pemberton hopefully.

'No she will - it's invaluable. One of the few emeralds to be cut on the cross bias, or something like that.'

'In that case, dear boy, don't give it to Lady Tizzy. She's so unreliable. You know how it is - she'll only put it in a pocket and send it to the laundry. Or give it to Oxfam because she can't find change for a pound. No, you keep it, as a hedge against inflation. You know, instead of an overdraft. You know what life can be like, one minute hey nonny no, and the next you're scrabbling around for three pence three farthings, and all ends to the middle.'

'Never mind that. I want to give it to the object of my love,' Andrew said. 'And she can do what she likes with it, bless her cotton petticoats.'

'How do you know her petticoats are cotton?'

'Because I do. She told me.'

'When?'

'Years ago. When we were at some fearful fund-raising for the new portacabins for the Vicar's modelling classes.'

'Vicars modelling, whatever next?' Pemberton muttered as the impact of the rather too early drink hit him somewhere between his recent alteration and his collar and tie.

'Not vicars modelling, people modelling for vicars.'

'That's what I mean,' Pemberton persisted. 'Whatever next?'

'No, they were modelling plasticine.'

'People will wear anything nowadays, you know,' said Pemberton, gloomily refilling his glass. 'Personally I like cashmere and lace, but plasticine - it wouldn't surprise me in the least.'

'Nothing's going to stop me getting down on one knee to the divine Lady Tisbury,' Andrew went on. 'But nothing. I am hers whether she wants me or not.'

'Which she won't,' said Pemberton quite firmly. 'She's got better things to do with her time, mark my words.'

He picked up his drink and knocked it back, dreaming of summerhouses and the kinds of things people could do in them, if like him they were lucky enough to own one. As he did so he watched Andrew scribbling a note on an old page of his racing diary. Right across Chepstow he was writing something that looked like *Meet me in the summerhouse after the last dance.*

'Can you read that all right?'

Pemberton stared at him.

'Perfectly,' he said.

'In that case she'll be able to,' Andrew said happily.

'Tell you what?'

'Mmm?'

'How about if I gave it to her, not you?'

At that moment the door opened once more and Bloss entered his own little kingdom, the kingdom of which he was the real and only ruler.

'Ah, Bloss,' said Andrew. 'The very man I want. Give this to Lady Tisbury, would you, there's a good fellow? At the right moment, of course.'

Bloss nodded.

'Of course, sir.'

'You're a good man, Bloss,' Andrew told him. 'Now I'm going to toddle off and have a kip before the roll of the drums. The Countess needs me to be on hand to take charge of her reticule, and I know not what. The sort of thing that keeps a fellow on his toes.'

He disappeared back into the hail as Pemberton's hand fell upon his butler's shoulder.

'You can give me that, Bloss, if you will,' he said.

'A gentleman's word is meant to be as good as his life, milord.' Bloss looked his lordship calmly in the eye. 'I promised Mr Gillott I would give this to Lady Tisbury personally,' he continued, looking down at the message scrawled over the page of the racing diary. 'And I must be seen to be as good as my word.'

'You know that new car of yours, Bloss?' Pemberton said smoothly.

'As I said,' Bloss continued equally smoothly. 'I promised I would give Lady Tisbury this note. What I did not promise was on whose behalf I would give it.'

Pemberton stared at his butler. He was the brightest thing out, he thought – and moral with it.

Meet me in the summerhouse.

It was just what he himself wanted to convey to Lady Tisbury.

'You know something, Bloss - you should be running the country instead of the shower we've got in at the moment,' Pemberton announced, slapping Bloss on the back. 'Singlehandedly you would see us through.'

Bloss couldn't help smiling, nor could he help silently agreeing with his master. After all it must be a lot simpler than running the Hall, he thought, but quite discreetly.

The Countess surveyed herself in the mirror. It was rather fun seeing herself once more decked out as a countess should be, tiara, rose *taille* - the dress was an old Molyneux but the cut was the newest around - long white gloves, everything as it should be, and nothing smelling of mothballs. She nodded to herself and to the man standing behind her.

'You'll do, you'll do very, very well,' he said.

She smiled at him before he faded from her sight.

Freddie. Her own darling Freddie. He always had said that to her, and it had been so nice.

'You'll do.'

It didn't need anything more - just that, and the look in his eyes. She still missed him. She missed him every moment of her day. One of these days she would be joining him in an eternal waltz and she would look forward to that, but meanwhile, thanks to the Empress's Box, she was giving a great ball in the old manner, and everyone was coming who could come. All Mary's friends had been re-routed, and all Jennifer's of friends, and even the miscreant Georgiana Longborough.

'My dear, you look quite, quite wonderful.'

The Countess stared at Georgiana. The ability to look perfect in jewellery and evening dress belonged to patrician Englishwomen. It was like that. It would always be like that. It was a fact. The rest of the world could look good in everything else but there was nothing like an Englishwoman in a beautiful evening dress, her family jewels gleaming, everything just so.

Georgiana's dress was pink where the Countess's was old rose. Georgiana's was beautifully wide, where the Countess's was figure clinging and cut on the bias. How perfectly they complemented each other they could both see. Georgiana brushed the Countess's cheek in the accepted manner. Georgiana's hair was folded into her neck, the Countess's brushed up. Georgiana's head shimmered, because the family tiara was made up of thousands of small stones, the centrepiece a rose for England which moved slightly as her head moved.

'What on earth is that?' asked the Countess as she peered at the decoration on Andrew's sash.

'It's made out of milk bottle tops. Rather good, don't you think?'

'I'm not sure. Depends what it's for.'

Andrew held out an arm to her.

'For surviving.'

'In that case you can leave it on,' the Countess smiled. 'As a matter of fact we should all be wearing one.'

Georgiana looked round her. The great room was festooned with fresh flowers, and the people with jewels. Perhaps because the Countess was in charge there was a definite aura of another era, and she had long ago lost count of the number of tiaras that had entered the room, and were now drifting in and out of the silk-lined tents as the orchestra played a medley of tunes. The faces were not much changed since she was a debutante. The general mix was not too different either, but she was – she was so changed and in only a few years that the sight of one face alone could make her feel that it was worth dancing life's insistent waltz. If he didn't arrive, if he had already left for Los Angeles, she didn't really care, she told herself as she laughed and talked to the whole world who jostled each other to be by her side, to pay her compliments, to stand near her. At the end of the famous day Kaminski was after all only Sasha. On the other hand if he arrived and headed straight for her he would be again the great Kaminski, whose genius and talent would shine as long as the stones in her tiara, perhaps longer, thanks to celluloid. And to be singled out by him, to be taken by the hand and led in to dinner would cause a scandal, but only of the kind that everyone liked and envied, in other words a scandal of the very best kind.

The stage was set in any case, with Nanny was waiting with George in a nearby hotel. Everything was set fair for them all to escape to the West Coast, to a warmer climate, away from the coming winter and the damp and the rain.

'May I take you in to dinner?'

Georgiana stared at the speaker, and her heart started to beat so loudly that for a second she imagined that it would be quite nice to forget about all the formalities, the dinner, the dancing, the breakfast served at midnight, and faint straight into his arms so that they could run away together that minute.

'I didn't think you were coming,' she said to him, quietly.

'For one moment,' he replied. 'Neither did I. But only for a moment.'

He smiled and held out his arm. Georgiana placed her kid glove on it, and as the orchestra played *Violets for Her Furs* as a special request for the Countess, it seemed to Georgiana that her fate was temporarily but gloriously sealed. They would run away together and it would be wonderful. No voice whispered in her ear *what if?* or *and after this?* but then with her it never did. To Georgiana life was something to be danced, and dance it she would.

'It's so nice to see all the young people enjoying themselves,' someone said en passant to the Countess.

'Do you think so, really?' the Countess replied, with a smile. 'I always find it somewhat ominous myself.'

THE END

Made in the USA
Monee, IL
16 February 2020